MW01443572

LIFE FORCE PRESERVE

LIFE FORCE PRESERVE

Book 1

Anna and the resurgent of the precious blood

by

COURTNEY LEIGH PAHLKE

eBooks2go

Published in the United States
by eBooks2go, Inc.
1827 Walden Office Square, Suite 260, Schaumburg, IL 60173

ISBN-10: 1-5457-4413-0

ISBN-13: 978-1-5457-4413-0

Library of Congress Cataloging in Publication

To my readers, may you find your way when uncontrollable moments toss you off course.

To my family and friends, thank you for lifting me up through the hardest time of my life. And Kat, *words* can't express my appreciation for your support when the physical pain took over me.

CONTENTS

CHAPTER 1

On Wednesday I stepped outside to grab my mail, and a bird pooped on my head. I managed to scare the crap out of a loitering rooftop pigeon. If I had a beak and feathers, I would fly south for the winter. I'd mingle with an outbound V—maybe join a bird posse in the Keys for a couple months while I contemplate the advantages of an early-bird retirement. I'd never lurk around on a rooftop during a snowstorm. I wasn't aware of the sneaky bird bomb until I was in front of a mirror, washing my hands. The smeary white patch caught my eye. It looked like a bleach stain in my auburn mane. Gross.

What are the odds of that happening twice in one week? Should I find my hat just in case? No, I'll spill my coffee. Forget the head armor. I feel a yawn coming and choke it down. Nah, it won't happen again—forget about the stinky bird.

I raise my smoldering mug of fresh brew up to my face and let the steam seep through my pores. The gentle mist soothes my dry skin. I close my eyes and inhale the traces of rich caramel and roasted hazelnut that exude from the foamy creamer. Just another minute until I sample this bold columbian brew.

The wood floors creak as I step toward the front door. Each footstep sounds like an old man rocking in a homemade chair. I can't help it; I stomp when I walk. Patches from the fuzzy morning light nudge through the blinds of the surrounding windows. I reach for the mail key, slide it in my pocket, and press my forehead against the front-door window.

The winter air tickles my face as it bleeds through the defective cracks of the old wooden door. I stare out the window. There're two lopsided circles of fog lingering on the glass from my nostrils. It's another frostbite-friendly morning here in the Windy City.

Inching away from the glass, I lift my coffee to my nose and smell the aroma once more. My sense of smell wants to selfishly strip the reigns from other sensory leaders. Go ahead, smell the potent coffee. I feel my salivary glands tap-dancing. The marks on the window from my breath vanish in the glass, revealing the clear reality of a gloomy morning. Naked trees aligning the sidewalk enhance the depressing still-shot picture through my window.

I stare across the street at the neighbor's front yard. Someone chopped the head off the neighbor kid's snowman. The head is smashed on the ground next to its beheaded trunk. Both eyeballs were removed and replaced as "snowman boobs" before the decapitation.

Without looking down, I stick my tongue into the coffee. Crap. Still hot. The frigid air will turn it down a notch. Making sure I have my phone, I grab the mail key and step outside. Grasping my coffee tight, I lunge out to the top of the stairs. My body jolts and shifts off balance. My stomach drops as I snap backward. I land on my back. Everything's going. Everything—gone.

CHAPTER 2

I see a snowman, he lost his head,
Snowman, coffee, now he's dead.
A scorched tongue and a whack on the ground,
Anna sleeps while evil surrounds.

There's an echo. Noisy traffic ricochets between skyscrapers, polluting the city. I sit up and open my eyes. Wait. I can't see anything. Where the hell am I? The echo transforms into a piercing elongated pitch and stops. I gulp down air. I think I hear my heart hammering around in my chest. I thought it's only possible to hear a heart with a stethoscope. The sound is faint, but it grows louder as the drum in my head magnifies. Am I sleeping?

I rub my eyes, and I'm able to see again, though things look off. Everything surrounding me is monochrome and pixelated, and I'm lying inside of a bubble. I'm in a bubble? It looks like I'm trapped inside a Halloween-themed snow globe.

A figure lurks past me. I sit up and watch. Is it a man or a woman? I can't see clear. The mysterious blur scampers across the street into the neighbor's yard. It bends over and gathers snow. Snow globe snow. Perfect packing snow.

Breathe a breath and hold it tight,
Don't lose your mind, you know you're right.
Wake up, Anna.

The wind whistles. A dead tree branch snaps and hits the ground. The stranger halts like a deer hesitating in an open field. Don't move. Don't breathe. Don't let it catch me staring. It's trapped with me inside the snow globe.

The figure moves. It lowers itself and grabs a chunk of snow. The two arms resemble tree branches. Tree branches? Odd. It packs the snow tight with its freaky arms until the snow looks the size of a soccer ball. It stretches its arms upward, raising the snowy sphere in the air.

Wait a minute? I squint. The sun beams down on the figure. It's a snowman. The neighbor's beheaded snowman. The snowman takes the ball and props it on its body. Did he just build himself a new head?

The figure spins in my direction and removes two lumps of coal from his chest. He wedges the coal against his head, creating eyeballs. The snowman whips around and stops so that he's facing me. I'm spotted.

My clothes are drenched in sweat, and I'm sunburnt. Wait—I'm outside in the snow, and snowmen can't move. Snowmen don't move. He takes a few steps toward me and stops. What's he looking at? This can't be real. Go away. I count the seconds. *One. Two. Three.* I breathe and blink. *Four. Five.* I better get up—something's not right. *Six.* The snowman turns and stares off. I feel wind. *Seven.* The wind blows, causing an icicle to shatter on the ground next to me. *Eight.* Get up, Anna. The sun vanishes behind a cloud. *Nine.* The snowman swivels around, facing my direction, and initiates a full sprint. He has legs? Stop it. I can't move. I'm stuck.

Anna Lynn Gibson, it's time to wake,
He's coming to get you, it's no mistake.
Hear the wind coil, feel the winter attack,
Snap out of this now, before there's no going back.

I gasp for air and flutter my eyelids. My mind feels mushy. Everything looks backward and duplicated as though I'm crossing my eyes while sitting in a circle of mirrors. Wind hurls at my face. I try to open my eyes, but I'm tired. I must sleep now. Now? Sleeping? Yes, sleep.

Anna, stop. Do not sleep. Dream a nightmare. What does that even mean? Stay awhile. Stop the spinning. Please stop the spinning. I'm in a pitch-black room, but I feel myself spinning. Spinning in left circles. I can't turn right. You're dreaming; get out. *Wake up.* I'm awake. The voices stop.

I open my eyes. I'm on the ground. What's wrong with me? What the hell just happened?

CHAPTER 3

A gust of nostril-piercing air burns the skin inside my nose as I inhale a stinging batch of bitterness. I'm on my back, and I'm not in the warmth of my bed. A second blast of wind catches my hair and whips it across my face. I pucker my lips and blow a strand of hair from my eyes. I feel the cold initializing a raid on my corneas.

Racket from an earsplitting sound of crunching metal makes me jolt on the ground. I lift my head and look around. The back of my skull feels like it's on fire. I lower my head and hear pulverizing sounds of melded steel prying apart. *What was that?* That's an accident. I know that sound—too familiar of a sound.

Sit up. *Sit up now.* I can't. *Has it happened again?* No—it can't be. Am I still in the snowman nightmare? I had a snowman nightmare, right?

I feel tears building along the rims of my eye sockets. I've lost control of my eyes like a river dam blasting open. I thought I had to be in hell to feel like I've been camping in Antarctica while rodents chomped away at my limbs.

Stop it. Calm down. Just do something—anything. I move my leg. A fiery prickle radiates up my calf muscle as though I'm being negatively charged by an electrical socket. I stop and listen to the noise. The surround sound shifts from crumpled metal to burning rubber. A second sound of shrieking brakes follow. The car accident is live and continues while I lay here helpless.

I move an arm and feel glass chards and cactus needles grinding around in my shoulder blades. What now? What do I do? The noise stops. I lay still and listen. I hear nothing but the wind.

The abrupt silence is off-putting. I close my eyes and wait. The wind hisses in my ears, driving chills up my spinal cord. I'm reliving my hell.

What are the odds? A second car accident? I've barely been inside a vehicle since the first accident. Wait. Is this the first accident?

My heart beats faster. It's as though I'm watching myself walk across a melting ice pond, the ice crackling with every step as I try to stay ahead of the breaking ice, knowing the outcome. I'm beginning to believe that it's possible for a person to be struck by lightning multiple times.

I squeeze my eyelids open and close, blinking away the winter dryness. I roll my eyes in circles and look up and down. I suck in air and hold my breath. I close my eyes. Calm. Gentle. Warmth. Think of comfort. I exhale. A long bubble bath while enjoying a crisp glass of wine. Warm slippers. Ordering takeout and binge-watching a new series. I must power down my mind and start over. Positive headspace—don't be a head case.

I force my head upward, lifting my shoulder blades off the ground. My vision is blurred in one eye. I force the bad eye shut and stare at a brass hanging lantern. It's my brass hanging lantern. I'm laying underneath the second-floor balcony of my three-flat. I recognize the brown discoloration in the ceiling from an old bee's nest.

I tilt my head to one side and stop. I'm at the edge of my staircase. Had I tipped a few inches, I would've tumbled down an entire cement staircase. I pivot away from the edge and flip onto my side. *Think, Anna, before the cold attacks your core.* The wind pries through my pant fibers, forcing goose bumps. The ache distributes down my spine, surging with intensity.

Life feels real. Staying alive feels real. An adrenaline junkie would thrive in this moment. The whack to my head must be preventing my brain from activating an acute stress response. I'm too frail to fight. I reach an arm up in the air and move it in a circle. I feel like a geriatric patient doing water therapy.

Sucking in air, I jerk my weight on my right forearm. "Son of a baseball," I cry. Son of a baseball? What the hell was that about? It's not even baseball season. My clothing peels from the ground as I stretch myself higher. I slap my right hand down and straighten my arm. I plummet on my shoulder. What is this? Ice? I force myself back up and peer around.

How? My porch—it's covered. Seldom do I get snow on the porch, as it's covered by the floor above. Every inch is flooded with ice. In some sections, the ice is thick enough for a person to successfully skate across. I've never had this happen before. What's with this?

The ice closer to the door thins out and is saturated with brown stains. I see perforations inside the brown spots from melting ice. There's shattered glass throughout the mess. *Great.* There's my phone. To the right of my phone—a broken coffee mug handle. My favorite mug. I get it now. The early morning hit-and-run—mere coincidence.

My porch looks like a crime scene. I open my other eye. The blur is still there. I feel like an annihilated bystander. The murky vision reminds me of what things looked like when I'd walk in my college apartment after nine hours of tailgating. Why was I outside in the first place? Did I eat breakfast this morning? Wait—what day is today?

I close my eyes. Make this go away. I crack an eyelid—yep, I'm still here. I would eat spiders if it meant escaping this moment. Quit wasting time with unrealistic thoughts, and get inside that door.

The stair railing is close enough. If I slide over and grab onto the side, I could pluck myself up to a sitting position. Yes, this could work. I drop on my stomach and exhale. I center my weight between my forearms and army crawl across the ice.

I hoist my right arm and whack the railing with my knuckle. "Brussels spouts," I yelp. What did I say? I didn't even say it correctly. Brussels sprouts are disgusting. I think I have a concussion. I cup the side of the railing, tug myself up, and twist onto my butt. I want to scream until my throat is raw. It feels like I lowered my tailbone against a razor. I chomp down on my lip and feel tears.

Who can I ask for help? It must be early—not a single person in sight. Pathetic how city society adapts to commotion in which a loud accident fazed no one. I suppose it wouldn't have bothered me either if I wasn't laying in the front row of the action. Come on, focus. I don't have time to wait for someone to walk by. I should yell. Nope—last resort. Only cause a neighborhood scene as a last-ditch effort.

There are parts of a broken taillight scattered across my street. The door of a parked car is bashed in. I was right about the crash—it happened right in front of my home. Bird shit doesn't seem so bad now.

I scoot across the ice. My palms are numb to the bone, and my fingers tingle as I slide forward. I snatch my phone. The screen's shattered—I can relate.

I brush away a layer of glass. Call Jessica. She could hop in a cab and be here in minutes. Hurry up and call her—she'll help. No, don't ruin her day. I put my best friend through enough this past year, and she has a life to live too. Has there ever been a moment where I had to take care of her?

I drop the phone in my lap and slide toward the door. The rocking motion is making me nauseous. I'm dizzy. A trip to the hospital may be happening soon. Just call her—she won't care. I stop and look at my phone. I bite at my bottom lip. Am I her deadweight? She's never needed me like I've needed her, starting from the moment we met.

* * * *

Jessica and I were little kids and had the same recess. It was the same year I watched a nice girl turn into a monster before my eyes. Her name was Scarlett, and she was a nasty little brat.

Scarlett was taller than most kids and would talk about her older sisters all the time. She was my first bully. I learned basic math while keeping an eye on the devious little shit while I sat at my desk. If the teacher would direct a question at me, I would slouch in my seat and pray for her to keep her mouth shut. It was worse when she did things in front of the entire class. Watching her act so nice to everyone else in school confused me, causing me to think I was the problem.

She wasn't always mean to me, though. Scarlett and I sat next to each other on the bus, even played on the same soccer team for a year. One day coach appointed me captain, which caused her to have a temper tantrum on the field. A first encounter with jealousy was all it took to wake the devil inside her.

The bullying began with a snarl during class. I'd get an answer wrong and hear her giggle in the background. I wouldn't react, so she upgraded to snarky remarks about me to others—my clothing, my posture.

She would give intel about what her cool older sisters did and wore, which ironically differed from me every single time. A few times I fueled her fire by showing up the next day in what she explained was "cool," only to hear her say, "Anna still doesn't get it." I was too young to understand why she did it and too afraid to stick up for myself. We don't learn this until later in life, but the manipulators of society begin to stalk their prey prior to their victim's loss of innocence. They feel powerful over the powerless, which changes once the powerless discover their manipulator's intentions.

I let things go too far while the situation paralleled with my tolerance. What did I understand as a fifth grader? One afternoon the snotty little brat girl tripped me during recess and made fun of my red hair. It was the first time she got physical. She walked up from behind me and kicked the book lying next to me on the ground. A little blond girl witnessed the scene and came to my rescue.

"Leave her alone," the little girl said.

The bully turned toward the little girl. "What did you say?"

"My friend says you're always picking on her. What did she ever do to you?" the girl asked.

I looked up in fear.

The bully walked toward the girl. "You want to say that again?"

"Yes, but get closer so I don't have to yell so loud." The blonde made a hand gesture, and a group of kids walked over.

The girl was from one of the other fifth-grade classes in our school. She glared at the bully. It was my first time witnessing a face-off. She was smaller than the bully, which made me nervous.

"Anna, right?" the little blonde hollered, ignoring the bully.

"Yes," I said.

"You okay?" the blonde asked.

"I'm fine, I swear."

The blonde walked my direction and stopped so she was face-to-face with the mean girl. Her supporters gathered around. She knew she was shorter but didn't care. "Anna, come over and join us. We don't treat people like she does."

"Redheaded alien," the bully muttered.

I got up and walked sideways toward the safety zone. The other kids from her class walked over in comfort. I wanted to cry.

"Did you make fun of her hair color?" the blond girl asked.

The bully rolled her eyes. "Yes, I made fun of her ugly hair."

"I thought so. I would've walked away, but you put her down again." The blond girl looked at the other kids. "Look how beautiful Anna's hair is. It's shining in the sunlight. Now look at hers." She pointed at the bully. "You have shit-colored hair, and you're just jealous. I have older sisters too, and they warned me about people like you. If I see you treat her or anyone like that again, you'll regret it."

"Grow up," another voice from the support group shouted.

"No, don't yell. We don't act like her—we don't bully. She just needed to be checked," the blonde intervened. She took a few steps in my direction and turned back toward the bully. "We don't leave people out, so if you want to be nice to everyone, you can play with us next time."

I was stunned and didn't know what to say. I watched my hero walk over to me.

"My name's Jessica," the girl said and put her hand on my shoulder for comfort.

"I'm Anna." I hugged her.

That was the most mature thing I ever witnessed a kid do.

* * * *

I bump my back against the door. I made it on my own.

CHAPTER 4

I swat at the handle and press my body against the door. The handle cranks to the right, and the door swings open. I fall inside. Warmth. The abrupt climate change startles my system. Lukewarm air feels scalding against my flesh.

I feel like a slug as I heave the rest of my body through the entrance. Pressing the arch of my foot against the door, I kick it shut. Whatever day it is—I'm not off to a good start. I pat the back of my head and feel a lump. My hand goes numb. I should get this checked.

I call my dad and hang up. Don't do this to him. Don't make him waste hours in a car for this; he's been through enough. My closest lifeline is Jessica. Her phone rings and goes to voicemail. I look at my phone; it's not even seven in the morning on a Sunday. Why would a twenty-four-year-old be cognizant and out of bed? I wouldn't be if I were healthy and had a social life. *Don't be a burden.*

What now? Do I call an ambulance and cause a scene? I touch the mangled glass on my phone—can't type messages. What are the odds that I'm okay, and this is all in my head? I don't need another damn hospital bill to pay off.

I dial Jessica and get her voicemail. Wait, didn't I call her already? I can't remember. I hold one eye shut and look through the shattered glass. I accidentally called her twice. Crap, two—calls in a row. She'll think there's an emergency. I'll call and leave a message.

The person you're trying to reach has a mailbox that's full. Please try again later.

"Of course your voicemail's full. The one and only time." I hang up the phone. I'll explain things once I hear back from her. I slump down and hug the cherrywood floors. The warmth of my home surrounds me.

There's an old green chair topped with the box I marked for Goodwill. It's within reaching distance. I can slide over and use the chair to pull myself up—simple plan. Now make a move and get up. Move it. I shuffle side to side and reach for the chair. I grab ahold of one of the legs and pull it toward me. The box slides to one side and topples to the ground. Some old sweaters and a load of books strike the ground next to my head.

A book lands in front of me, and an old fortune cookie message slips from the pages. *Today's an improvement over yesterday as well as the next day after that*, it reads. *Your lucky numbers 13, 54, 27, 38, 12, 48.* What kind of a message is that? Stupid cookie. I remember saving the little piece of paper and using it as a bookmark a while back. I felt inspired by the words as my health improved. I slap the message facedown.

My arms shake as pull I the chair toward me. I stop to scratch my face and sneeze. The piece of paper flips over. I grab the taunting slit of paper off the ground, wrinkle it up, and pop it in my mouth. I chew it down to the size of a pea and spit it on the floor.

The wood drives hard against my bones as I center my weight between my forearms. The rubbing sounds like someone winding a salt grinder. I drag my legs toward my stomach and bend my knees. I lean back and propel my arms at the sides of the chair. I heave myself onto the edge of the chair and stand up.

My inner thighs feel warm—I've peed my pants. I remember learning about paralysis and *cauda equina syndrome*—uncontrollable bladder and lumbar disc herniations are two major symptoms. I close my eyes and lift a leg. I twitch forward from an internal electrocution. I grab my phone.

"Call Chicago Cab," I say.

"*Calling Chicago Cab.*" The phone rings.

"Thanks for calling Chicago Cab. Is the number you're calling from Anna?" the operator asks.

"Yes."

"What's your last name?" the operator asks.

"Gibson. I need a cab sent to my home address on file in ten minutes," I say.

"The one off Madiso—"

"Yes. And I'll be heading to Rush Hospital." I hang up.

How am I going to get out of here? I didn't think this through. Another fall could be all that it'd take to drive me to the ground and finish me. I imagine what the final spill would look like—something out of an overdramatized slasher film. My tailbone will burst through the skin, leaving me dead in my tracks. The event will mimic a plug being ripped from an outlet. My lights will go out and my vertebrae will clatter to the ground, leaving me brain-dead and defeated.

Maybe I should call the paramedics. They'd come in and assist me out the door. I grab my phone. No, don't do it. They'll send an ambulance, but with a fire truck and a few squad cars—cause a scene and rack up a tab. I turn and stare at the back door. Bingo. I grab one of the sweaters from the scattered donation pile and tie it around my waist and look for my purse. It'd take too long to change my pants.

Having not been out the back door in over a month, I pray the back stairway is clear of ice. I shuffle through my kitchen and stop at my back door. Why's the dead bolt unlocked? I cover my bad eye—yes, it's unlocked. I always keep this door locked. My heart beats faster, and I turn and around to check for intruders. Everything's in order.

The door blows open with a slight push. The screen door's unlocked. "Jessica." I shake my head. She was here recently and should know better. I plant one leg outside the door and look down the steep staircase. I hold on to the wooden railing, drag my other foot out, and push the door shut.

I stop on one of the snow-filled steps and cover the blurry eye. There're several large shoeprints up and down my stairs—the remnants of my dad's and brother's hard work from their last visit. I bet my brother left the doors unlocked. He's done it before. There's a blue tarp covering my future back patio. A stack of plywood and a plastic storage bin lay next to the tarp.

The pain infects my mind. The wind enhances the infection as I continue down the stairs. "Think positive," I mutter to myself. I used to love the winter. I look ahead at my obstacle course. The untouched snow glistens under the morning sun. The snow is fresh and unpolluted.

There's something about the look of snow that triggers childhood nostalgia. The way it glistens as it drops. Each snowflake distinct, like a fingerprint. Some fall fast, clustered with the droplets of moisture they accumulate on their way down, turning to slush as they land. I prefer the snowflakes that are massive and feathery, where the air swirls them sideways. Every kid yearns to stick their tongue out for a sampling. I still hold my mouth open for a taste during the first snowfall each year. I find it soothing when I step outside and feel as though I'm in my very own snow globe.

Mornings when I'd see a bright-white coating, I'd take off out the back door, occasionally forgetting my jacket, and create a mess of the untouched layers. I liked to run as fast as I could through the snow with our dog, tasting the glittery gleam of white until dog would turn it yellow. My brother would join just before the yellow stains multiplied.

We played relentless games of tag and hide-and-seek, as we never minded the cold Illinois winters. We would be outside until my cheeks were rosy and my lips were blue, fingers and toes frozen. Mom always baked her cinnamon-raisin oatmeal cookies on frigid winter days. I can still smell the spices.

I inhale the fresh air. The imaginary scent of spices vanishes when my nostrils fill with needle stings. My nose is running, and my eyes are tearing. I'm a few steps away from the finish line.

There's a large wooden hammer with blue-and-yellow paint splattered across the middle of the shaft. The hammer's laying horizontal across one of the footprints—one step down on the other side of the stairwell. Shouldn't it be buried with snow? Weird. I don't recognize the hammer. When were my dad and brother here last?

Warmth edges across my forehead. My cheeks heat up as though I have hand warmers taped on each. The skin around my ears feel like someone's bearing a flame to the back of both sides. No, I believe my dad brought his tools up recently. It's simple—he left it on the stairs. But I've never seen this hammer before. What if someone was trying to break in?

My phone rings.

"Hello?"

"This is your taxi. I'm out front by the coffee shop," the driver says.

"But that's down the street a little way. Can you come to the front of the address I requested please?" I ask.

"I can't get down that one-way street right now. The police have the road closed. Some sort of incident on your street," he says.

"So the police were called there, then? The accident?" I ask.

"What?" the driver asks.

"Never mind. Please wait there for me—it's an emergency. I'll need you to drive me to the ER."

"I'll wait here."

The throbbing's growing worse by the minute. I walk through the back alley and turn down a side street. Two blocks—I can do this. I'm not sure how I'll respond if that driver bails on me. There'll be loud noises and swear words.

I can't help but think about the hammer in the snow. What were my dad and brother doing to my place last where they left behind a hammer? The two of them were covering up the patio before the first snowfall. I stop. Before the snow. It's been way longer than I thought. Those weren't their footprints on the stairs. There must be a logical explanation—a utility issue, gas meter, or my cable company could've been back there while I was out. Calm down. Everything inside my place was in order.

The raw weather isn't supporting my case right now. My shuffling's decelerating, and I'm running low on fuel. If a person walked through globs of quick-drying cement, they'd still beat me in any race. I cross over to the next block and see early risers walking about. I'm almost there. One woman turns the corner, power-walking toward me. She's fit and full of energy—I want to look happy like her.

I wait until the woman's closer and straighten my posture. I screech in pain. She jumps and veers off the sidewalk, passing me from the road. I'm not sure if I should feel bad or angered by her body language. To an onlooker, I'm sure I stand out. Most women in their early twenties wouldn't be out in freezing climates, staggering down a sidewalk, unless they're coming home from a crazy all-nighter. I'm walking down the sidewalk like Shrek after eating a jar of bath salts. The sun's barely up, and I've scared a pedestrian—good for you, Anna.

A cab's parked in front of the coffee shop window. Please be my cab. A woman crosses the street and runs toward the entrance of the coffee shop. Great, there's already a line out the door of the local shop. A man exits with coffee and jumps in the cab. The cab drives off. "Wait. That's my cab," I say, picking up the pace.

A woman leaves the coffee shop and jumps in a car that's blocking traffic. The emergency lights turn off and the car speeds away. Another cab parallel parks in an open parking space. "Please, please be him." Two women leave with coffee and approach the cab. One of the women opens the door and slides in the back of the cab. Her friend helps her back out. "That must be him."

I cross the intersection and look down my street. Two squad cars block the one-way street. The driver was right—if only they were sooner. I hold the back of my leg and massage the nerve pain as I approach the local coffee shop.

I lurch past the window. There're people cozied up at the bar aligning the window. A mom with two little boys sits next to a group of girlfriends having coffee post yoga class. I feel their eyes on me as a limp by like a strung-out zombie. I'm sure my pee stain's showing, and my lips are blue. I wonder what they'd do if I turned and yelled, "Braaaaaiiinnsss," at them in the window. That'll teach them not to stare.

I pass the coffee shop and lock eyes with the cabdriver parked up ahead. From my miserable-looking appearance, the driver realizes that I'm his ER customer. He backs his cab out of the parking spot and pulls alongside me with his flashers on. The driver hops from his vehicle and runs over to assist me. He reaches out his hand.

"You okay, miss?" A tall, lanky man helps me to the cab.

"I need to get to Rush Hospital right away."

"You need a bag to puke in?" he asks.

"No."

He looks at me. "Oh, water broke—going into labor?"

I peek at the bulge from the sweater and the frozen stain. "No, it's my neck and back … and head."

"Your back?" he asks. He scratches his head.

"Yes, and I can barely walk. I think I'm going into paralysis—please get me there quick." Tears begin.

"Should be a quick ride. Roads are clear—besides your street." The driver follows me to the side and opens the door.

I bend forward and cry out.

"Hold on to the handle and slide in. I had back surgery twice."

I look over to him.

"Squat a little, then use your legs—hold the door handle." He reaches out his hand to assist me.

I follow his lead and squat down. I grab the handle and pull myself onto the seat.

"Just a moment." He opens the front passenger door and slides the seat forward. "Do you mind if I grab your legs?"

"No."

"Hang tight." He lifts my legs and swings them in front of my body.

"Thank you for helping me, and thank you for waiting," I say.

The driver runs around his vehicle and slides in the driver's seat. "Not a problem. I'm a patient man."

"Thanks again."

"Some people won't understand the pain you're in unless they've lived it. A few years back, I remember calling my wife to get me out of my car. She had to go and grab the neighbors." He puts his seat belt on. "Rush Hospital?"

"Yes, please."

"We're you in that accident on your street?" he asks.

"Me? No, I'm like this from another car accident."

"That's a shame. You're too young for back problems."

"I hear that often."

"Distracted driver? I see it all the time. Stupid people," he says.

"I'll never know."

"Oh." The driver stops talking.

I see the bright lights shining from the hospital. Here I go again—this time I'm heading to the hospital in a conscious state.

CHAPTER 5

Waking up in a hospital bed was horrifying. I heard sounds over a loud speaker—thought I was in a shopping mall food court. The echoing pages would sound at random. I didn't know if they were talking to me or what they were saying.

The first time I opened my eyes I was blinded by a light. I saw a man's face—thought someone took a wine bottle and cracked it over my head. I went back to sleep. The second time I opened my eyes I was wasted and passed out on a bench in Union Station. I heard names being called over a loud speaker, and I didn't know why I was there or if I was alone. The light was too bright, so I went back to sleep.

It became a pattern. I'd be somewhere around the city, and I'd open my eyes to the same damn light. Every time I saw the blinding spectacle, I'd close my eyes and reset my mind. I knew what was coming before it happened. I would escape the light and started over.

I was in a zipped-up tent in the middle of the woods, looking through a translucent window. I heard muffled sounds outside the tent, but when I unzipped it and peeked out through a corner, I was in a shopping mall food court. I popped my head outside the tent and saw the light. It didn't make sense—I was camping in the woods.

I fought the bright light by staring at it as long as I could. The light suddenly faded, and I saw white ceramic tiles. I was stuck there.

"She's awake," a woman said.

"She's responding to tests," a man said.

"She should be in a coma. She's making me nervous," she said.

"We can't now," he said.

"She looked right at me and closed her eyes. She didn't want answers," the woman said.

"Let her adjust. She can hear us. There wasn't damage to the occipital lobe," the man said. "It's the neurogenic shock."

"Her body fought off the pentobarbital and thiopental. I'd never seen anything like it," the woman said.

"Keep an eye on her, and let her take her time," the man said.

I realized I was in a hospital bed. How did I get here? What was I afraid of facing? The longer I laid there like a coward, the longer I was prolonging inevitable news. Maybe the sooner I addressed someone, the sooner I could get the hell out of here. The next time she came into my room, I decided I'd talk to her.

I waited for her to come back, ready for the question-and-answer game. My eyes felt heavy from the drugs. I closed my eyes and dozed off. I felt someone lift my arm.

Come on. Wake up. You need answers. I opened my eyes and looked at the nurse, bent over alongside my bed. She was folding a washcloth as she swung over to face me in a chair.

"I have a few questions," I said.

"Christ almighty," she shrieked and shot backward. "You scared the shit out of me." The nurse grabbed her chest, holding herself from keeling over. "I'm so sorry; I didn't mean to swear. You've been sleeping since you got here, and I didn't expect that to happen."

"No, I'm sorry," I said. My voice was raspy, and my throat felt dry.

"Now that you're up, I'm your nurse, Kathy." She stood up and readjusted my pillow. "You need to stay in this position for the time being, so please try not to move around."

"What's wrong with me?" I asked.

"You were in a car accident a little over a week ago. Do you remember anything?" she asked.

"No, I don't think so. Maybe? What's wrong with me? Maybe I'll remember."

"We were about to do an MRI on your spine. Your x-rays revealed multiple spinal fractures and disc herniations. The first MRI showed severe bleeding into your spinal cord." The nurse fidgeted around the room.

"What does that mean?"

"On the first MRI, you were so inflamed, several of your discs moved far enough that they were pressing through your spinal cord," she said.

"Am I paralyzed?" I started to cry.

"No. Just try to relax and not work yourself up. You'll be okay—keep still. You came a hair away from the disc moving through the entire cord, but you're not paralyzed," she said.

"I don't understand."

"Here, take this." She held a pill up to my mouth and waited for me to open.

"What's this?"

"For anxiety. The doctor said to give it to you if you happened to wake up while he was unavailable."

I opened my mouth and let her pop in the pill. I looked up at her as she lowered a water cup toward my mouth. She bent the straw and slid it against my tongue. My throat felt dry, and the water felt soothing. I gulped down as much water as I could. I had never been so thirsty in my life.

"Once the swelling comes down, you'll be able to do a little more. We're doing the second MRI soon to check the progress. We've been pumping an anti-inflammatory through your IV, so hopefully the inflammation has come down," she said.

I let go of the straw. "Can you please start from the beginning and explain what happened?" I bit the straw so she wouldn't take the water away.

"Sure, I bet some answers will help. I'm able to tell you the info Doctor Bertain approved me to discuss with you. You were in an accident, and we're treating you for cervical and lumbar trauma. The good news—"

"There's good news?" I spit out the straw.

"The positive news—you're in good hands with Doctor Bertain. He's handled a lot of spinal cord trauma and has been at this hospital a long time." She put the cloth across my forehead. "I'm administering a second calming agent into your IV. You need to stay calm and sleep some more. Doctor Bertain's in surgery but will be here later to disclose everything."

"I don't want to sleep right now."

"Count to ten with me?" she asked.

I gave in. "One, two, three …" I closed my eyes and fell asleep.

When I woke up from Kathy's forced sleep cycle, I did not know if I was asleep for a few hours or a few days. Out of the corner of my eyes, I saw my dad and brother walking toward my room from a slit between the curtain and the wall.

"Dad, in here," I said.

My dad and brother made their way into my room.

"Sleeping Beauty arises," my brother said.

"Daniel, hang on, let her breathe a moment. She's just waking up," my dad said, swatting at my brother, Dan.

"She's comfortable right now," Nurse Kathy said, entering the room behind them. "I was talking to Anna earlier, before her MRI—Doctor Bertain will be in shortly. He's just wrapping up surgery in the third wing." Kathy walked in with a syringe and administered more drugs. She smiled and backed out of the room.

"What hospital am I in?" I asked.

"Saint Mark's Hospital," Dan said.

"I'm in the suburbs?" I asked.

"Yes, you are," my dad said.

"We've been here since the accident pretty much. You've been sleeping." Dan walked over to the side table and grabbed a vase filled with roses and a balloon that read "Get Better Sister."

"I bought you these."

"Those are lovely—thank you. How'd you know I was here?" I asked.

"A man called us after your accident. Said he saw the entire thing and that you were in an ambulance heading to Saint Mark's Hospital," my dad said. "That was over a week ago now."

"You were in a serious hit-and-run," my brother said.

"Dan." My dad snapped his fingers at my brother.

"Guys, I'll be okay. I'm not in pain right now." I forced a smile. "Who was the guy—the one who called you?"

"A witness. Someone hit you at high speed and took off. The guy told me he called the police and ambulance and helped you get out of the car. What did he say his name was again—uh, I scribbled it down. It was Bryan something …" My dad searched his wallet.

"Who cares right now. She's awake finally," Dan interrupted.

My brother had bags under his eyes. He clearly hadn't been sleeping. He had the same droopy look on his face—the one he bared the months following our mother's death. It was hard to look at him. It was just over a year ago. My mom and I were out riding our bikes for ice cream, when someone jolted out and backed over my mom, killing her instantly. We were told it was a drunk driver leaving the bar next to the ice cream shop. The driver never stopped.

We had to relive the incident all over the news. The case still comes up on various networks. They use the same picture of her—one we took on her birthday, where she was beaming from ear to ear. The vehicle knocked me down with her, cracking my head. I could only identify that the car was a black four-door sedan with tinted windows.

"I'll be all right. I'm tough and young," I said.

"It's all just so messed up." Dan shook his head. "Another stupid fucking driver who was probably drunk or on drugs or texting—who the hell knows. It's just not fair. They can't get away with this."

"I know. It's unfortunate," my dad said. "I'm just glad you're alive."

"How did that Bryan guy get ahold of you?" I asked.

"I received a call on my cell."

"How'd he get your cell number?" I asked.

"The police department, I'm certain. He made sure I had his number to call him for our insurance and as a witness to the scene. Nice guy."

A tall, lanky man walked into the room and looked around.

"Are you my hero? You Bryan?" I asked the man. Whatever drug Kathy gave me was strong. I saw double.

"I'm sorry—wrong room," the man said.

"You're not Bryan?" I asked.

"I'm sorry. She's on a bunch of drugs," my dad said and walked him toward the exit.

"She is, and so is everyone else around here. Good luck to you," the man said and walked out.

"Why'd you make him leave. Tell him to come back. He saved me."

"I think we should let you rest and come back in a little while," my dad said. "Come on, Dan. She needs to sleep."

"Yeah—she's freaking me out," Dan said.

"I'm fine. I'm fine." I closed my eyes.

"She's not going to remember anything right now," my dad said.

"My memory's exquisite," I chuckled.

"What else do you remember, then?" my brother asked.

"Huh?" I opened one of my eyes. I fell back asleep.

I woke up an hour later and saw my dad reading on a chair.

Nurse Kathy walked in the room with water. Dr. Bertain walked in behind her and startled her. "Sorry, Kathy, I was right behind you. Let's go over the report."

"Let's hear it," I said.

My spine was severely herniated from my cervical 3-8 discs. Two of the herniations he pointed to appeared to have passed through the spinal cord, but since I could prove feeling during tests, I was walking a fine line with paralysis, according to imaging. I remember observing Dr. Bertain while he scratched his balding head and remarked on how lucky I was. My mid to upper back, identified as the thoracic vertebrae, recorded as bulging discs with slight herniations. My lower back L2-S2 reported as extruding, with a potential fusion surgery for correction.

"You'll need to remain in my care for a while. We'll transfer you up to another room in the neurological sciences building. Spinal cord injuries are very serious, especially where your MRI is showing the bleeding."

As Dr. Bertain continued with my diagnosis and treatment plan, I mentally muted him.

CHAPTER 6

The cab driver veers around the emergency entrance and parks. He hops out of the vehicle and flags for assistance. "She needs a wheelchair," he shouts.

I barely have time to swipe my credit card before the driver opens my door. A man runs over with a wheelchair, and the two men help me out of the cab.

"Thank you. You've been more than kind and helpful," I say.

"You take care of yourself," he says, running around the cab.

"Let's get you checked it," the hospital attendant says, wheeling me inside Rush.

With the number of people scurrying around, Rush Hospital is more intimidating than Saint Mark's Hospital. Maybe the reason no one witnessed my pitiful fall this morning is because everyone hangs out here on Sunday mornings. Crowds of people from every direction wander to their destination. Where's everyone going? Are they visiting a sick loved one? If someone is checking in, what led them here?

The ER attendant wheels me through the hallway as I gape at all the people I'm joining in agony for the day. A rosy-cheeked woman with striking long blond hair stands in the patient-filled hallway, crying next to her companion as two nurses guide him onto a wheelchair. The man is bleeding down his left leg. At a closer glance, during my wheelchair-express guided tour, I sneak a peek at the man's wound. Gross. I draw my eyes back into their sockets and try to forget what I'm looking at. I saw bone—pukity-puke. I may hurl. It looked like he jammed his leg in a lawn mower and turned it on. The poor guy's quiet, while his wife cries hard enough there's snot running out of her nose. She blows a snot bubble, and I gag.

"I'm fine, honey. Calm down," the man says to his wife. "It's just some stitches, and then we can head home." He grips her hand.

Wow, she's an ugly crier. I blink a few times, and we reach the next display of the hospital exhibit. I watch a woman in her early thirties stand next to an open room. She looks to be waiting around for her loved one to get back. I wonder who she's waiting for and the reason she's in the Sunday exhibit. She bites the sides of her cheeks as she texts on her phone. There's a large tattoo on her arm—whiskey-brown ink swirling up her forearm and a DNA strand with an arrow striking through the center. I find the art interesting.

We roll by a few other rooms, continuing my moving tour. Many have their heads poking through curtains, bending forward to follow what their nurses are saying. When they step out of the room, they bear the same lifeless expression—eyes widened and an upside-down smile. They play it calm on the sidelines as curious observers and guardians of their loved ones. Some lack the poker face, nervously pacing in front of their loved one.

Should I have called my dad or brother? It's not too late to call them. Not so sure I want them joining the production crew of this depressing exhibit. The Saint Mark's meeting was scarring enough. Their faces looked just like each of these highly stressed individuals scattered around me. As the patient—I saw right through their poker face.

We brush through curtains and into a hospital room—my very own display case. My temporary accommodation reminds me of an oversized supply closet. The attendant wheels me toward the bed and parks the wheelchair.

"I'll be okay from here. I'd like to wait for the nurse before I get up," I say.

The attendant releases the brakes and darts out, leaving the plastic curtain of a door open—let the show begin. I'm being brought to light in my own pain-filled exhibit as the live audience in this circus of suffering passes by. I feel lonely as I stare out the curtain.

Entering the next room across from me is a little boy and his young mother. It must be his first trip to the ER, as he's expressionless. He's maybe three years old. The twentysomething-year-old mom looks terrified, struggling with exposing her feebleness in presence of her son. She's biting her nails and doesn't realize she's about to lead her son past the bleeding leg-wound man. The little boy gazes at the blood, and it's too late. She grabs his head and pulls him to her side, but his little brain soaked it all up like a sponge. A nurse brings them into the next room and shuts the curtain as the young boy lets out a high-pitched screech.

A man walking between our rooms jumps up in the air from the little boy's squeal, suddenly transforming into squawk-like shrieks from behind the curtain. I'm sure the miserable little kiddo thinks they'll cut him up like the bloody man in the hallway. The startled man drops his phone from the scare. He snatches up his phone and crouches upright as he looks in my room. The man clutches the phone in both hands and stares in my eyes. I shoot him a grin, hoping to ease the tension. He drops his phone a second time.

"Sorry, didn't see you there," he says and darts away.

What was that all about? My cheeks feel warm, and I feel a sense of uneasiness from the bizarre interaction. It looked like he recognized me. I must have seen him around the city somewhere.

"Morning, Anna, sorry for the delay." An out-of-breath nurse comes staggering into my room.

"Everything always happens at once—started as a normal Sunday, and then it went wild with accidents and the winter flu virus."

"I understand."

The nurse walks around the wheelchair to help me get up and over to the bed. I try to shove myself up somewhat to help the nurse, but my arms are limited. I let her do most of the effort.

"I went down hard on ice this morning and think I cracked my head," I say.

"We'll perform a few tests shortly, after I check your vitals," the nurse says as she prepares to take my blood pressure.

"I was practically paralyzed over the summer from a car accident and spent a month in the hospital."

"Any surgeries?" she asks.

"No, my neurosurgeon says I was a miracle case. But I'm certain my luck has worn off." I start to cry. "I can't feel my arms right now."

The nurse hands me a tissue. "It's okay; we'll have you checked out."

"This is it. I'm going into paralysis. I know it—I can feel it, I guess." I look down at my tingling limbs.

"It wouldn't happen like you're expressing. You're moving around still, even though it hurts," she says.

"I know, but my body was almost paralyzed, and I was able to move at that point."

"We're very thorough here—one of the best in the country and won't let you walk out of here without some answers," she says.

"Okay. But everything from my neck to my tailbone hurts."

"Let's start with some deep breaths," she says.

"When will the pain stop?" I ask.

"Try to relax. It'll release some of the tension."

"I'll try."

The nurse lifts my unwashed auburn locks of wavy hair and glances at the back of my neck. "There's some visible swelling. I'll snatch the doctor quick, so we can get you set up." She takes out her blood pressure monitor and works through her routine. "Geez, honey, I really need you to keep your stress level down. Your blood pressures at a dangerous level."

"I'll try."

"Your body temp is at ninety-five point nine," she says. "I'll have to—"

She's cut off by the sound of the plastic curtain sliding. The doctor steps in and grabs the nurse's notes. "Hello, Anna, I'm Doctor West. Let me skim through these notes here really quick."

"Her blood pressure is alarmingly high—her temperature is ... well ..." the nurse says to the doctor as she points to her notes.

"What's wrong with me?" I ask.

"Are you a negative blood type, Anna?" Dr. West asks. "The Rh negative blood type is rare, but we see a common correlation in these two traits."

"I'm not sure. I didn't know there was a positive and negative," I say.

"We'll be blood typing you in case of an emergency, and I'm ordering an MRI scan on your neck and lower lumbar vertebra," Dr. West says as she hands the notes back to her nurse.

"Okay, whatever helps," I say.

Dr. West lifts my hair. "Yeah, you're pretty swollen back there. In the remarks, it states here you can't feel your arms?" she asks and reaches out a pin. She begins a quick nerve-functioning process by poking each of my fingertips. "Can you feel that?"

"Barely. Not the pinky finger," I say.

"Okay, we'll get you set up with an IV and get some anti-inflammatory pumping through your veins—let's get the swelling down first," she says to the nurse.

"I'll get her set up." The nurse steps out of the room.

"Once we're finished with blood-typing and have your CBC results, we'll send you for an MRI." Dr. West holds out a light and shines it into my eyes. "I need you to hold your head straight and follow my finger. Keep your head straight, using your eyes only."

I follow instructions, but the urge to move my head takes over.

"Stop. Let's try once more." She holds her finger out.

I follow her finger. "Did I do it right this time?"

"Not even close. You may have a concussion. Try to keep your head straight, and use your eyes only, please. Try once more."

"Now?" I ask, following her finger.

"Nope." She clicks off the light and scribbles "minor concussion" in her notes. Dr. West leaves the room.

The nurse walks in carrying a tray of tools. She holds up a syringe. I take a few deep breaths and find something around the boring room for distraction. I peek at the syringe and look away.

I bite my lip and look down at the ground. My nurse is unquestionably wearing two different socks. Her right sock is navy blue, with a sturdy, upright pleat-looking hold around the lower ankle, while the left is loose fitting, with a faded appearance as though it's begging for retirement. She's dressed as though she's been working back-to-back shifts, which undoubtedly caused the sock malfunction. I feel her hand on my arm as she nudges around for a vein.

"Try to hold your head up and straight," the nurse says, interrupting my stare. She looks down and crosses her feet—she seems to notice her mismatched socks.

From across the way, there's sharp-pitch squeaks and hollers from the boy. "I hate you mom," he shouts. He turned on his mother as though she betrayed him. Every scream turns into a choking cough. Poor little guy.

"Almost set. I'm adding the anti-inflammatory through your IV now and another for the pain. You'll feel a slight burn at first," the nurse says. She pulls off her gloves and lays everything back onto the tray.

I feel an immediate release of pain and close my eyes. I remember this feeling. I lost track of days in this sedated state.

* * * *

"We'll learn how you're improving as soon as I get today's MRI disc up," Dr. Bertain said.

"Yeah. Improvements," I said, agitated. I reached my five-week mark at Saint Mark's.

"The sensations you're experiencing in both arms are a positive sign. It's a sign the inflammation's decreasing. In your case, it's improving substantially. The epidural must be working," the doctor said, lifting my arm up and moving it around.

"I still feel like shit." Rolling my eyes, I glanced away from Dr. Bertain and out the window, avoiding eye contact. I felt weak and constipated from the pain medicine—all doped up.

"I know you hated the side effects, but I think the spinal epidural did more than you realize. Anna, you listening? Your therapist agrees," he said.

I closed my eyes. I didn't wish to talk anymore. By the end of the fourth week, I decided on autopilot responses. I had pain, despite the heavy drugs, both mentally and physically. Hearing my therapist tell me "Good job" for raising my arm up over my head was the final straw. Why did someone do this to me?

"You passed the EMG test yesterday. There's something to be grateful for," Dr. Bertain said.

"Whoopie," I said.

"You're depressed. We talked about this—I'm sending your counselor up later today." He strolled around me and slid his glasses on.

"A bilateral laminectomy and fusing your L3-L4 and L4-L5 is a better verdict than last month—the artificial disc samples for your neck will be ready tomorrow morning. We'll know more from this MRI. Remember, we've got plenty of time—months, if needed—to get your discs back on their own."

"I know. All we do is talk about it."

"I understand. Just remember—you'll recover. I've had to operate full spinal fusions on women your same age. There's many out there who weren't as lucky as you," he said.

"I understand," I said.

"Let's look at your improvements; then I'll call your counselor." Dr. Bertain grabbed the disc.

I peeped over Dr. Bertain's shoulder as he inserted the MRI disc. I felt bad for being so rude to him. I was on so many drugs. The lower the dosage, the more I was able to reason. He was a nice man. His hair and short beard were white as snow. When he put his smaller glasses on, I swear he could pass as Santa's half brother. He smoothed his beard as he opened the file. Dr. Bertain removed his specs and wiped them off with a towelette. He flipped his glasses back on and moved his chair as close as he could toward the screen.

"I'll be a monkey's uncle …" The doctor stood up and popped the disc back out. "I'll be right back—grabbing another doctor."

"Where are you going? Is something wrong, Doctor Bertain? I'm sorry for being mean—it's the drugs." I heard the doctor talking outside the door.

"I'll accept your apology." Dr. Bertain popped his head back in the room and smiled. "Give me a moment."

"I'm going to kill the guy who did this to me as soon as I get out of here if something else is wrong. Doc?"

"Forgiveness, Anna." The doctor popped his head in the room. "We talked about this too. Forgive him—or her."

Three doctors followed Dr. Bertain into my room. The radiologist soon after.

"I got your message," the radiologist said. "There wasn't movement during the MRI."

"I want to see the order of people you imaged," one of the doctors said.

"That's Anna. Look. See? She has no wisdom teeth. The female before her should have two wisdom teeth." The radiologist clicks through the images. "Okay, now look *here*. On the lumbar MRI—she has an extra lumbar vertebra. See the lordosis? Those are correct. That's Anna. Trust me—I've done most of her imagining, and I almost fell out of my chair."

"I'd like you to redo the MRI immediately, please." Dr. Bertain flagged a nurse.

"What's going on? Is something wrong with me?"

Dr. Bertain pulled up a chair next to me. "Honestly, between you and me, since we've become acquainted with each other through your recovery, and I've always been straight with you …" He cleared his throat, scooting his chair closer to me.

"Go ahead, Doc."

"If this disc is correct, and there are no errors, which we are going to be sure of right now with another MRI—"

"What is it?"

"I've heard of cases where there's just something you can't explain—this will be my first experience. I don't want to jump the gun here by telling you this, as I've watched your MRIs closely—"

"What'd you find?"

"If this was an initial MRI, I'd just tell you they're large herniations. But given you're young, this could be corrected without surgery through continued therapy."

"Wait. What?" I asked.

"You're young and in great shape. Your body's healing itself, but remarkably faster than anyone I've ever had as a patient. I'm not saying that this MRI is accurate, but if this MRI we're about to do shows the same, you'll be able to continue your healing at home and with therapy."

The nurse walked in. "You need me?"

"She needs to go back for another MRI—lumbar and cervical, with and without contrast, please. I want to make sure I'm not losing my mind." Dr. Bertain exited the room.

The nurse hurried behind him with questions.

CHAPTER 7

Anna, Anna, get some rest,
Allow the drugs to manifest.
If your minds on overdrive,
You will fail, instead of strive.

Rustling around the hospital bed, I open my eyes from my induced nap. I stop moving. How long was I out? I look for Dr. Bertain.

"Doctor Bertain?" I ask.

"Why're you doing this to me?" screams a little boy. "Momma, I hate you."

I remember that voice. I was only out a few minutes. I doubt the little boy's been crying for hours. I'm not at Saint Marks. I'm at Rush Hospital, and Dr. West is my doctor. Morphine always knocks me on my ass. Will there be a second miracle today? Do people get two miracles? I feel nothing from the unremitting amounts of morphine infectiously flowing through my body. My nurse runs in the room, carrying a container. She stops and holds her chest.

"Am I on a lot of drugs?" I ask.

"You scared me—you're definitely reacting to the drugs," the nurse says. "You fell asleep for a few minutes and kept trying to face yourself toward the ground. I had to move you on your back. That won't benefit your spinal situation."

"I'm really sorry. I thought I fell sound asleep," I say.

"Some people react when it enters their system. You made me nervous for a few minutes," she says. "You watch any scary movies?" she asks.

"I do."

"You know the *Exorcism of Emily Rose*?"

"Of course," I say.

"Well, the movie came to mind, watching you move," she says.

"Seriously?" I ask.

"No, you weren't like that—only teasing. Your body was adjusting to it, though," she says. "Everyone reacts differently."

"I was going to say—if I pulled myself into a back-bend when I fell asleep, no wonder why my back's hurting," I laugh.

"At least I got you to smile. I'm leaving you some water. Try to rest, and I'll be back in a bit." She walks out of the room.

I stare at the curtain and listen to the people pitter-pattering down the hallway. I listen for the little boy. Things are quieting down.

Someone pops their head around the corner into my room. This must be the emergency room's creeper. He has a mustache and a half goatee, thick-rimmed glasses, and large purplish bags under his eyes. I stare back at him and raise my eyebrows. He pokes his lanky arm through the curtain and slides it over. He bears a clipboard in the other hand. There's a pen tied to a string that's dangling around, slapping his legs as he walks. He looks clumsy. He confirms this by tripping over the bottom of the curtain.

"Can I help you?" I ask.

"Evening, Ann … *a*, is it? Not Ann. Okay. All right—want to make sure I had the right room. My name's Tom, and I'll be taking you up for your MRI," the man says.

"I'm Anna," I say. Wait. Maybe I should've lied?

He walks to the bed and stomps down on the wheel locks. I feel the goofy kick from the top of the bed. He uses his foot to thrust the Doctor's chair across the room. The chair crashes into the wall. "You ready?" he asks.

"Do I have a choice?" I ask.

"What's that?" he asks.

"I said I'm ready," I brace for the ride.

Tom must be coming from the overnight shift. His eyes are red, and the pearls of sweat seeping out of his pores intensify his five-o'clock shadow. He rolls me into the hallway and grazes an elderly woman sleeping on a chair. The woman doesn't move.

"Whoops," he says. "Give me a moment. I'll snag you an extra blanket. It'll be cold up there," Tom says.

If there were a moment in my life, I wish I could just tuck and roll, this would be one of them. He left me in the middle of the hallway, with my face in reaching distance from an old woman he nearly decapitated.

I stare at the woman and make sure she's breathing. The woman lifts her eyebrows and pops open her eyes. She's alive. I look the other direction.

I look for the people I saw earlier. The woman with the ugly cry is now at ease. Her husband's sleeping. She's reading a book and sipping a steaming cup of coffee. Every room down the hallway is occupied. Most of the curtains are pulled shut. I look for the little boy. His curtain is shut. Hopefully the little nugget is homeward bound.

A frantic-looking man dressed in dark jeans and a black hooded sweatshirt is down the hall from me, intently talking on his phone. He strides back and forth. From his strut, he's very engaged in his phone conversation. An old woman with a cane is gawking at him from her seat in the middle of the waiting area. Her head bobs side to side, following his nervous tread. The man turns like a soldier, pacing the other direction. He's the man who dropped his phone and fled earlier.

Where's Tom? Why am I here? I hope this MRI goes quick. My thoughts are spewing recklessly from my brain—it's got to be the drugs. I'm ready to get the hell out of here. Maybe I freaked out over nothing. Maybe I'm whining over a minor herniation. No. No, I could barely walk. The morphine is clouding my brain. But what if I have a concussion? I've heard grotesque stories of people dying from untreated concussions. People can die in their sleep because they fail to go in and get checked out. You're in the hospital, stop it. Stop it. Calm down. That's it. I'm losing my mind.

The guy on the phone throws his hand up in the air, grabbing my attention. What's with this guy? I feel off about him. There's something about the way he hesitated when he looked at me. He has thick black hair with patches of gray through the sideburns and he's dressed down, as though he just hopped out of bed. I wonder what brought him here. The man skims my direction and slows his pacing. He wanders over by the elderly woman and squats next to her, continuing his phone call.

Why did he do that? I'm certain he saw me and walked away.

"Sorry—very busy the past several hours," Tom says.

"I know. A Sunday turned crazy. Hey, we heading in that direction for the MRI?" I point toward the mystery man. "I've got to ask that man something."

"Yeah, is that your dad?" Tom asks.

"No, but I think I know him. Can you slow down when we get over to him?" I ask.

Tom rolls me toward the man. The man peers down at his phone midconversation and puts one call on hold to take another. He stands up and walks around the corner.

Tom walks faster, and we turn behind the man. There's a familiar scream mixed with soft, pattering footsteps. It's the screaming little boy from earlier. He swings his elbows furiously side to side, breaking free from one of the rooms. The little boy's making a run for it. He's running for his life.

"It's just a quick shot, Jimmy," his mom cries out as she runs after him down the hall.

His little sneaker falls off as he clears past the nurse trying to stop him. The boy has his head spun back to his mom and the nurse as he gains momentum. The boy turns forward, driving his face sideways into the rear end of the mystery man. He bounces off and hits the ground. The man whips around, startled by the little boy.

Tom rolls me to the side of the hallway, next to the scene. I stare at the man. He has a narrow slit like scar from his left eyebrow to his scalp, causing some of his hair to thin out in the region. He looks at me and lowers himself next to the boy, helping him up.

Jimmy's mother catches up. "I'm so, so sorry, sir. My son's never been in the hospital before. He didn't want a shot." She slows her breathing.

"It's all right. Glad I could serve as the bumper." The man lifts the boy up.

The little boy smears the snot from his nose with the back of his hand and reaches out toward the man.

"Jimmy," the mom scolds. "I'm terribly sorry for his behavior. I'll get a tissue."

"It's all right," the man says.

"You must have kids—thanks for being so understanding." She bends over with a tissue and hands it to the man.

"Nah, never had the chance," the man says. He looks at Jimmy.

"Then thank you for being so patient," she says.

"Everything's going to be all right. Okay, little man?" he comforts. "Just follow what they need you to do, and then you get to go home."

"Hang on, Annie, I'll be right back," Tom says. "I'm going to escort the little guy back to his room." He cups his hand on the boy's shoulder. The boy, defeated, treads back with his head hunched, holding his mother's hand.

"I'll be here," I say.

The man turns and walks down the hallway.

"I recognize you," I say to the man.

He twists around. "You recognize me from where?" he asks.

"You're friends with my dad, right?" I ask.

"I don't know you, miss. I'm sorry," he says, searching over me.

"What are you in the ER for?" I ask.

I follow his eyes and tilt my head as far as I can without causing pain. He makes eye contact with a tall, slender woman in a business-casual outfit. Her long dark hair is tied neatly in a ponytail. She adjusts her black-framed glasses as she struts down the hallway toward the man. The woman stops, causing the person behind her to jump out of the way. Her heels tap the ground as she strides the opposite direction.

The man turns to his phone and types frantically. He stops and stares at me. I try to look away, but he draws me in with his eyes. He's creating a diversion for the woman. She vanishes. The man taps his phone. Two phones chime at the same time. I search for the culprits. Most people in the hallway are on their phones.

"You know them, don't you? You sent a message—I saw the whole thing. Who did you send it to?" I ask.

"You're mistaken," he says.

"What are you? You an off-duty security officer or something?"

"It seems you're confusing me with someone else. We don't know each other. My wife's in the hospital." His phone buzzes. "Pardon me, I've got to take this call."

"Then why aren't you wearing a wedding ring?" I yell to him as he walks away.

Tom walks back. "Let's try this again, shall we?"

"I asked you a question, Mister. Where's your wedding ring?"

"Okay, Ann—Anna. That kind of approach won't win you any dates," Tom says as he rolls me past the scene.

The man walks away on his phone.

What was that all about? How the hell do I know this person? The scar, eyes, and that voice. We live in Chicago—an enormous city. Maybe I pass him all time? But what about the woman and the in-sync text messages?

As we continue down the hallway, I look at Tom. I want to slap him right now. I've never hit anyone in my life, but I would swat him for the embarrassing remark about me winning dates. I would hit him a second time for removing me from the situation. That guy back there was lying about something. Lanky Tom blew it.

"You guys have undercover security here? It's a huge hospital," I say.

"There's our security," Tom says, nodding to a guard in uniform as we pass.

"That man was lying," I say.

"Some people don't wear wedding rings," Tom says, holding up his hand. "Mine's in my locker."

"Yeah, but you wear one. You're working and had to take it off. You know what, never mind," I say as we make our way through a set of doors. Beyond the doors, I see a bright futuristic-looking space room. MRI machines resemble what I picture a time-warping machine would match.

"I'll be waiting right outside the exit. Gary here will get you set up," Tom says.

"Hey, I'm Gary, your technician. Any metal on your body?"

"I know the drill—no metal," I say.

"All right, then you know to remain completely still, I presume?" Gary asks.

"Yep," I say.

"I have headphones for you. What station would you like me to play?" he asks. "You have music at this hospital?"

"Yeah," Tom says, "and you get to choose what type of music. I'm your technician and DJ rolled into one for the next twenty minutes."

"Alternative, please?" I ask.

I'm finally getting an MRI. I close my eyes and the music starts. I lie still—doped up. The music is a nice touch and nerve settling—I've never heard this song before. I wait for the next song to begin. I'm at ease.

A familiar drumbeat begins—*Alive*, by Empire of the Sun. The song takes me to a place of summer concerts and dancing around with friends. Smiles and laughter. No. No. Wait a minute. Hang on. I feel off. The tune changes, and it slows down inside my head. I remember. I don't want to remember, but I remember now. Sweat forms across my forehead, and the song continues in slow motion. I open my eyes. Make it stop. I wish I could make it stop, but I can't. I think of green grass and walking around in the summertime, but it's too late. I remember now. I remember my accident. The reason why I'm like this in the first place—forget today's spill. Make him stop the music. No. Listen to the music. I deserve to know. I want to know. I must know who did this to me—tried to break me and get away with it. I close my eyes.

* * * *

I drummed my thumbs against the leather-wrapped steering wheel to the energizing chorus and fast-paced beats of *Alive*, as turned on a shortcut. I remember the smell of freshly cut blades of crabgrass mixed with lingering hints of the hot summer sun beaming down on dry cornfields. There was a muddy, wheat-like, cornstalk odor that would quickly go away if it finally rained. As I continued down the road, the smells turned into an intoxicating combination of BBQ sauce, sweet onions, and hints of bacon.

Earlier I had worked up an appetite, as I accomplished my ten-mile mark in my marathon training. With hair still wet, I had hopped in my car, excited to get out of the big city, and catch up with my dad and brother. *I hope Dad is grilling*, I remember thinking as I gripped the wheel, excited for the day. As I made my way down an old country road, I imagined the taste of a medium-rare, horseradish-crusted filet melting in my mouth, with a sip of a bold red blend. Dad always buys steaks when I come home for a night. I rolled down the windows, hoping to catch more hints of bacon.

As I passed by each house, I noticed everyone was out doing yard work. The more I drove down the country road, the more the houses grew further apart, and the more the population decreased. There were two kids running up and down a driveway, shooting each other with squirt guns as I drove by one of the houses. It reminded me of my brother and I running around in our backyard. I remember feeling carefree, like a child who hasn't experienced the horrid reality of evil happening around us every day.

I saw a little old man and his wife walking together, holding hands down their gravel driveway as I passed their house—the last home for miles. I glanced in my rearview mirror and saw a black car gaining speed behind me. I slowed down, hoping he'd pass me. The car reduced speed and drove to the back of my bumper, forcing me to gain speed. I felt my heart pounding faster than the beat in the song. I forced my foot as hard as I could on the gas and sped up down the road. The car swerved to the gravel shoulder and stopped, leaving a cloud of dust. I stepped on the gas, flying over a set of railroad tracks.

A second sedan peeled out from a side street and swerved into my lane. The driver sped up, driving towards me head on. I slowed down and steered to the side of the road. I heard the music once more and blacked out.

They're here Anna,
This is it.
You've had your time.
You should quit.
Up Anna. Wake up now.

A sharp sensation engulfed my body. The back of my head felt like someone stuck me in an oven. I felt a pulse in my neck, and the pain engulfed my entire body, like I was thrown on top of a hornet's nest. I heard metal crushing as if someone smashed a heavy can into the back of my head.

Everything went blurry and muffled. I couldn't open my eyes. I wanted to sleep. What happened to my body? It hurt everywhere, like I was dropped inside a volcano. I sunk into the lava—if went to sleep, it would go away.

I heard voices from afar, and a warm hand brushed across my face.

"I told you they were less than thirty seconds this time," said a woman. "Our life's work."

Who said that? Where am I?

"She's breathing," one man said.

"Keep her awake; I'll make the call," a deep voice said.

"Can we slide her out?" the woman asked.

Slide who out? Me? Am I dead? I hear you.

"Just don't let her sleep—she'll die," the man said.

The man with the deep voice put his hands around my neck. "You guys go now. Get the hell out of here and find the others; she's waking up."

I rolled my eyes inside the sockets. I felt the eyeball brushing against the lid, trying to flutter my eyelids wide. Orange lighting turned to yellow-and-green colors, with some specs of copper-colored dust. A blurry face appeared through the dust.

"Miss, I need you to stay with me and stay awake. Try to open your eyes," the deep-voiced man said.

I'm trying. I heard echoing sounds of sirens from afar.

"Stay with me Ann—young lady. You were in a serious accident."

"Where am ..." I uttered.

"You need to stay like this."

I fluttered my eyelids open and saw a face blocking the sun. An orange glow looked as though it was blaring out from behind his head. It looked like he had a blazing fireball mane.

"How did I—"

"Please just stay calm. The ambulance is pulling up right now. *Everything's going to be all right.*"

CHAPTER 8

I flip my eyes open. "I need to get out of here *right* now. Get me out of here." I kick and thrust my arms as hard as I can. "The man in the lobby. I remember his voice—he said it to the little boy! The little boy in the hallway. That man. My Name. He knew my name—"

"Anna?" the technician's voice streams through the speaker. "You okay?"

"No. No, I'm not. Someone downstairs is following me. A stalker or something. I'm being stalked."

The technician stops the machine. "I'm not sure I understand what you're saying."

"Tom, the guy who brought me up here, saw him too. There's a guy following me downstairs. I need to get out of here," I plead.

"Anna, I need to finish these MRI images. You need to take a break?"

"Yes. I mean, no," I say.

"Yes, you need a break? Or yes, you're okay to finish the MRI?" he asks.

"I don't know."

"No one can enter the room without me buzzing them in," he says.

I hold my breath.

"I can see the hallway through the monitor. I'm able to see who's at the door," he adds.

"You have a camera on the door?" I ask.

"Yes."

"But what if that man's dangerous? What if he's got a gun?" I ask.

"He can't get into this room," he says.

Maybe I should stay in here? I hold my breath. It may be safer in here than out there.

"I'll call down to security and make them aware of the situation. Okay?" he asks.

"Yeah, tell them he's the man on the phone, pacing around my room with a scar on his face. Tom saw him too," I say.

"Give me a minute to call down. Hang tight," he says.

I wiggle my toes. It's cold in here. I'm not sure it's the climate or my fear causing the hairs to raise on my arms. I try to remember more of the man. I can't. Just mainly his voice and the sun beaming around his face, which was blurry from going in and out of consciousness. Dare I question myself? Are my facts straight?

A voice comes on through the speakers. "I notified security. You okay to finish your imaging?" he asks.

"Yeah, let's get it over with. Keep the music off, please," I say.

"All right. No movement. I'll make sure Tom's here to bring you down when you're done," he says.

The bleeping sounds from the machine begin again. I close my eyes and count the seconds. I get to 322, and the machine stops.

"I think I got what we need. You're all set," Gary says.

"Okay."

"Be right there to get you out," he adds.

"Okay," I say. He walks in the room and slides me out of the machine.

I feel embarrassed. "Sorry for causing a scene," I say. "Don't apologize. Claustrophobics cause the biggest scenes," he says.

"I can imagine." Gary wheels me to the door. "Tom should be outside to take you back down. The doctor will have your results shortly."

Gary opens the door, and I see Tom blowing his nose.

"Ready?" Tom asks.

"Anna told me about the man downstairs who's making her feel unsafe. I notified security," Gary says to Tom.

"What man?" Tom asks, looking at me.

"She said there was a man down by her room," Gary looks at me.

"Wasn't that the same gentleman you were questioning about his relationship status on our way up here?" Tom asks me and turns back to Gary.

"I'm not sure what happened but called security," Gary says.

"Anna, you were yelling at the man on our way up. Don't you remember?" Tom asks me.

"So, is this man a threat?" Gary looks at Tom.

"From what I saw, I think the man had no clue who Anna was," Tom says.

"Morphine effects each person differently," Gary says, looking at me.

He had to throw in the morphine factor. Great. Now I look crazy. They'll never believe me. Give it up. Give up; you've already caused a scene.

"You know what, maybe you're right. I thought I knew him. I'm sorry for all that."

"I have the next patient coming through," Gary says, looking over to the next hospital attendant.

"So you're okay with me taking you back down?" Tom asks.

"Yes, I'm fine."

"Your doctor will be in shortly with the results." Gary nods at Tom and walks back into the room.

We head back toward my room. The man and woman are gone. Maybe I imagined everything from the morphine. I could be in the middle of a bad trip from the drug. I look around. Everything around me is slowing down. Tom's dragging his feet when he walks. I hear his shoe swiping against the tiles with every step. I no longer recognize sole round me. Not one person from earlier. Even Tom looks different from before. Is that even the same guy who brought me to the MRI? We're almost to my room. I close my eyes and pretend to sleep. I fall asleep.

The nurse comes waltzing in and administers more morphine. I feel a burn inside my vein. Hello, I'm Anna. Have we met? I stare at the nurse. What's going on? I battle to keep my eyes open as I peer at my room's entryway, bracing myself for something. What thing? Wait. It's coming back now. Intruders. There may be intruders. How long was I out?

"Evening, Anna." Dr. West comes walking in with a disc in her hand. "My apologies for the delay."

"Huh? It's evening?" I ask.

"Yes, we've been backed up with patients all day."

"Oh."

"I looked at your disc, and I'd like to review it with you," Dr. West says as she pops the disc into the computer.

"How bad?"

"You have several herniated discs in your cervical and lumbar regions." She clicks through the MRI images. "A small one at C4-C5 and the one causing most of the pain right now in your neck, C6-C7. Lumbar region—it's your L4-L5. I'm seeing nerve compression here."

"So not nearly as bad as before?" I ask.

"That I'm unable to determine unless I had the previous MRI results for comparison. I wouldn't say you need surgery, just rest and therapy. I'll have a list of recommended neurosurgeons for you to follow up with."

"I was doing so well. I don't want to start over again."

"You're young. Try everything to prevent surgery, even if you have setbacks. It'll be worth it in the long run."

"I understand."

"Would you like me to go over the images in more detail?"

"No, I understand the results."

Dr. West clicks out of an image and into a new one. "Did you know you have an extra vertebra?"

"Yeah, and I'm aware of its rarity."

"Well, sounds like you had a very thorough doctor. Many doctors fail to notice this in imaging. It's uncommon."

I think of Dr. Bertain's Santa beard. "Yeah, he was great."

"I'll have a copy of the written report for you to take with. Bring it to your physical therapist. Rest three weeks before starting therapy. Oh, and I'll have a few scripts ready before you check out. For pain and inflammation. You have any questions?"

"So, what do I do now?"

"We can keep you here and continue to treat the inflammation and pain if you'd like, or you're free to go home," she says.

"I'm ready to leave."

"All right, let me get you the printout and scripts, and we'll get you checked out in no time. You have a friend or family member to help you get home?"

"Yeah, my friend told me to call her when I'm ready to leave," I lie.

"Great, be back shortly with your scripts." She nods and walks out of the room.

I look around for my phone. I should call Jessica. No. I should wait until I'm home. The doctor mentioned prescriptions. Every time I leave a doctor, she'll ask about pain meds—if they forced meds on me. I'll see tears form in her eyes.

Feels like yesterday—the devastating moment from the time I had to pry Jess from her boyfriend's arms while the cops searched his college apartment. Her three-year relationship went to shit the day we learned the man she wanted to marry was secretly dealing narcos and heroin throughout campus. Campus police found four students dead following several late-night parties because of drug overdoses. Every person pronounced dead in each case tested positive for the same unknown compound laced with the drugs her boyfriend was selling.

Jessica slept at my apartment every day for the six months following his arrest and refused to get out of bed. Once her grades slipped, I'd leave a class and dart across campus to sit through some of her lectures. I'd try to write everything word for word as I didn't know what the hell her professor was talking about most of the time. I refused to watch her fail out.

I slither upright and peek around the room for my phone. I feel a pull from the IV holding me hostage. I'll give Jess a shout as soon as I get home.

CHAPTER 9

When Dr. West said, "no time," I almost believed her. It's been another hour and a half. A different nurse, who looks to be starting the evening shift, walks in to remove the needle from my arm. I have no words. Get me out of here, lady. Get me out. She hands me the paperwork, and I crinkle it up and tuck it away. No more for today. I'm over it.

Paranoia has me on my feet and ready to react in the event of an attack. The last dose of morphine gave me the spins but has provided me the opportunity to walk out of here on my own. I look at the clock. Thirteen hours passed since my initial arrival.

I feel like I'm floating as I trudge down the hallway. One slow stride at a time, I look around for the man with the scar on his face. Peeking into every room, I'm on a hunt for anything out of the ordinary. I make sure each room has a patient and a person accompanying it. With all the rooms occupied with new cases of sickness and trauma, I realize my emergency wasn't as urgent as the others. Approaching the front entrance, I scout around once more, making certain no one was following me. The attendant at the door hails a cab for me.

Getting into the back of the taxicab, I hear no one. No car lights, people, other vehicles. I feel as though I'm carrying out a strong run for it. Operation hospital escapee to home. I can't help but feel I'm being followed. Maybe it is the drugs. But what if I'm right?

The car ride home from the hospital is quiet. No conversation. I like it. Aside from me giving my address, there's no exchange between myself and the driver.

The cabbie turns onto a main road and stops. I see lights from vehicles in every direction. Taillights, angry drivers honking horns, streetlights, people jaywalking, a group of drunks walking out of one bar and into the lounge next door, and drivers blocking the street as they wait for parking. Everything feels normal again. Cluttered and out of control, but normal.

"Home is close?" I ask the driver.

"What?" he asks.

Nope. Everything's not normal yet. I'm still a little messed up from that last injection. Maybe I was way more messed up than I thought. I may have made the entire stalker scenario up in my doped-up little mind. I don't have proof to support my allegations. I recall the look the man gave me when he looked at me in the room—could've been an honest reaction to my appearance.

I'm embarrassed. Of all the exhibits featured in today's show I somehow forced my way up as the headliner. The audience will remember me from my disturbing display as Dopey McDoperson—specializing in calling out married men not wearing a ring inside emergency rooms. I wish I could tuck and roll out of this cab. Who knows what I look like to the cab driver.

The cab drops me off in front of my home. Every home on the street has a light on except for mine. When I came home from the hospital after the car accident, my dad and brother painted signs and taped them all over the house. They turned our family room into my personal healing space. The two of them painted *Anna's Healing Cabana* on a banner and hung it over the family room. They even moved around furniture to accommodate for my injuries.

The wind stings my nostrils as I shuffle across the sidewalk. I stick my hand in the air and flip off my front porch as I establish my path around the side and to the back of my house. There's no way in hell I'm falling twice today. I trail across the wintry ground and freeze. A spotlight shines. I'm in the center of the blaring light. My heartbeat picks up pace. Stop freaking out, you triggered your own light sensors dummy.

Using the light to guide my course, I work my way through my path from earlier. The snow crunches with my steps. I feel the wind at my face and it feels refreshing. I'm sweaty from the morphine, almost feverish. A serious swing from my experience earlier.

I come face-to-face with my next obstacle—the staircase. I need to move quick before the morphine fades. The sensor light beam is bright as it reflects off the untouched parts of the snow, displaying a glisten of shimmering sugar-like frosting. If I wasn't relying on the drugs to get up the stairs, I could stand and stare at the glimmer the next few hours. Come on. Get a move on.

I place my foot on the first step and stop. The hammer from earlier is gone. It is a fact: the paint-covered tool was on the stairs this morning. I grab the railing and force my way onto the next stair, looking as far up I can see. With ease, I'm able to pinpoint the exact spot on the step the hammer was laying. There it is.

I haul myself onto the next stair. There's a shadowy impression, the remnants from the head of the hammer still engraved in the snow. I look to the right of the tool imprint and detect a fresh footprint pointing upward. I glance at the other shoe prints from earlier, each facing away from the building, now bearing a layer of snow dust from wind gusts. The new shoe print differs from the others. The size of the imprint is even different. Both prints are comparable in one entity, for they are both large enough to be men's shoes. Someone's been back here while I was gone.

I look around the rest of my yard, checking to see what else is out of the ordinary. When was the last time my dad and brother were here? Think. Was there snow? Leaves were on the ground. I remember. Yes, they came here to put away my patio furniture. It wasn't that long ago. I exhale. The release of mental tension takes pressure off my spine. I straighten my stance.

I take another step. Wait. That doesn't explain why the hammer from earlier went missing. Think about it. Stop.

My dad and brother were here to move the patio furniture and cover the deck. What does that even matter right now? Dopey McDoperson strikes again. Forget the stupid patio furniture. The hammer is gone, and your dad and brother didn't drive out here to pick it up while you were in the hospital. I feel sick. The cold air welcomes its way back to my skin.

I adjust my grip on the railing. I feel the crisp air entering through the bottom of my pants, slithering its way between my skin and fabric. The reality is sobering, and the cold has made it through my drug induced numbing agent. It's a bitter one tonight. I squint, struggling to get a clear view of the top of the staircase and entrance. The doorway is dark, with a large shadow blocking my view.

I need a light—fast. Where's my phone? I pat myself down. I fumble around and find it tucked inside a pocket. My screen lights up. Incoming call. Shit, it's Jessica. I forgot I tried her twice this morning.

Jessica and I have a pact: If we call each other twice in a row, the call is urgent. This doesn't mean there's an emergency, but to call back when you have a chance. If there's an actual emergency, we text each other 911. If one of us receives a 911 text, it means, "I don't give a shit if you're in the middle of the best date of your life. Pardon yourself and call immediately." I've only sent Jess one 911 text, and it was to tell her my mom died. On the other side, she misuses the codes and what defines an emergency, unlike me.

I'm about to take the call when I notice my phone will die upon answering it. It will be better to wait to call her once the phone has battery life. That would be a perfect call. "Hey, Jessica, I'm just getting out of the hospital, fell on ice, and—" phone dies. Realizing I've neglected my phone all day, I scan the screen. I have thirty-nine missed calls and forty-two text messages. Great.

I look up and pull a piece of my hair off my face. Something moves on the stairs and catches my eye. As the wind hisses, it whips a layer of snow across the light sensor, causing the thing on top of the stairs to shift again. Someone's watching me from the corner—I can feel it. I'm paralyzed with fear.

The wind rustles once more and thrusts frozen snow particles into my ears. Fear has me anchored to the cement step, bound by the freezing ice. I squint my eyes at the dark silhouette in the corner. I'm glued to the shadowy outlines of a stranger hiding in the dark. The light sensor shuts off.

Where's the damn hammer, Anna? I watch for body movement. *Mom, if you're up there watching, protect me.* Wind roars through the bare trees and stops. I hear snow grinding. Where's it coming from? Who's out there? I bite my lip.

My legs throb as I lower myself into a squatting position. I feel the misaligned vertebra colliding as I move slow enough to prevent the sensor from triggering. Feeling a flame rising through my leg and into the center of my back, I force past the pain and, continue to crouch. It feels like there's a person inside my lower back with a death grip on my muscle and cord, yanking them like reigns as I bend.

I reach my free hand toward the ground. Deep breaths. I touch the ground and grasp for a wad of snow, setting off the light sensor. Using the railing, I hoist myself to a midstance and launch a wad of snow at the shadow. I hear the snow clack against the wall. I hold my chest. What if something lunged out at me? Who cares now; just get inside.

I walk into my home and flip on the lights. I'm home. I turn around and lock the door behind me. I jiggle the dead bolt to make sure it's tight. Loud pounding startles me.

The sound is light at first. It's coming from the other room. I turn around and unlock the back door.

I pull the door open and flip off the light. Feverish heat enters behind my ears and seeps up to my forehead. I step back outside. This is the last thing I want to be doing right now. Where will I go? My phone's dead, and it's cold. I should've stayed in the hospital bed. The pounding turns into sounds of loud kicking. I hear yelling.

"Anna," a muffled voice shouts from behind the door. "Anna, please open. Anna, it's Jess. Open the door. I saw a light on."

Shit. Jessica. I wipe sweat from my forehead.

"Anna!" Jessica yells again.

"One minute," I shout. I slide back in and shut the door, locking it tight. I flip on the lights and stagger to the front door. I flip on the porch light, immediately shooting a spotlight on a hotheaded blondie.

"Ann—"

I open the door, revealing a spazzed-out Jessica. "Hey, I'm so, so sorry."

"What the hell is wrong with you?" Jessica thrusts the door open. "You called me twice—no, three times—scaring the shit out of me when I woke up this morning. I called you several dozen times. Even sent you a 911 text so you'd call me back, and nothing."

"I can ex—"

"Shut up and let me finish," she scorns.

I nod for her to continue.

"Then I came over this afternoon and banged on your door like a psycho, since your brother hasn't given back my spare key. After twenty calls and many painful slivers from pounding on your door, I had no choice but to get your family involved." Jessica stops to gasp for air.

"I just—" I begin and pause, seeing if she would let me talk yet. "I—"

"Did you know if you didn't answer this trip to your house, your dad was about to get in his truck and head over? I was told to call the police." Her face turns red. "You can't scare us like that."

"Can I please say something?"

"You've been bad about the phone lately, which I get. You're going through some heavy stuff, but why is it so hard to send a text?"

"I'm sorry. I'm just getting home." I look over her shoulder. "Wait a minute—how the hell did you get up here without slipping on the skating rink?"

"What? Quit changing subjects and apologize," Jessica says.

"I'm sorry."

"I spent the entire day worried. I woke up and saw your calls—"

The porch light flickers, diverting my attention. The ice. What happened to the ice? The words spewing out of Jessica's mouth muffle off in the distance. Everything around me moves in slow motion. A car driving with a headlight out inches by. I move my head with the vehicle. I no longer hear her voice. I hear nothing. The vehicle stops at the end of the street. Its brake lights snap me back in the moment.

I look at the ground. The ice is covered with rock salt and sand. How? I don't understand.

"Are you listening?" she asks.

"Jess, shut up, please. When you were here earlier, was my porch salted?" I ask.

"Yeah. Why?"

"I just got back from the hospital. I slipped and cracked my head right there this morning." I point to the top of the stairs.

"You hit your head? Wait, your back. What about your back?"

"Come in. I'll explain everything."

"Are you okay?" she asks.

"Yeah, just startled."

"Sorry if I'm being hard on you. You make me worry."

"I know, and I want to talk about it when I'm thinking clearly, okay?" I ask.

"Did they shove a bunch of narcos down your throat?"

"Can we please not go down that road right now? It's been a long day. Trained professionals monitored every drug administered, not a creepy doctor." I avoid eye contact. "So please, can we not?"

"You're right. I'm sorry. I've been following the stories on the doc a little too much. It's been stirring things up again," she says.

"I've noticed, trust me. Surprised it took this long to put him behind bars." I lock the door and shake the knob. "But before you think I've lost my mind, I have to ask: was anyone following you here? Anyone around my place look suspicious?"

"No. Why?"

"I feel like I'm being followed."

"Followed? By who?" she asks.

"A person. People. I'm not sure. Today's been rough."

"I'm sorry. You've lost me. You didn't answer my question. Are you okay? Physically?"

"I unwound months of physical therapy this morning. So that's a hard no. No, I'm not okay."

"What can I do?" she asks.

"Not yell."

"Fine. I'll try not to get so worked up. Can I see your paperwork from the ER?"

"Of course." I grab the wrinkled wad of papers from my pocket and hand it over to Jessica.

"You had some spill," she says, skimming through the report. The doctor's scripts fall from the pages.

"I wasn't planning on filling those."

"It's okay. I'm okay. I know you're not abusing this stuff. You don't have to hide anything from me."

I raise an eyebrow.

"I'm being serious. It's only a reaction from the news reports. Want me to drop these scripts off on my way to work?"

"Nah, I have plenty of pills left." I study Jessica's reaction.

"So who's following you?" Jessica asks.

"I'm not sure."

"Then how can that be?"

"I'm recognizing people. Random people. And now my porch is salted."

"I'm going to stop you there. That doesn't make any sense, love. How does that relate?" she asks.

"I don't know how. I'm spilling thoughts." I stop and see if she has anything to say. "Someone salted my porch. Don't you find that a little odd?"

"Maybe someone wanted to be kind. Did you think of that? A neighbor, the building association …" she lists off. "You're not making any sense. None."

"I can tell you're still upset with me."

"I'm frustrated with the situation, not you. I know you wouldn't do this on purpose. I was seriously worried."

"I'm sorry. I hate making you feel like this."

"I know you do, which is why I'm here. And I know you don't mean it. You remember my worst self?"

"I could've double majored—actually learned a lot from your business law class. No, but you're right about the porch. Not sure what got into me."

"Do you really feel like someone's following you?"

"I'm coming clean. I'm on a lot of hospital drugs," I say.

"Yeah, the drugs are making you crazy."

"Can we just talk about this more tomorrow? I'm exhausted and not myself right now."

"Of course. What can I do to help? Think you should stay with me tonight?"

"I'm okay. I'm fine here."

"I have a lot to prep for work tomorrow and can't stay over, so you should stay at my place. You can sleep, and I'll get my work done."

"Thank you, but I can't. I need my bed right now. Can you help me up the stairs? I just want to watch a movie and go to bed."

"Of course, I understand."

"I'm sorry again; I hate burdening you. That's all I've been the last year and a half."

"I didn't apologize to you over and over like this so shut it with the burdening shit. Here, grab on to my arm so I can help you." Jessica escorts me and stops. "Wait. I have a better idea." She steps behind me and cups both arms upward underneath my armpits, lifting pressure off my spine. "Take baby steps."

"Thank you." I tear up.

"Stop. Don't you dare start crying."

"When will this stop?" I ask.

"You're stronger than this. That's the drugs talking."

"I feel awful."

"You're nowhere near your worst. Remember when I used to hold you up behind your armpits to pee in public bathrooms?"

"Yes, unfortunately."

"At least you're not that bad; you couldn't get upstairs then," she says.

"Remember my first night out after the accident?" I ask.

"When you wore that baggy moo-moo-looking dress to cover up your brace?" Jessica asks.

"Ha, yeah." I stop. "It hurts to laugh. Don't make me laugh."

"There's nothing funny about dropping the back of your moo-moo in a toilet at a Michelin-rated restaurant," Jessica says.

"I wasn't ready to be out in public."

"No, but you wanted to get out of the house," Jessica says.

"I peed on my dress. In a public bathroom. At a Michelin-rated restaurant."

"No, you peed in the toilet that you dropped the back of your dress in. There was nothing we could do."

"I was mortified."

"You yelled at me like there was something I could've done. I was holding your lifeless body over a toilet in a stall meant for one person."

"You almost fell into the wall," I say.

I feel her hands shake as we get halfway up the stairs. They feel warm underneath my arms. I try to take more weight off Jessica.

"Stop doing that. You'll make the pain worse if you keep fidgeting around. We're almost to the top," Jessica says.

"I know. I'm sorry. I swear I saw that Bryan guy at the hospital today."

"Can we please get you to the top? You're not helping me when you stop to talk." Jessica grunts.

"Sorry. One more step," I moan.

"Now, what were you saying?" she asks.

"That man from my accident. I swear I saw him today. I know it was him at the hospital." "Why would he be there? You're not making any sense."

"It was him," I say.

"How could you be so sure?"

"I know what I saw. It was the man from my accident. The one who called my dad, remember?"

"You're going backward with healing, love. Why would that guy follow you from hospital to hospital?"

"Can't you just pretend to believe me?"

"Fine. Then did you at least ask him why he gave your dad a fake phone number? You're still dealing with insurance issues and no witness. Please drop this."

"I'll drop it for now, but what if I see him again?"

"You weren't coherent then, and you can't possibly remember him now on morphine."

"I remember him," I say.

"You need to sleep. I see that now. Keep walking—you're making me sweat."

"Sleep sounds nice."

"I feel bad I wasn't with you at the hospital today," Jessica says.

"I wouldn't have made such a scene."

"Exactly. And I could see what you're talking about. The guy from the accident," Jessica says.

"I shouldn't have brought it up."

"I'm sorry I'm acting pissy with you. I got none of my work done today, and I was scared something happened to you. You need to get better at using your phone, like you used to."

"Oh, so I can see the things all my fake friends are doing on social media without me over and over."

"I'm not a fake friend and have gone through this with you from the beginning. Please, out of respect for me and your family, keep your phone on you."

"I promise."

"Where's your phone right now?"

"It's dead. I forgot to charge it last night. Sorry," I say. I grab my phone and hand it over to her.

"My point exactly. Give me your phone."

I fidget around for my phone.

"Yikes, your screen's shot. You went down hard," she says.

"I feel the way the screen looks." I plant my arms on the edge of the bed and wait for Jessica's aid.

"Let's get you to bed. Hopefully this mangled up phone charges." Jessica plugs my phone in and walks over to me. She lifts me into bed.

I watch her walk around my room. It's comforting to see her pull my clothing from the drawers. She knows her way around, like my mother once did. Forcing my eyes to stay open, I watch her stagger out of my room. She races back in with a cup of water, toothpaste, and toothbrush.

"I picked your mom's shirt," she says.

"Thanks again. Sorry for being a big pain in the ass." I watch her pull my legs out of my pants.

"Quit thanking me and try to lift your arms up."

I turn and force my arms up as high as I can, letting out a little yelp.

"Wow, you must have taken some spill. I see the swelling in your neck." She gently touches the back of my neck. "You call me if you need anything. I'll be up working."

"Promise. I'll call you."

"I'll call your dad and brother on my way home and tell them what happened." Jessica flips on my TV and hands me the remote. "Toothbrush and water are next to the bed. Just spit in the cup."

"I know the drill. Please downplay my story so they aren't worried, okay?"

"I will," she says.

"Love you," I say.

"Love you back." She flips off the light. "Oh yeah, and to give you something to look forward to, if you're up to it, I got a reservation for next Saturday at that new restaurant you've been telling me about."

"Hopefully I've got a clean moo-moo."

"Just lay on ice all week so you can hobble out for a good meal," Jessica says.

"Okay, I'll try."

CHAPTER 10

I stare out the window, ready for Jess to pick me up in a cab. With a nice dinner being the highlight of my week, I made sure I was ready, with time to spare. I feel like a lonely dog in the window, with nothing to do but wait. I'm desperate for a night out of the house.

The monotonous week finally ended when I opened my eyes this morning. I made it to Saturday. Jessica's plans for tonight helped me gain momentum midweek at moments of struggle. This week I thought about those who wake up for their full-time jobs, head to the gym from work, and maintain a social life. I was dry shampooing, ordering takeout, and spending over a half hour per sock and shoe.

I feel stronger than last week but look like an animated stick-figure drawing walking barefoot on glass with a Skip-It on my ankle. I can imagine myself walking into my old marketing firm with my unwashed hair and crooked hobble. Maybe I'd get my old job back out of pity.

On Thursday I was aching to lie down in the tub, take a hot bubble bath, and read. I was able to sit in a slant, upright position, but I couldn't move my neck much. I improvised with household items. I filled eight large Ziploc bags with air and spread them across the bottom of my tub for cushioning. Filling the tub with water, I stretched apart the Ziplocs. I failed. The pitiful sight resembled a kid trying to plunge in a pool of small flotation devices and landing everywhere in-between. I managed to pull myself out of the tub but grew more determined for that hot bath.

I grabbed an airplane neck pillow and a memory foam pillow off my bed. Filling up the tub once more, I used the neck pillow as a donut for my butt and the pillow off my bed for my legs. As soon as I propped my body into an L-shaped angle, I realized I forgot a pillow to support my neck. It was too late. Thanks to Jessica's rant on Sunday, I set my phone next to the tub. I even got my chance to prove my promise to keep my phone by my side when I called her out of work Thursday morning to get me out of the tub. I cringe and hope this won't come up at dinner tonight.

My phone rings.

"I'll be outside your place in a few minutes," Jessica says.

"You're early," I say.

"I was going to see if you needed me to help you put your clothes on," Jessica says.

"Hang on." Her voice muffles. "Sir, I see you staring at me in the mirror."

"Jessica, what's goi—"

A man's voice trails.

"No, we're not picking up a drunk girl. She has a spinal cord injury. Can you please just keep the meter running? She can't dress herself."

"Jess," I yell out.

"Sorry about that."

"First off, I heard that. Second, I've been dressed for hours," I admit.

"Oh, great. I'll be there in exactly two minutes. I'll run up and help you down the stairs," she says and hangs up.

She always hangs up the phone. No goodbye nor proper closure at the end of a phone conversation. I've continued conversations in the past, only to discover I was talking to myself. At least when we were kids using landlines, I'd hear a dial tone and realize she was gone. Her mother even does it. I guess the sour apple doesn't fall far from her family forest.

As the cab pulls up, a smiling blonde pops out, gracefully jogging toward me in neon-yellow heels. Her hair's curled loosely and bounces as she dashes my direction. She's wearing a pair of trendy denim pants. I can imagine how beautiful her top is underneath her lint-free, dry-cleaned dress coat.

"You look gorgeous," I shout from my doorway.

"You cleaned up well since your Thursday-morning mishap," Jessica says.

"I thought we agreed not to talk about that tonight."

"I had to get one out of my system before we're among friends. Shall we?"

I see swirls of energetic lights from the cab. Radiant rose reds crisscrossed with sweet-corn yellows glistening from afar. I'm in awe. As the cab pulls up to the restaurant, I notice stripes of lime-green fluorescent lights braided with zigzag streaks of lavender. The colors decorate the egg-white contemporary structure. People exit the establishment wreathed in smiles as they walk by. I feel pain from the cab ride but sense the ambiance of the restaurant will be contagious.

The wind carries aromas of caramelized onions and fresh garlic as I step out of the cab. I feel my taste buds dance. Each time the door pops open, I feel gusts of heat brush against my face. The patches of warmth are bundled with savory spices, exploding into my nostrils when I inhale.

"I'm so excited," Jessica squeaks. "Look, my heels match the lights."

"Slow down. I can't walk that fast."

"Sorry about that." Jessica takes my arm and guides me.

"I don't want my limping to turn heads."

"You turned heads before the accident, Anna." Jessica turns to me and shoots a warm smile. "You need to get your confidence back. Let's find you a boyfriend tonight."

"Ha. Absolutely not. A priority before a man would be a job."

Jessica pushes open the door, revealing a full house.

"Wow. It's beautiful in here." Jessica's jaw drops.

"Pictures didn't do this place justice," I say.

"So we're a little early. My friends from work aren't here yet. Let's snag those two seats at the bar." Jessica points to a couple paying their tab.

"Drinks?" I ask.

"Yes, please. Grab the first round, and I'll check us in."

"I'm on it," I say, hobbling to the bar, ready to snag the two seats. I pull myself onto a stool and watch Jessica glide through the crowd.

Glowering upward, I first notice the shimmery, diamond-like flickers reflecting off one chandelier. Prismatic glitters of ruby red and amethyst purple brush across the bar. There are at least thirty chandeliers filling the ceiling, each unique in style and incorporating all the contrasting colors from outside the restaurant. Each fixture is dazzled with highlighting pieces contrived from random fabrics, beads, and splattered paints. Accents are subtle on each chandelier, baring plentiful contrast to draw one in.

The tables and chairs compliment the brilliant lighting made up of various shades of reds and yellows. I notice the furniture is simplistic enough to highlight the lengthy electric-green fabric that's draped over each table. The plates, from what I gather, look custom made. Every dish is matched with either a chalk white or mustard yellow, featuring artwork of the chandeliers at various angles on each plate. The gleaming from the light reveals gold silverware at each setting, pulling the matching gold rim of each plate.

I adjust my focus to the bar and realize I've passed up several chances to order drinks. I realize Jessica will be back momentarily, and I haven't done a single thing but gawk around.

"Can I help you, miss?" the bartender asks.

"Can I have two dirty martinis—your recommended vodka, please?" I ask.

"And make them super dirty, please," Jessica says, startling me from behind.

"Sorry, I was busy checking out the place. I never looked at a menu," I say.

"The bartender's very handsome," Jessica says as she smiles at him from across the bar.

The bartender comes back with two glasses in his hands, bringing the shaker and jar of olives with him. "Where you ladies from?" the bartender asks.

Jessica disregards his question. "This is my friend Anna," she says.

"Anna, I'm Jordan," he says, reaching out his free hand.

"I'm going to use the ladies' room really quick," Jessica says and gets up and walks away.

"Sorry about her. That's my friend Jessica."

"You live in the city?" he asks.

He smiles at me in a flirtatious way, revealing his perfectly aligned sugar-white teeth. Dimples appear on both cheeks. I feel my cheeks getting warm as I smile back. His voice is almost raspy enough to hide his southern accent.

"I'm from the burbs but live close to here now. I can tell you're from the South," I say.

"I'm from Boston," he says as he prods the shaker.

"Really? I never would of thou—"

"I'm only kidding, Anna. I'm from Austin." He reveals his dimples once more. "One moment," Jordan says as he sets down the shaker to start another order.

He holds his smile at me as he walks over to help another customer. When I'm not distracted by his perfect smile, I notice he has large blue eyes. He walks back over and starts the next drink order in front of me.

"Surprised you chose the Windy City," I say with a smile.

"My dad wanted to open up this place, so I came with him for now."

"I can't even find the words to describe how beautiful the decor is." I smile and look around.

"That would be my mother's doing. What do you do?" he asks.

"How's it going?" Jessica comes up from behind me.

"You need to stop jumping out of nowhere," I say.

"Geez, woman. You were jumpy before the accident. You're unbearable now."

"The bartender, whose name is Jordan, just asked what I do for a living. What do I tell him? That I'm recovering and have been unemployed over a year?" I frown. "I shouldn't be doing this right now."

"Anyone who cares will look past that, Anna."

"I want my old life back so bad. I was getting there, but I had to fall and crack my head," I say as I smack the martini glass, shattering it over the bar.

Jordan comes running back. "Did you cut yourself?"

"I'm so, so sorry. I didn't mean too. I haven't even had a thing to drink yet," I say.

"She can be a little clumsy," Jessica says. "Our table is ready too."

"Go ahead to your table, girls. I'll bring your drinks to you," he says.

"Again, I'm so sorry," I say as Jessica helps me off the stool. "I'm mortified," I mutter under my breath to Jessica.

The host guides us over to our own green-cloaked table. We're being seated below one of favorite chandeliers yet—an oversized clover-green antique twinkles above our table. It's dusted with bright-yellow paint splatters dappled with differing shades of red, purple, and yellow jewels.

"Before your work friends sit down, I know how much you love me and want me to find someone, and I wish the same for you, but I can't date right now," I say.

"No one's ever ready for love." She smiles.

"Cute. Nice talk," I say.

"Seriously, why not put in some practice instead of shutting yourself out completely?"

"Yeah, okay. I get your point. Look, I see your work friends." I point and change the subject.

Two girls walk through the restaurant and wave at Jessica. They're wearing long, sleek business-formal dresses with high heels. I can't wait for the day I get to strut around in a fresh pair of heels. I will splurge on some fresh pumps.

"Anna, you remember Elle and Andrea?" Jessica asks. She jumps out of her seat to greet them. She presses on my shoulder, so I stay in my seat.

"Yes, of course." I stick my hand out, grateful I didn't have to waste strength standing up.

"Anna's recovering from a bad back and neck injury. It's her first night out in a while, so I've been trying to force her to relax," Jessica says.

"Oh my, I'm so sorry to hear that," one girl says.

"My mom just had back surgery. I can't even imagine," the other girl says.

"I'm doing okay. Jessica babies me a bit," I say. I feel a hand on my shoulder and turn to see Jordan run by.

"Jordan's swamped and short-staffed tonight, so he wanted me to make sure you had a first round on him. I'm your waiter, Darren," he says. "I believe these martinis are for you." He sets two dirty martinis in front of me and Jessica.

"Oh, that was so nice," I say.

"Tell Jordan thank you," Jessica adds.

It only takes five minutes until the three of them banter about work issues and the lunchroom creeper. Even the negative stories make me miss my job. I miss using my mind for design and creativity instead of watching others accomplish it on TV while I struggle to get dressed every morning.

I glance around the restaurant and notice a line has formed in front of the joint. It's unbelievable how long people wait for a taste of the latest trend. Everyone's all dressed up for the night, looking their best, ready to have a nice meal before they head out to live it up in Chicago.

I attempt to join the conversation at my table but know nothing about the food in their office. I'm about to chime in with an appropriate story to relate when Elle interrupts.

"Oh, I forgot to mention. Emily Anderson is quitting next week."

"I have to use the ladies' room. Excuse me for a moment." I place both hands on the sides of my chair and use my body weight to pull me up, trying not to let out a groan of grief.

"Anna, you need me to help you?" Jessica asks.

"No, no. I got this," I say. I take a large gulp of my martini.

I make my way around the restaurant and see a traffic jam in front of the bathroom. I found the first flaw of the restaurant—the lack of stalls.

There are two independent women's bathrooms. I know I'm not a record breaker with the time it takes to pee in this physical state, but I'm much faster than the two girls going into one bathroom. By time they're done gossiping and refreshing their makeup, I would be back at my seat.

The bathroom line wraps around a wall, placing me in close radius to the back end of the bar. I glance over and see Jordan, turning away immediately. *Don't* look over, *don't* look over … Shit, he's looking right at me. I shoot a warm smile and wave discretely. Two girls come out of the bathroom, bumping me further from the bar. I wanted to wait until after dinner to thank him for cleaning up my mess and giving a free round of drinks, but I'll feel like a jerk if I don't say anything.

Fifteen minutes later, I get to use the women's bathroom. I'm anxious to get back to my seat and have a nice meal, though I feel the appropriate thing to do is tell someone thank you for their generous act. The guy could be married for all I know and was being a sweetheart and saving me from embarrassment after I shattered glass across the bar.

I look around the bar area as I make my way out of the bathroom. I feel like I'm going to be really pissed at Jessica after the conversation I'm about to have with Jordan. I squirm between two people sitting at the bar, hoping I'd get his attention by eye contact once more. He was busy lighting a cocktail on fire, with two eggs lined up as a next step. I take in more of the ambiance.

Everyone at the bar smiles as they sip their drinks, appreciating the kaleidoscopic glimmering above. I look over to the woman sitting in the stool next to me, her back turned toward me. The woman is alone, sipping on a large glass of ice water. She reaches her arm out for a napkin, stretching her arm beyond her sleeve. I see a sizable whiskey-brown tattoo starting at the base of her wrist and coiling up her arm as she stretches out further. She uses her fingertips to pinch at a napkin. Squinting my eyes, I tilt my head and stare at the art. Wait a minute—I've seen this before.

Suddenly, the music evaporates, leaving me with echoes of my heartbeat pumping as if it were located behind my ears. I hear muffled sounds of dings and clatter from the silverware accompany the thumping. As the woman brings her arm back, her sleeve covers the giant DNA-strand tattoo on her arm. The arrow is precisely how I remember it, plunged through the center. I devour a gulp of air, trying to keep my martini in my stomach. This woman was standing alone in the hallway at the hospital. She's a part of it. That man sent a message, and she was the other receiver. Why is she here?

Taking two slow steps back, I reverse shuffle my feet. I look over her shoulder and realize she has a direct view of my table. I need to leave. Right now. How do I go about telling the girls? Taking another step back, I freeze. I don't want to drag those girls into whatever the hell this is.

I move back toward the bar to gather my thoughts. There were a few of them. For all I know, they're placed around the restaurant, watching me this very second. The more I look concerned, the more I'll reveal myself. I skim the crowd and see if I recognize anyone else from the hospital. I can't see anyone, but I can feel other's watching.

I'm going to excuse myself out of this situation and make a run for it. No. Wait. Stay calm. Remain calm. As calm as I can, I'm going to make it look as though I'm going out for a smoke. Yes, a smoke may work. My jackets at my table. A real smoker would bring their coat. Come on, Anna, think. You're smarter than this. I could walk up and tell the girls I'm not feeling well and leave. Bad idea. I don't want to give these shitheads any time to plan. Slow your thoughts. What are the chances of someone having an identical tattoo like that? Slim. I need to get out of here.

"Hey, Anna." Jordan appears. "Darren just walked off with a round of drinks for you and your friends."

"I came over here to say thank you. That was sweet of you," I say. I try to speak up loud enough for the tattoo woman to hear.

"So I was going to ask you—" Jordan begins.

"Oh—Jordan, it's my mom calling. My grandma's been sick," I say, holding my phone. "I've got to take this call. Be back."

"I'm sorry to hear that," Jordan says.

"Hello? Mom? One minute, okay? I'm stepping outside so I can hear you." I grab my wallet, taking out a credit card. "Here, Jordan, I want to buy my friends' the next round." I slide the card over to him.

Good plan. Keep going. Now she thinks I'm coming back. Get out of here. Walk. Now.

"Sure, hope everything's okay," Jordan says.

Out of the corner of my eye, I see the woman rustle in her seat. I return to my performance. "How's Grandma doing? I'll be outside in just a moment," I say as I feel adrenaline oozing through my veins. It's as though I'm injured prey. I've been gashed badly, but they continue to stalk and wait until they can finish me off. Every step I take, I feel as though I'm out in the middle of an open field, with the hunters hiding.

I step outside and hold still for what marks the longest five seconds of my life. I turn to the left and make a run for it, walking as fast as my body will allow. As I walk out into the dark, gloomy night, I hear the wind whispering. The cold attacks me at every angle as I search through my purse for disguise. Finding a hair tie, I throw my hair into a ponytail on top of my head.

Changing hairstyles, unfortunately, doesn't change my bright-auburn hair. I pull out the hair tie and clamp my hands on the top of my head. I realize I'm desperate and throw my hair on top of my head once more, this time twisting it into a tight bun. Well, this will have to work. I look around cautiously in every direction and feel sick, as though I'm sitting in a carnival teapot ride. I lift my shaky arms up to my cheeks and press tightly. *Think, you idiot. Come on, Anna.*

I pull myself close to what resembles a vacant retail space spanning out the length of a full city block. Draping my hands against the frigid cement building, I try to blend into the darkness. The sidewalk slowly turns into a slight upward slant. I spot a little neighborhood bar the next block over.

Mismatched strands of colored lights highlight the bar front, flashing every other second and begging me to walk in. The upward slant in the sidewalk flattens out as I inch closer to the illuminating safety zone. I run my hand down the back of my leg and feel the nerve pain threatening the muscle. Carefully making it to the end of the old building, I shuffle past a vast murky glass window. Crossing the window, I slowly read "Family Owned and Operated" in barnyard-red paint.

Square-shaped headlights shine into the window from behind me, revealing the inside of the old family empire. I watch the car slow down behind me through the window's reflection. I see the exhausted trickle out into the black night. I thrust myself to move faster, but my body gates me. Just beyond the sparkling lights, a red door opens. I see the door staff member step outside of the bar to light up a cigarette.

"Help me. This car's following me," I shout out at him. I walk into the street dividing the two blocks.

"You need me to get the police," he answers back, signaling at two men from inside the bar to step outside. The man drops his cigarette and runs toward me, glaring at the front windshield of the vehicle.

The car speeds off.

"Thank you so much. I have a back injury and can't run," I say with tears of joy as I walk up to the man. "He started following me from that new restaurant right down there."

"Come inside. You can get a ride from here. Been doing security here for fifteen years," he says.

"I can't even tell you—thank—"

"Don't thank me," he interrupts. "Any man ignoring a cry for help is a loser."

"My name's Anna." I shoot him a warm smile.

"I'm Chris," he says and pulls the door open.

"I'm going to make a call from here and be on my way," I say.

"Take your time. I'll keep an eye out for the car. It's odd—I've got no idea what type of car that was, and I'm a car guy," Chris says.

"It looked like a squad car," I say.

"I couldn't tell how many people were in the car when it drove under the streetlights. Windows were tinted dark. Did you see?" he asks.

"No."

"Come in. Hopefully it's not some sick freak trying to pull some Jeffrey Dahmer shit." Chris waits for me to walk in and shuts the door.

A bright light blares through the shattered screen of my phone. It's Jessica. I scramble to the back of the bar and spot the women's bathroom. I look to the bar entrance. No one followed me in. There's a back door exit close to the bathroom. I guess I have an emergency escape route. I slip inside the restroom and take a deep breath. Jess will yell. She's going to kill me. This looks bad. I look bad. I call her.

"Hi, I can ex—" I start. Jessica's voice takes over.

"Anna, where are you?"

"Okay, give me a second to process, please," I plead.

"Process?"

"Yes," I say.

"I'm trying to process what your new boyfriend Jordan just told me," she says, raising her voice.

"What do you mean?"

"He said you had to take a phone call from your mom and took off," she says.

"Yeah, I said that."

"Well, you and I both know you can't possibly take a call from your mother—"

"Jessica, I need you to listen to me right now. Please let me explain," I interrupt.

"What? You poop your pants or something? I'd let that slide."

I grit my teeth. I want to smack the sarcasm out of her.

"Answer me. Because I don't know any other reason a normal person would bail on her best friend. We're sitting around waiting on you to order food. Who does that?"

I look around the bathroom stalls. I search for feet and push the stall doors open. I'm alone. I'm alone and losing my mind.

"You there?" she asks.

"I'm here," I say.

"Wait a minute. What's that sound? Did you peace out and go to another bar? I hear music."

"I'm in the bathroom. The music's loud in here."

"Wait. You still here? The bathroom here?" she asks.

"Uh, not exactly."

"These bathrooms don't have the Metallica *Black Album* blaring when you walk in the ladies' room. Where are you?"

"If you'd let me get a word in, I could explain," I snap.

"Fine. Start talking, and make it quick. I've got hungry friends ready to order food at the table," she says.

"Where do I begin?" I ask.

"Anna, you just said you wanted me to shut—"

"Stop! Enough talking. Just listen to me. Where are you standing right now?" I ask.

"I'm by the women's bathroom. Why?" she asks.

"Oh no."

"Why?"

"Okay. You need to listen to me. Follow what I say."

"Now you're freaking me out," she says.

"I need you to look for someone. But you need to act causal," I say.

"I'm getting nervous. What's your deal?

"Don't talk right now. Stop talking about feeling nervous. Just listen to me and act natural," I say.

"Okay."

"Don't do that concerned motherly look you do all the time," I say.

"It's kind of hard not to. You're making me feel uneasy."

"I saw someone, and I need to see if they're still sitting at the bar. So stand there and try to look natural."

"You drunk or something?"

"I'm being dead serious. Please do what I say."

"Geez, Anna."

"Don't say my name aloud. I'm going to describe the person to you, and I need you to tell me if you see them," I say.

"Yeah?"

"Was that a question or a yes?" I ask.

"No?"

"Loosen up a little. Pretend you're flirting with some hot guy and put on a smile."

"Okay," she says.

I hear heavy breathing.

"Jessica, seriously? I can tell by the amount of air you're pushing through your nostrils that you're doing your creepy smile thing."

I hear heavy breathing.

"Wow, I can actually hear you smiling through the phone. I can't believe you don't snore at night. Stop that," I order.

"Ummm. What is it you want to *tell* me, dear?" Jessica asks.

"Oh my God, I can only imagine what you look like right now. I bet you look like the clenched-teeth emoji."

"Okay, what do you want to tell me? I have friends waiting for me at the table, and this is weird," she says.

"There's a woman at the bar—".

"Thanks, Jordan. I've got her on the phone now … okay …" Jessica says.

"Holy cow, you're really taking me seriously I see. Chatty Kathy, I *really* need you to focus here," I shout into the phone.

"I'm here, sorry," she says.

"It's that Bryan guy again from my accident. They're at the restaurant," I say.

"He's here?" she asks.

"Well, not him. There were two other women with him at the hospital. One's sitting at the bar. Her hair is pulled up, and she's wearing a black leather jacket. Second stool closest to you. Jessica? You hear me?" I ask.

"Yeah. Yeah, I'm here. I was nodding and trying to decide if you've lost your mind. I'm starting to worry about you," she says.

"You're such a smart young woman, Jess, but I swear you'd make the world's worst agent. I'd feel unsafe around you. And I'm fine, I swear." I scratch my forehead. "Jess? You still there?"

My screen goes blank. What's happened? This couldn't be one of her normal goodbyes. What if the woman did something to her? Do I call the police? Maybe call the restaurant? Both?

My phone makes a ping sound.

Jess: *It's me … Agent Jessica.*

Me: *Oh thank God! I thought something happened! I can barely read my screen.*

Jess: *I'm in the bathroom and there's a line behind me so make it quick. You were scaring me. Seriously???? What's up with you?*

Me: *Okay. I want you to look for that woman. Hair pulled up. Black leather jacket. Seat #2 at the bar. … Tell me if she is still there please????*

Jess: *I already checked when I hung up … There's a guy in that seat now.*

Jess: *Wait a minute …*

Me: *… ?*

Me: *It's been over 2 minutes. You're worrying me now!!!! JESS!*

Jess: *Okay. So, she had a tab left on the bar where she was. She must've gotten up right before I came over …*

Me: *Jess go look at the name on the receipt!!!!*

Me: *Jessica?*

Where did she go? Breathe. What do I do now? I call her. Voicemail. I call her again, voicemail. Think Anna. I slide my fingers across the shattered glass and search for the restaurant's phone number.

My phone pings.

Jess: *She paid with cash. I asked Jordan what she ordered and if he's seen her before Hang on … I'm still talking to Jordan.*

Me: *Okay. TY so much. Sorry about this. I know how this sounds.*

Jess: *Your soon to be boyfriend and I both forgive your crazy ass! You're cut off. You're smarter than this.*

Me: *???*

Me: *I'm not following.*

Jess: *You shouldn't be drinking on pain meds. Very stupid.*

Jess: *You on your way back then? You need to eat. Your man says he's holding your card hostage lol.*

Me: *I'm not on pain meds FYI and you sound drunk!*

Me: *I didn't mean that. I'm not so sure I'm ready to be out. Tell your work friends, I'm sorry for leaving. I need to go home and rest. Xoxo text you when home.*

Jess: *I'm sad, but I totally understand love ... You're not acting like yourself tonight. I'm worried.*

Me: *I know.*

Me: *PLEASE. PLEASE. GET. MY. CARD. FROM. JORDAN.*

Me: *Jessica?*

Me: *Don't forget to get my card!*

She's going to forget.

I walk to the hand dryer and stand under the heat. Not sure I feel the conversation with Jess went well. She doesn't believe me. Would I believe her? Nope, I'd think she's mixing pain meds too. I squint and skim over her texts through the glass cobwebs. I sound unstable. Great.

I lean against the door and press it open. Everyone's fixated on what looks like an overtime Bull's game. The bar is silent. Eyeballs gridlocked to the game. I step out of the bathroom and walk past the crowd. No one flinches from my presence. I watch the timer on the screen as I sneak by. Thirty-four. Thirty-three. Thirty-two. Thirty-one. Time-out. Foul. Swear words echo from fans around the bar. I step outside.

"Everything okay?" Chris asks.

"Uh, yeah. That was nerve-racking," I say.

"The manager's filing a report regarding the incident." Chris pulls out a business card. "I said I'd go in and give details in the morning from what I saw. If you want to add anything, here's his info," he says, handing me a business card. "Want me to grab you a cab?" he asks.

"Yes, a cab would be nice. Make sure its identifiable."

Silence.

"Sorry, bad joke. I'm exhausted," I say.

Chris signals to a cab from across the street.

"Just so we're clear, you saw what I saw, right? A car? Someone following me?" I ask.

"Yeah, why?" he asks.

"It felt like a nightmare. Never thought something like that happened in real life, but it does," I say.

"Buy one of those mace key chains," he says.

I nod. "What would've happened if you weren't there?"

"You scream at the top of your lungs and do what you can to strike first," he says.

The cab pulls up.

"Good advice," I say.

"I've got two younger sisters." He signals for the cab to roll down the passenger window.

"Hey, Chris, tell your manager I'll be in touch in the morning. And thanks for the advice," I say.

"Anna, right?" he asks.

"Yeah."

He waits for the driver to roll down the and takes out his phone. "I'm taking a picture of your cab. Get her where she needs to go safely please," Chris says.

"Sir, I drive for a cab company. I don't need an app to get around," the driver says.

"I'm fine," I say and slide in the cab.

"Fair enough." Chris shuts the cab door. "Night, Anna."

CHAPTER 11

The cab rolls up to my home. I look at the stairway leading up to my front porch. I feel cemented to my seat. What happens when I step out of the cab?

"Your stop?" the driver asks.

"Uh, yeah." I fumble around for my wallet. "Will you make sure I make it inside?"

"Is this the right home?" the driver asks.

"Never mind. I'll be fine." I press my face against the window and check the sidewalk. My surrounding neighbors' lights are on. I step out of the cab.

The taxi zips away, leaving me in the street under a flickering light post. I turn around and patrol the street in-between steps as I make my way to my front door. I hear rustles from the bare trees. Nothing looks unusual. Nothing out of the ordinary.

The warmth inside my home feels comforting as the heat coils around my body. It feels good to be home and away from chaos. Part of me wants to ignore my fearful intuition of being followed and give my battered body a night of rest. What if they know where I live and are watching me this very second? Maybe I shouldn't be here.

I take out my phone.

Me: *Hey Jess, would it be okay if I stayed at your place tonight? You can grab me on your way home …*

I walk in my kitchen, put my finger on the light switch, and stop. I look out back. The back-porch sensor lights are on. I rub my eyes and walk to the back door. Who's there? I press my face against the glass and feel hairs raise on the back of my neck. The darkness surrounding me in the house makes me feel like a stranger in my own home. It's too quiet. My thoughts feel like someone's standing behind me in the kitchen, whispering behind my shoulder. *Get out, Anna.*

The wind coils a heap of snow against the window. I pull back. Through a streak of light, I spot the hammer on the steps. How? The light sensor shuts off, leaving me standing in fear, all alone, in my pitch-black kitchen.

My heart beats faster. It may burst through my chest. I feel dizzy. *Mom. Hammer. Hospital. Car accident. Car crash. Mom. Hammer missing. Taunting. Stalker. Black car. Bryan. Scars. Hammer not missing. DNA tattoo. Hospital. Pain. Pain. Pain.* It feels as though I have an atrium of butterflies flocking around inside my stomach. Their wings brush against my heart as they beat their wings, tearing through the muscle, dying to break free. I feel them shudder through my rib cage as they burst through the slits between each rib. *No. No more. No more pain. No more taunting*. I've had enough.

Beads of sweat force through my pores. The fright inside me now feels like a fireball working through my system as though I swallowed hell itself, chewed it up, and spat it into a garbage can. Adrenaline consumes me as though I self-administered it with a needle. I want to take the hammer and whip it through the window.

I grab my phone.

Me: *Hey Jess. You're probably finishing up dinner. I'm already in bed. Good movie on. I think I need a good night's rest. Disregard earlier message! Xoxo I'm not crazy, I swear.*

I step back from the door and lean against the wall. If I'm going to outsmart these psychos, I must act normal. I need to make the stalker feel like they're hunting and catch them when they least expect it. Why should I run if I don't know what I'm running from in the first place? My phone vibrates.

Jess: *You're always doing that lately lol. Just wrapping up din din and going to grab another drink from here. Get rest xo*

I set my phone down and close my eyes. Deep breaths. I tiptoe through my kitchen and reach for a knife. I grab a dish towel and wrap it inside. The light sensor flashes on. Out of the corner of my eye I see a shadowy figure step out of the light. Okay. Here it goes. Act normal. I dial 911 and lock my phone. Hiding the knife, I walk over to the light switch. And action. Remain calm.

There's a faint sound coming from the laundry room. Scraping sounds like a raccoon climbing around on the roof. I walk over and flip on the light. The noise stops. Maybe the wind? I grab a spray bottle of cleaner and a bottle bleach from the laundry room. I grab a bucket and lay the chemicals and the knife inside. It's ten o'clock. Now what do I do? What would I normally do? Popcorn and a movie would allow me to dim the lights and sneak over to a window.

I grab a bag of popcorn and put it in the microwave. Each second feels like five. Whoever's out there has a clear view of me from the window as I stand here in front of the microwave. I'm like a deer in an open field. The pop from the first kernel startles me.

I bring the bowl of popcorn to the living room, turn on the TV, and look around. The blinds are closed. No one can see me from the living room. They'll see the lighting from the TV and fall for my stunt—I hope.

I turn off the kitchen lights and grab the bucket. A commercial brightens the TV screen. I slip into the living room and hide against the wall. The TV screen goes dark. *Now*. The next commercial starts. I missed my moment. Even if I wasn't injured, I don't think I could dart across the open space in one second flat. The screen goes dark. *What are you doing? Go. Now.* I hold the bucket handle and thrust myself past the window and onto the first stair. I feel my right leg drag lifelessly behind my body. I hug the wall tight. The TV screen lights up with people dancing in bright-color onesies. I exhale.

The stairs look like a painful climb. I can do this. One at a time. Climb a stair and take a break. Slow and steady. What if I need to get back down? This plan has flaws. Wait a minute—I don't really have a plan, and I'm holding a stupid bucket. What's upstairs? A window? I plant my foot on the first step and climb.

CHAPTER 12

An orange glow from the streetlight shines through a bent blind. I shuffle through my dusky bedroom, using the light as my marker. The bucket clunks against my bedpost, and I stub my toe on the edge. "Oww!" Gritting my teeth, I feel around for pillows and slide two of them off the bed in front of the window.

I kneel on the pillows and fold the end of the bent blind in half, giving me clear vision of the street. It looks like a quiet night. A long, boring night. Better than what could be at the opposite end of the spectrum. How long do I sit here and watch?

I remove the knife and chemicals, twist off the tops, and set the bottles on the ground. My nostrils sting from the bleach. What would this do, if I shot it into someone's eyes? The spray-top shoots like a squirt gun and may reach further than my mace. I run my finger across the bottle-rim and pour the bleach into the other chemical bottle. I'll regret pouring this in the dark. A few drips leak through my fingers and down the side of the bottle. I shake the bottle and set it next to the knife. Now, I wait.

Time's ticking slow. Not much happening this Saturday night. A couple holding hands. A man and his dog. A drunk staggering home. I yawn. Three of the cars parallel parked on the street are buried with snow from plows. An interior light turns on and off in a car parked behind one of the snow-packed cars. I lean closer to the window.

Someone in a baseball cap scampers down the sidewalk and enters the passenger side door of the car. What the hell? The car sits. No exhaust. No headlights. It remains parked in the cold during the middle of the night.

Almost an hour has passes. My eyes feel heavy, and I my limbs tingle from nerve pain. The passenger door opens. Someone pops out and runs to the trunk. The light from the trunk shines bright enough, revealing a woman under the baseball cap. She bows in the trunk and pulls out what looks to be a large jacket and a blanket. She's close enough to the light, where I see her breath in the cold air. I squint my eyes.

The woman rips off her jacket and tosses it in the trunk, revealing a T-shirt. She lifts her hands to her mouth and attempts to heat them up. A car drives by, and she lunges. Odd. She leans toward the light and reaches for the jacket. As her arm brushes across the light, I see the DNA strand tattoo. My heart accelerates.

I reach for my phone to call the police. No. Not yet. I have a chance to confront her. Find out what the hell she's doing. Maybe they're confusing me with someone else? I grab ahold the window ledge, force myself upright, and tuck my phone in a pocket.

I sit on top of the stairs, with both weapons, and slide down on my butt. This is it. I wasn't losing my mind. I'll catch them off guard. A knock on the window and a spray to the face if they try stepping from the car.

I lay down on my stomach at the bottom of the stairs and slide across the floor, sliding the knife and bottle to the back door. My teeth clatter uncontrollably and I'm tight in the chest as though I'm wearing a corset two sizes too small. I'm trembling but feel feverish. Hidden by the kitchen island, I crawl on all fours to the laundry room and force my body up to the switch box. I use the light from my phone to find the master switch for the back sensors. Got it. I pray my dad labeled the switches correctly.

With a knife in one hand and the bottle latched to the back of my pants, I slip out the back door. The sensors are off. I step down to the second stair and flail an arm. The sensors are still off. The imaginary death-grip corset now feels one size smaller around my chest. I wrap my armpit over the side of the stair rail as though I'm using a crutch and slide down. My heels slam hard onto the concrete and I clasp the railing, catching myself from landing on my back. The nerves connecting to each of my limbs, feel like they've been electrocuted.

Snow trickles inside my shoes as I tread to the fence surrounding my yard. The slush melts through my socks, gluing gravel particles to my feet. The ice-cold liquid rises through the fibers of both pant legs, causing the fabric to stick to the skin of my calves. I'm halfway there. I feel like a creature prowling through the night as I sneak against the fence toward the front of my home. I feel in charge. I feel ready. I'm in my element. I'm hunting my hunters. I'm in control. I jab the knife outward. *One. Warm-up.* I jab it again. *Two.* I take a step and thrust the knife forward.

Three. In case I must use this thing. The wind blows snow at my face. Breathe. Keep walking.

A light pole highlights the street and sidewalk. I see the parallel parked cars from afar. The medium sized evergreen trees between my house and the neighbor's, skewing my view of the crazy lady in the car. I grip the knife tight and grab the spray bottle from my pocket. A large shadow darts at me from the bushes.

I point my knife and shuffle backward.

The man stops and backs in one of the evergreens.

"Anna, stop," the man says.

"How do you now my name? What do you want?" I ask, waving the knife around in the dark.

"Please, Anna, you don't know what you're doing," he says calmly.

"Help! Help me!" I scream.

The man lashes forward, and I whip the chemical bottle, hitting him on the leg. He runs behind me. I turn and hold my knife out in the dark and jerk it around in front of me, ready to stab him.

Sounds of rapid snow crunching grow louder. The man springs at me from the side. He swivels my body sideways and catches me in a cradle-like position. He cups my mouth. I bite down on his hand like a wild animal.

"Anna, I'm not going to hurt you. Calm down," he says, gritting his teeth.

"Help!" I cry. I violently drive my body side to side.

"You're in danger," he says.

I bite harder on his hand. My teeth chomp through his flesh like a fatty piece of steak until I taste his blood.

He rips his hand away. "I'm here to protect you. I can explain everything. Just keep your voice down, or they'll hear you," he says.

"Who? The deranged woman in the car?" I ask.

"Just don't scream," he says.

I relax in his arms and wait for him to loosen his grip. I hold my breath and yank my body hard to one side, swiping his stomach with the knife.

"Shit." He jolts back. "I can't believe you stabbed me." He grabs his side. "You got me good."

"Stay back," I say.

"You're in grave danger," he says.

I hold the knife in front of me, facing him. I recognize his face in the hazy moonlit sky. I see the scar.

"It's you. I knew it—from the hospital." I say.

"I can exp—"

"From my accident. You were there. Tell me you were there," I demand.

"Anna, calm down."

"You were at my accident. You were at the hospital. You lied to me. You're a dirty liar." I clench my teeth.

The neighbors turn a light on.

"The neighbors are coming out. They'll call the police. One's a Chicago cop."

"Anna, please let me explain," the man pleads.

"Stay back—I'll stab you again."

"I'm an undercover agent, and you're in trouble. I can prove it to you. Watch, I'm laying down. You can stab me to death if you'd like." He lays facedown on the ground.

"Prove it, then. You have seconds."

"I'm with the Life Force Preserve. I'm not going to hurt you. We're not safe out in the open like this." He lifts hands over his head. "I pulled you out from the car. Me and other agents."

"I'm supposed to believe that? I'm an agent too, then. I can't prove it but believe me when I say it."

"Miss Gibson, please don't get smart with me. We're running out of time."

"No, you're running out of time," I say, watching a second light turn on. "Who's that woman with the DNA tattoo?" I ask.

"Leslie. Another agent on the team," he says.

"There was a second woman at the hospital," I say.

"Cindy—another agent. They were guarding the wings at the hospital."

"You're full of shit."

My neighbor steps outside. "Hello? Someone need help?"

"I was there when your mother was killed. We all were. It was a setup, not an accident. Remember you couldn't identify the type of vehicle they used?" he whispers.

"It's me, sorry," I yell back to the neighbor. "I slipped on ice but I'm okay."

"You need help?" the neighbor asks.

"I have a friend here now. Thank you," I shout.

"Okay. Goodnight, then," the neighbor says, shutting the door and flipping off the light.

"You're saying, my mom's death was a murder? How do I know it wasn't you people?" I ask.

"Your mom was killed by a Stag. My guy Hank took off in our ops car after the vehicle … he was posted across the street. I called the police while another agent stayed with you and your mom," he says.

"I'm not following. The woman—"

"Theresa. A tall, beautiful African woman. Remember her?"

"Yeah."

"She was an LFP agent, not a witness. I had no choice but to discharge her from all public duties after she breeched the rules and jeopardized our operation to comfort you."

"She was an agent?" I ask.

"Yes. Can I stand up?" he asks.

"No, I don't believe you."

"Look, I was with your mom and dad the day you were born. You—"

"Impossible. Keep your hands above your head."

"It was my first week out of training, and I was driving behind our squad leader, tailing your parents in a cab. We were in gridlock traffic on Lake Street and Upper Wacker Drive. Can I please stand up? We should discuss this inside, we may have an unwelcomed audience."

"Not yet. Keep going with your story."

"You were born in a cab. My squad leader fled his car in the middle of traffic and helped deliver you in the middle of the traffic jam. I'm sure you've seen the article from the paper. That man in the photo led my squad. He told your parents he was a retired officer from—"

"The East Coast," I say.

"Yes, I'm sure your parents told you the story many times."

"It makes sense now—why Phil never gave them the exact state and city he retired. My parents said they couldn't find him to send a card."

"He was right about the retirement. Main headquarters dissolved him from the squad after his very public appearance. Now he's chief officer at the US headquarters."

"You can stand up," I say.

"Can we go inside? It's safer. We shouldn't be having this discussion in the open. They may be watching," he says.

"Who's they?" I ask.

"The Stags. I know you have questions. Just ask them somewhere safe." He stands up.

"You're scaring me. Why are people—"

"They're not a group of people," he says.

"I don't feel well. I'm light-headed."

The man runs over to me and holds me up before I faint. He puts my arm around his neck and walks me to my back door.

"I'm Bryan."

"So you gave my dad your real name?" I ask.

"I did. But now you understand the fake number."

"What you said about me not knowing the car that killed my mom. A similar car followed me from the restaurant tonight."

"Leslie, the agent with the DNA tattoo, couldn't tail you. For the first time you went off our radar."

"Because I was running from her. I think I'm going to puke." I lean over the side of the stairs and vomit. My back spasms. "Did they do this to me? My spine?"

"Yes. I'm sorry."

"But why?" I dry heave over the railing and jolt the knife upward. Tears emerge.

"Deep breaths. You'll only make your spine worse. Can I take this knife from you before you accidentally kill me?"

"I'm sorry I stabbed you." I hand him the knife and cry.

"It's fine. I'd let you stab me as many times you need to if it meant keeping you safe." Bryan says, opening the back door.

I flip on the kitchen light. "You're bleeding through your shirt and jacket."

"That was an impressive move for an injured young lady."

"There's a first aid kit under the sink," I point, hunching over the kitchen island. I can't control my tears.

"Stay there," Bryan says.

"Why? Why did this happen? My mom. My accident." I cry harder.

"LeeAnne was an Interhybrid."

"I don't understand."

"The Stags know Interhybrids possess something in their DNA—proteins in the blood that can revive a sick human."

"I need a bucket. I feel it coming up again." I dry heave on the counter.

Bryan walks over and rubs my back. "I understand this is difficult to process. I always wondered how you'd handle the news. There will be a moment soon where the LFP must reveal this info to their Interhybrids. I thought, I'd have a script or something prepared for you."

"What am I? What am I?"

"You, like your mother, are an Interhybrid."

"No, you've got that wrong." I feel my eyelids filling up.

"No, Anna, you're an Interhybrid," he says.

"I can't be."

"You don't even know what it is. You possess the most precious blood on earth."

"I'm a human. Stop calling me that. I'm human."

"Breathe for a moment and listen. It's not a bad thing. There's nothing wrong with you. The Stags are trying to kill off your kind because they know you're the key to human existence."

"Who are the Stags?"

"Sit down for a moment." Bryan pulls out a stool. "Stag is slang for Astargarians. They're from another planet resembling Earth."

"You mean aliens?"

"Yes, though according to them, we're the aliens. They've been living on Earth for a while, blending in. Creating viruses such has West Nile and AIDS, to name a few. Our scientists have traced each virus to the same source of origin."

"This is insane. You sound insane. If this is true, why aren't you alerting the world."

"And cause an uproar? What would you do if you discovered there may be a real apocalypse?"

"I feel like I just did. I'm scared to death. You're telling me the truth."

"My point exactly. Imagine every culture and the entire world learning this at once. We have another strategy." He lifts his shirt to look at the wound.

"Oh my God, it's pretty deep. You need stitches." I open the first aid.

"They can stitch me back up at our Chicago warehouse." He pulls his shirt back down and closes the first aid."

"So, what's your strategy with the Stegosauruses—"

"Astargarians." He nods at me.

"Me? What about me?"

"Your blood. Some of our leading scientists overseas created a concentrate. Each of the proteins in your blood, mixed with the concentrate, can be injected to fight off infection."

"How many out there are like me?"

"Only a few thousand left that are known Interhybrids. The Stags are killing you off one by one. They stage it like an accident, blending in with society. Once you're all gone, they'll release a potent virus, killing off humanity."

"Why like that?"

"They need to evacuate their planet and bring their kind to a planet with intact resources."

"I don't know what to say. I believed in aliens, but this is uncomfortable."

"Sorry you had to find out like this."

"How did you know I had this blood?"

"A hospital's database is how we track Interhybrids, and unfortunately it's how our enemy locates you too."

"When was I tracked?"

"When you went to the ER after your mom's accident, you were blood typed and flagged in our system. We were packing up when we were informed," Bryan says.

"So they do it in hospitals?"

"At birth, babies are blood typed and entered in a database for donors. You were born in a cab and skipped the process. We should've figured you were one, as looking back you've never been sick with so much as a cough."

"I wonder if my brother is—"

"Dan was flagged as RH positive at birth. He's not an Interhybrid."

Bryan's phone lights up.

"I've got so many questions," I say.

"And we'll answer them. Leslie's calling from out front. I must take this."

I nod. Bryan answers the call, placing the phone on speaker mode.

"How's it going, Leslie?" Bryan answers the call.

"Jack noticed one of the screens on the side of the house has been removed," she says.

"Go on," Bryan says.

"He's arguing with me and says the screen was like that before I left for the restaurant. It wasn't," Leslie says.

"Now she has me second guessing myself," a guy's voice takes over.

"Give me a few minutes and I'll be over." Bryan hangs up.

"That's my laundry room window they're talking about. I heard sounds coming from the laundry room a few hours back," I say.

"Let me look," Bryan says, walking to the laundry room.

I follow Bryan. "What are they talking about?" I ask.

"Did you notice anything with the window earlier?" Bryan asks.

"I only heard scratching sounds. It was dark outside."

"Stand back." Bryan flips on the light.

"What's that?" I ask, stepping behind Bryan.

There are two handprints smeared against the dirty, snow-filled window. The prints run along the sides of the ledge. They came from someone with narrow hands and elongated fingers.

"Any of your agents extra skinny NBA players?" I ask.

"Stag prints," Bryan says.

"Is that an extra finger? Do they have six fingers?" I cover my mouth. "I feel sick."

"Stay calm," he says.

"I don't want to be here. I'm scared."

"I think you better come with me," he says. "The ice trick didn't work, and now they're getting desperate."

"They did that to my porch?" I ask.

"And I came by and salted it," Bryan says.

"So that was you?" I ask.

"That was me," he says.

I look at the imprints on the window. "I'm going with you."

"I'm not sure if this one got in in," Bryan says.

"The window's unlocked. What if it's in the house?" I ask.

"We need to get you out of here."

"But what if they're inside?"

"Grab the knife—stand behind me. I need to be sure I didn't put my squad and the entire operation at risk."

"Okay. I'm scared."

Bryan places a call. "Leslie, any action around the house?" he pauses. "No, I'm fine. I'll be over in a few. I'll explain when I see you."

"Everything okay?" I whisper.

"Yes. Just stay close behind me." Bryan pulls out a gun. "After I clear down here, I'll hand you my phone, and you'll wait by the front door."

"Why?"

"I need to clear the upstairs too, and you can't run. If you hear anything from upstairs, you call this number and head out the door, screaming," he whispers and hands me the phone. "Got it?"

I nod.

I stay close to Bryan as he turns a corner, pointing his gun in front of the wall dividing the kitchen and living room. He opens the bathroom door, and I jerk backward. I feel a shock of nerve pain from the sudden move. We approach a closet, and I hold my breath and grab the back of Bryan's jacket. I hide behind him, clenching tight with my sweaty hand. He opens the door and points the gun. Nothing.

"Good thing we're in the city. There's not a lot of space to clear. Stay here." Bryan hands me his phone and takes off up the stairs.

I see my bedroom light go on. *One. Two. Three. Four. Five. Six, Seven.* It shuts off. I breathe. The bathroom light turns on. I hold my breath. The light goes off. He walks to the top of the stairs and turns to the window behind him. He walks up to the window and peers out.

His phone lights up in my hand. "Bryan, you're getting a call."

"We're clear. Coming down." Bryan appears in the light halfway down the stairs. He's holding his side.

I hand him his phone. "Hey, Leslie." He pauses. "Yes, I'm aware." He shakes his head at me. "Her lights were turning on and off?" he asks. "Stay there. Don't do anything."

"Your agents are efficient," I say.

"You okay to come back with us?" Bryan asks.

"Yes, definitely. I'm permanently petrified to go anywhere in my house now. How could I ever go back to living a normal life after what you've told me?"

"I'm sorry you had to learn like this. In your case, I think it's now or never to get you out of here alive."

"Yeah, I guess."

"Come on, let's get you out of here. You can leave the knife behind," he says.

"You think the Snags—"

"Stags," Bryan interrupts.

"You think they'll come back tonight?"

"If they're ripping off window screens in order to get you, they would've been back."

CHAPTER 13

We slip out the back door.

"Did you cut the light sensors?" Bryan asks.

"I did," I say.

"Smart. Quick thinking." Bryan holds his wound and assists me with the other hand.

"You have to get that taken care of."

"I will—back at the warehouse. Follow behind me. Poke me in the back if you hear something," he says as we reach the bottom of the steps.

I walk inside his footprints and stay close behind him. The wind rustles through the naked trees and the temperature has dropped since earlier. I spot the same car from my failed sneak attack. What would've gone down with the agents had I made it to the car?

"Stay behind me," Bryan says, walking up to the car. He knocks on the window.

The woman with the tattoo rolls down the window. "We've got a problem inside. Something's up."

The wind blows my hair.

"What's that?" she asks. She sticks her arm out the window and shoves Bryan. "Are you serious?" she blurts out.

"Holy shit. But how? She sedated or something?" the driver asks.

"Put her back," the woman scolds.

"She's coming with us," Bryan says.

"No, you're putting her back," the woman says.

"She's not a toy. What do you mean 'put her back?'" the driver says.

"You're on my last nerve, buddy," the woman says to the driver.

"You realize she can hear you? She's just injured, not deaf, dummy," the passenger fires back.

"I'll explain everything. She's coming with us," Bryan says.

"What the hell's wrong with you?" The woman raises her voice. "She can't come; it's against policy."

"We'll get canned for this," the driver says.

"What does she know?" the woman asks.

"Enough. The LFP, Stags—"

"You realize you've ruined her life by telling her," the woman says.

"If she's not sedated, she's seems to be taking the news well," the driver says.

"We had a confrontation, and I told her. Stags were almost inside. She had hours, maybe another night. Unlock the door—that's an order."

Bryan opens the door and guides me in.

"How bad is it?" the driver asks.

"They've progressed to breaking and entering. It's bad. I think something's happening sooner than we've expected," Bryan says.

"If she took the news this well, maybe it won't be that hard to bring them together after all," the woman says.

"No, she didn't take it well at all. She stabbed me."

"I'm sorry," I say.

"Stop apologizing," Bryan says.

"Anna stabbed you?" the woman asks.

"While you two were bickering in the car, I had an encounter with Anna. Now drive," Bryan says.

"What do we tell headquarters?" the woman hesitates.

"I need to think this through, but I think it's time to go to the board and request initiation for Z to A," Bryan says.

"They told me we had years left back in training. Maybe another five," the driver says.

"Well, you're wrong, kid. Use some common sense here." Bryan ignores the driver. "Sorry, Anna, he's new to our squad," Bryan says.

"It's okay," I say.

"This is Leslie, and she's normally not this difficult." Bryan glares.

"I'm caught off guard is all," Leslie says.

"And what's your name?" I ask the young driver.

Bryan leans over and murmurs, "Jack."

"Seriously? I was minding my business and following your orders, and you had to out my name?" Jack asks.

"Well, nice to meet you too, Jack. I'm Anna," I say.

"We know," both Leslie and Jack say at the same time.

"Whoops. Sorry, that was stupid of me. This may take some adjusting," I say.

"Quit apologizing. We understand it'll take some time. We've talked about this day, with you, and how we thought you'd respond," Bryan says.

"Well, I lost the bet," Leslie says.

"No, you didn't. She stabbed him," Jack says.

"Stop talking and focus on the road," Bryan snaps.

We take off in the dark. I stare up at a bright sliver of the moon, feeling the car gain speed. I have no idea what to expect, but feel satisfied in a way, learning I wasn't losing my mind and do serve a purpose in life, given the hell I've experienced. I haven't felt needed in a long time.

I feel a tug at my spine as we make a sharp turn. He gains speed and makes another sharp turn. He flips the headlights off and circles the block a little over halfway and turns down an alley. We pull onto Ashland, a busy street, and turn back off two blocks down. He drives around a few blocks and then crosses Ashland again. Bryan and Leslie stare out the window in opposite directions. Their eyes glued to their surroundings.

"Why does he drive like that?" I ask.

"That's how we check for tailing," Bryan says.

"That's how a new graduate checks for tailing," Leslie says.

"You have a problem with the way I'm driving?" Jack snaps at Leslie.

"I'm sick of listening to you two. We're going back to original rotation again, starting tomorrow. You're sloppy together. I was wrong. Leslie, you're back with Hank," Bryan intervenes.

"Thank you. She's bossy," Jack says.

"No, I wouldn't have to question you all the time if you'd follow through. You're a lazy millennial," Leslie barks.

"I see things differently than you, Mom," Jack mutters.

"You make me thankful I never had kids." She smiles.

"Well, you would've been strict, let me tell you that," Jack says.

"I agree," she says.

"We've been living together now for way too long," Bryan says.

"I sense that," I say.

"Jack joined us a little over a year ago, which snapped Leslie into the motherly caretaker she never knew she was," Bryan says.

"Thanks for the narration. Meanwhile, we're trying to keep everyone safe up here," Leslie says.

"Now you protect him," Bryan laughs.

"Love you, Leslie," Jack says.

"Enough. When we get there, you guys say nothing. I'll deal with the others," Bryan says firmly.

We pull up to what looks like a home crossed with an old warehouse.

"What neighborhood are we in?" I ask.

"Pilsen," Jack says.

"I've been over here for art shows and passed right by this spot. Never saw it was here," I say.

"Good," Leslie says.

"How'd you find this spot?" I ask.

"We didn't—the CIA headquarters did. They do a lot of research before we move in," Bryan says.

"Why don't you give her your social security number, badge, and guns, too, while you're at it," Leslie says.

"So you're with the CIA?" I ask.

"A division," Jack says.

"What does it matter right now? We've got Anna, and everyone's safe and sound," Bryan says.

"I'm taking it in. I bet you have some crazy technology in there," I say.

"We're set up with cameras, scanners, motion-detection devices, and user-activated infrared technology," Jack says.

"You forgot the pit bulls," Leslie says.

"We have both pit bulls and robot pit bulls," Jack says.

"Jack, stop." Bryan swats the back of his head.

"Wow, Bryan—can't we have a little fun?" Jack asks.

"Imagine what Anna's dealing with. Show some empathy," Bryan says.

"I can't imagine, and I've been an agent now over half my life. Most of the time was for your mother. I'm sorry, Anna," Leslie says.

"It's okay. I'm jumping into your world—I get it. Don't act different because of me," I say.

"If anyone bothers you, don't hesitate to shut them up," Bryan says.

"I won't. Trust me," I say.

Jack pulls up to the end of the driveway and stops.

"So you guys know pretty much everything about me, then, huh?" I ask.

"Ah. We ha—" Bryan begins.

"Relax, the LFP doesn't listen to your calls and gossip. A system pulls in key words We're not creepy stalkers; we only track what pertains to your safety. It's not *The Truman Show*," Jack says.

"Wow, what's with you?" Leslie asks.

Bryan stares at Jack.

"Was that supposed to make me feel better, Jack? It's my life we're talking about."

"No, I'm sorry," he says.

"I think we're all tired, on edge, and caught off guard," Bryan says.

"I agree," Leslie says.

"I'd like to keep everything off the grid with headquarters until tomorrow," Bryan says.

Leslie hands Bryan the blanket she pulled from the trunk. "Here, cover her with this," she says.

"Sorry, Anna, it's only through the gate," he says, holding the blanket.

"It's okay," I say. I cover myself with the blanket.

Jack pulls forward and stops. "Hank's on duty tonight, right?"

"Yeah, why?" Leslie asks.

"Nah. Never mind," he says.

Jack drives forward. I hear the city noise in the background as he rolls down the window. I peek through a crack in the blanket and watch as he flips open a kiosk. He holds his thumb to the pad and waits for his fingerprint to activate, then pulls the kiosk over to Leslie. She enters a password, and the gate opens.

We pull up to the building, and Bryan slides the blanket off my head. It looks like an old industrial building bound for demolition. A light sensor beams on, revealing red brick with green window trim. The window trim looks worn, and I can see rust around the windowsill above the large garage doors. We pull around the corner and face the garage. The dark green paint on each door is chipping and discolored. The rust stains seep down from the top of the wood on each door. It looks like blood-orange paint oozing down.

"It's an interesting place to live. Never knew this was back here," I say.

"Yeah. It's an old factory. Was vacant for fifteen years. It needed a little love," Leslie says.

"You guys must be like family, huh?" I ask.

"Yeah, we're all tight. You get close when you see what we've seen. Processing can be difficult," Bryan says.

"I can't imagine."

"It's not always negative. We have our fun," Leslie says.

"Ready to pull into the Batcave, Anna?" Jack asks.

"Seriously? It's like that?" I ask.

The car is silent.

"Nope. But we have a cool butler," Jack says.

"Really?"

"Nope. But we do have a cool garage."

"Come on. You're testing my patience," Bryan says.

"What? Like you said, we're all safe. Just trying to make light of the situation," Jack says.

"Why don't you bother Hank with this nonsense when we get in. Leave us alone," Leslie says.

Jack hits a button for the garage. "What'll Hank do when he sees we brought Anna home? I was thinking we could get him back," Jack says.

"It's late. Wait for him to come down," Bryan says.

"I swear, if he's done something to my room or toilet, I may shoot him tonight. I need sleep," Leslie says.

"I don't know how he can outdo last night," Jack laughs. "Your face, though. You looked … well, he got you good," Jack says.

"Who's Hank? What did he do?" I ask.

"Hank put plastic wrap on the outside of Leslie's bathroom door. She walked out of the bathroom right into it. He said she looked like a gremlin," Jack laughs.

"I couldn't see. My contacts were out." Leslie stops Jack. "You know what, I'd like to get him back for once."

"That jagoff lit a bottle rocket under my door this week." Bryan smiles at Leslie. "You have less than a minute until he's here. What's the joke?"

"Everyone hop out, and let Anna pull the car in," Leslie says.

"His face. He'll keel over," Jack says.

"Toss him the keys like he's valet," Leslie laughs.

"Me? Wait. What?" I ask.

Bryan's silent. "Yeah, not so sure—"

Leslie and Jack hop out of the car.

"Come on. Get out. Anna, you're cool with it, right?" Jack asks.

"You remember how to drive?" Leslie asks.

"Yes, I remember how to drive. I didn't lose my memory," I say.

Bryan sits in the car with me.

"I'll do it. I'm fine with a prank," I say.

"Fine," Bryan says, hopping out of the car to assist me. "Wait for the door to go up and then slowly pull in. He can see you through the window tint, so—"

"I'm good. Just go with them," I say, watching the garage door go up. It feels good to be a part of their prank. I haven't had fun in a while. The three of them hide behind a bush, ready for the excitement.

As the door rolls up, I see two white gym shoes. This must be Hank, the prankster. The door rises like a curtain. I see he's tall and bull-legged like a cowboy as the door travels upward. I see his face. Holy crap. No way. I quint and cover my mouth. It's Michael Douglas. His awkwardly tall doppelganger. How's it possible? This man's been able to blend in around me for who knows how long. How can someone live covertly and look like a celebrity? *Good for you, Hank.*

I shift the car in drive and pull forward. He looks tired, as though he was in the middle of a movie and was interrupted to answer the door. Aside from his autopilot appearance, there's a mischievous look about him. Maybe it's Leslie and Bryan's side stories about the guy, but I can imagine what he's like full of life.

Hank waits for me to pull all the way in and walks to the garage controls. He turns to press the button, and I pull forward. He stops and looks my direction. I freeze. I watch him turn to the button and pull the car in reverse. He spins around and crosses his arms. I put the car in park and wait for him to walk over to the car. He walks my direction. I hear a deep, muffled voice and clench both hands on the wheel.

He lights a cigarette and points to his watch. "Quit dicking around, kid. I'll lock you inside for the night." He grips his hands in the air as though he's holding a steering wheel and imitates a bad driver.

Ready to meet a cranky Hank, I roll down my window.

He drops his arms and stares at me. The cigarette falls from his mouth onto the concrete floor.

I turn off the car and hold the keys out the window. "Do I get a valet ticket or something?"

He stares at me.

"Aren't you going to help me get out of the car?" I ask.

Hank steps backward and grabs his chin. His celebrity status went from Michael Douglas to Lurch from *The Addams Family*. He doesn't blink.

"So you want to have a staring contest?" I ask.

"Wait there. Right there. Don't get out of the car, Ann—I meant to say animals. We have an animal loose in the garage." He reaches for his phone.

A high-pitch laugh and a snort trails in the wind. Leslie steps in the garage. Jack walks in and falls to his knees, laughing. Bryan walks over to Hank and puts his hand on Hank's shoulder.

"You should've seen your face," Bryan says and smiles at me.

"I can't wait to rewind the tapes," Leslie laughs.

"You look so pale-faced, man," Jack says.

"Someone mind telling me what's going on?" Hank asks.

"I'll explain inside. Hank and Leslie, get everyone up. Emergency meeting in the kitchen. Do not mention Anna," Bryan says.

"Anna stabbed Bryan," Jack says to Hank.

"Please stop talking," Hank says.

"Come on. Come with me, Hank. Everything's fine," Leslie says, taking Hank's arm.

"It was nice to meet you," I call out to Hank.

Hank turns and waves at me. He staggers up a steep flight of stairs behind Leslie.

"I was hoping you'd introduce yourself again." Jack shakes his head.

"Well, I didn't. Any normal human being would introduce themselves when meeting someone the first time," I snap back.

"But you're only half-human. You set yourself up for that one." Jack smiles.

"Leave her alone," Bryan says.

"How many of you are there?" I ask, ignoring Jack.

"Currently, six. We're expecting two more agents on this squad next month. The time between Stag attacks is narrowing worldwide," Bryan says.

We walk to the staircase.

"Too many stairs for her condition. Should I take her up the elevator?" Jack asks.

"Good idea. I'll head up and get this gash taken care of." Bryan stands on the first step and turns. "If you act like a smartass to her—"

"I won't."

"Good. Because I'll make sure you understand what the word humiliation stems from." Bryan turns and walks up the stairs.

"There's an old manufacturing elevator at the other end of the garage. Wait here a minute. I'll need the key," Jack says. He turns away.

"Jack?" I ask.

"Thanks for thinking of me. The stair situation," I say.

He walks to me and stops. It's the first time we meet face-to-face. I forget what I said a second ago and stare into his piercing eyes. My stomach feels feathery, and I want to run away. I didn't realize how attractive he is.

"Sorry if I came off as a jerk. I feel I'm losing my social skills this first year in the field."

"What do you mean? Don't you get out and have fun?"

"I hang out with my squad and stay in touch with friends from training."

"Wait. You mean you haven't gone out to meet people around our age?"

"It's not that I don't want to; I can't right now," Jack says, removing his eyes from our lock.

"Interesting," I say.

"There's bigger things to focus on, like keeping you alive. Not sure what Bryan's told you, but you've had some close calls this month, and I'm exhausted from pulling double shifts."

"Well, I'm here. I'm safe, so get rest."

"Stay here. I'll be right back."

I look around. The garage could at least, fit forty cars inside. There's over a half dozen vehicles parked in a row. Half the garage resembles an old manufacturing plant, and the other side has new construction. I smell the fresh plywood. I see a wall of bikes ranging in color and a bookshelf filled with every color helmet imaginable. I feel like I'm looking around a sporting goods store.

I feel my phone vibrate and grab it from my pocket.

"Is that your phone?" Jack asks, walking back.

"Yeah. Why?"

"Did Bryan say you could bring that?' he asks.

"I had it in my pocket. Why?"

Jack runs to me in a full sprint and rips the phone out of my hand. "Oh my God."

"What? I hid it—didn't think it'd be an issue."

"You can't have this. They may be tracking you through it. I'll be back." He sprints to the bike wall and yanks one down. He reaches for a helmet, knocking several on the ground. Running with the bike in hand he runs to the side door, placing his hand into a pad to unlock the door.

"Stay there," he says, slamming the door.

What just happened? I stare at the door. I wait. Should I yell? Would anyone hear me from upstairs? What if he doesn't come back?

I wait twenty minutes and walk to the stairs. If another five minutes pass, I climb this mountain. I hear the door rip open behind me. In walks an out of breath, messy looking guy. He turns around and locks the door with his palm print.

"You okay, Jack?" I ask.

He folds over, puts his hands on his knees, and motions for a moment to catch his breath. The bike falls to one side. Removing the helmet, Jack positions it in front of him and drop-kicks it across the garage.

"Did you see anything out of the ordinary while I was gone?" he asks, walking toward me.

"No. Nothing," I say.

"Do I need to pat you down?" he asks.

I shake my head. "Come on, let's get upstairs. Everyone's waiting."

"Can I ask you what happened back there? Why'd you do that?"

"Our tech department's unsure, but it may be possible, they're using the subject's phone with the new technology location services, to track."

"Don't ever refer to me as the subject again," I say.

"I didn't mean to, sorry. They use the term a lot in training."

"Well, it's offensive, so stop. The phone you swiped, is old. My phone's three years old."

"It's likely, it's the newer phones with the latest location services, but that doesn't mean it's okay to rule out your old phone."

"It's fine. But at some point very soon I'll need a phone to contact my family. You have no idea how they—"

"Yes, I know what you're about to say. We know how they are," he laughs.

"Yeah, I guess you do, then." I shake my head. "It's weird—you know everything about me, but you're a stranger to my eyes."

"If it makes you feel better, I'd rather ask you questions you can answer yourself, rather than reading reports."

"That's fine. But I get to ask personal questions in return. I should get to know the people keeping me alive."

"Seems like a fair trade," Jack says.

"So, where'd you go with my phone?"

"I went to the movie theater on Roosevelt. Found a plastic bag in a garbage can, wrapped it up, and hid it in a mound of snow outside emergency exit eleven."

"Why there?"

"Because if they're tracking your phone, I can check for snow prints or anything out of the ordinary." Jack leads me to the elevator.

"Clever thinking."

"Thanks. At least the phone will create a temporary diversion."

"It would, had the theater been open."

"Shit, you're right. But movies get out late in the city. Doesn't matter now, as long as they don't follow you here," Jack says.

"True."

"Plus, you haven't been here long enough. If anything, your phone will show you migrating at different speeds, and you'll appear like you're sitting in traffic," Jack says.

"Late at night? Heading to a theater when all the last shows are wrapping up?"

"It's Chicago, so yes, it's all possible. And if they're able to track you through your phone as well as we're talking, you'd already be dead."

"True again." I stop and look at Jack. I take a deep breath and stare at the ground.

"What's wrong?" he asks.

"I'm fine, though I just had a thought—it's chilling that people are walking around enjoying life, as aliens roam around them. They're able to walk around a movie theater and other public spots without drawing attention."

"It's funny you say that. I find myself watching people walk around Chicago, worrying about the little things like counting calories and the latest yoga trend. If only they knew how fast they'll lose everything."

"I can imagine it's irritating, though imagine a world living in fear?" I ask.

"It'd be outright chaos." Jack walks me to the elevator doors. "The key takes a second. I have to jiggle it."

"When was the last time someone used the elevator?" I ask.

"Bryan and I used it when I moved in." He jiggles the key until it clicks and forces the cage-like door open, exposing a second door.

"You're young so I'm sure it wasn't too long ago," I say.

"If it helps—if we get stuck—we're in a safe spot." He forces the second door open and straightens his arm, pointing inside the elevator. "Welcome aboard."

CHAPTER 14

The elevator door opens. It looks like we're in the living room of the house. I stare through tarnished elevator bars, waiting for Jack to jiggle the door open. The inside's inviting compared to the deteriorating warehouse vibe below. I step out of the elevator and stare across the room. A bright light shines from the ground onto an exposed brick wall. There's something artistic about the way the light strikes against the old marbled brick. I didn't know there are so many shades of one brick color that could fill a wall tastefully without a distracting piece of art. Four massive wooden beams surround the living room, separating it from the kitchen, dining room, and back porch.

We take a few steps, and I stop to look around. It's beautiful. I like the variety of grays used in the furniture. The vanilla and sunflower-yellow accent hues pop from the decoration pillows and surrounding décor. Pictures of different cities align the halls, separating each room. Different size plants fill the room and empty spaces.

I look up and see a cluster of lights. The hanging fixtures are unique, as they're a sequence of varying styles, only matching by the copper base. Jack walks inside the room and taps the light switch. The lights glimmer. This is a unique touch. I've never seen anything like this inside a home.

"You like the lights?" Jack asks.

"They're amazing," I say.

"Six people with different styles, under one roof. Everyone chose their own style of light then we mashed them together."

"Well done. Which one's yours?" I ask.

"The simple one with the Edison light." Jack points.

"That's my favorite one. Good taste."

"You're saying I have good taste?"

"Just your taste on one light fixture. The rest of you so far—debatable."

"Ouch. Thanks. I'll accept the compliment over the insult," Jack laughs.

"I'm only teasing. You weren't the friendliest at first."

"I apologize. I was caught off guard."

"You and I both. Wait a second." I stop. "There's one, two, three, four, five, six … seven?" I point at each light. "There are seven."

"Oh, that one's Theresa's." Jack looks around the room. He faces me.

I see his eyes shift several inches above my head. He stands on his toes and looks around. I blink and force a smirk, hoping to divert his attention back to our lamp conversation. Jack ignores my gesture. What on earth is he staring at? I consider turning around to peek. I stop myself. No. Don't turn.

"And where's Theresa?" I ask, trying to keep the conversation flowing.

"She passed away a little while back," he whispers.

"Oh—sorry. I'm so sorry. I didn't mean to pry. I'm sorry for your loss, as I'm sure it's been hard. You all seem close."

"Actually, I never got a chance to meet her. I was her replacement. But I hear a lot of stories."

"It seems like you're adjusting well with the group, at least from my observation. It'd be difficult, moving in with a grieving group."

"At first. But everyone's great. I wish I wasn't the youngest of the group sometimes, as they love offering life lessons even if I don't ask." Jack signals for me to follow him. "Can I get you anything? A glass of water?"

"I'm fine. Where's a bathroom?"

"This way. Follow me." He directs me to the kitchen. "Walk straight ahead. It's through the kitchen. I'm going to see where everyone is and will be right back. Help yourself to anything." Jack jogs the other direction.

"Okay. Thanks," I call back.

I step inside a chilly room. Unable to find a light switch, I feel around the kitchen in the dark. There's a flushing sound close by. I pat around the exterior of the kitchen and find a light through a crack, at the bottom of the door. Bingo. I shuffle to the door and stop as the handle clicks, popping the lock open. I brace the door with my hand before it cracks me in the head.

"H—"

The kitchen light flips on before I get a word out. The person stomps on my foot.

"Ouc—"

"What the—"

"Sorry, didn't mean to startle you," I say, rubbing my foot against the floor.

He stares at me like he's seen a ghost and backs into the wall.

"Sam, it's okay," a woman says, walking in the kitchen.

He points at me.

"Anna knows about us. Bryan brought her here. That's why they woke you to come down," she says.

"I thought I've lost it," he says.

The woman walks up to me and smiles. "Hey, Anna, I'm Cindy." She reaches out her hand. "This is Sam."

Sam walks up to me and shakes my hand.

"Nice to meet you both," I say.

"Sorry—stepped on your foot pretty hard," Sam says.

"I'm sorry I startled you," I say.

"All good. I don't normally walk around in the dark late at night, as I suffer from sleep inertia," he says.

"Sleep inertia? What's that?" I ask.

Cindy raises an eyebrow at Sam. "You'll have to excuse him. Everyone's exhausted," Cindy says.

"I can imagine. Where's Bryan?" I ask.

"He's in the lab," Cindy says.

"Lab?"

I call it my lab. It's my little office," she says.

"Did you see his gash?"

"You got him pretty good, my dear." Cindy turns toward the door. "Follow me."

"What happened to Bryan?" Sam asks, rubbing his eyes.

Cindy ignores Sam. "So how are you feeling?"

"I'm doing the best I can."

"You're a strong woman. Give your body a chance to heal itself," she says.

I stop and stare at Cindy. "Wait. You look familiar. Pull your hair back for a second?"

Cindy pulls her hair back.

"Were you the woman in the hallway? At the hospital?" I ask.

"Yeah, it was me. I was wondering if you'd remember. We knew we'd have issues from the scene at the hospital."

"I thought I was losing it. I saw your face, you turned, and took off."

"The way you looked at me, I could tell something in your mind triggered. Good memory, by the way," Cindy says.

"That's when Leslie said she saw a crazy kid run full speed into Bryan's ass," Sam says.

"That definitely happened. I saw it too," I laugh. "Bryan would've escaped my little interrogation if it wasn't for the kid."

"Well you're handling the situation very well. If you need to talk to anyone, I'm here," Cindy says.

"Thanks. Everything feels weird right now. I feel like I'm in *The Twilight Zone*. I guess if anything, I'd like to understand what makes me different."

"I can help with that. I spent most my career in a lab. Initially, I was a geneticist for the LFP, and when I witnessed what your blood and proteins are capable of, I trained to be out in the field with other agents," she says.

"You chose to put your life at risk for me?"

"I choose to every day. I'm protecting what I believe to be sacred," she says.

"I don't feel special. Just beat up."

"You're a fighter, and so's your body. Be excited. How cool is it? You're a superhuman with super-healing strength." She smiles.

I see Jack inside a bright-lit room.

"In here, Anna," Jack says.

"Welcome to my lab," Cindy says. She steps aside for me.

Hank, Leslie, and Jack circle Bryan on a table.

"I thought I said meet in the kitchen," Bryan says.

"Everyone wants to check out your stab wound," Jack says to Bryan.

Jack and Hank press down on Bryan's shoulders, holding him intact, while Leslie stitches him up.

"I see you've met Sam and Cindy," Bryan says through clenched teeth.

"Any deeper than this we'd have to take you in," Leslie says. She pulls the thread tight.

"Nice shot," Hank says.

"You did this?" Sam turns to me.

"Where've you been? That's old news," Jack says.

Sam rolls his eyes. "I've got iner—"

"Quit with the inertia shit," Hank says.

"Meerkat—Hank," Cindy says.

"I know it's late, but we've got Anna here with us now. I'd like to show her something with some of the concentrate in my fridge," Cindy says.

"How? You'll waste it. He's not infected with a virus," Leslie says.

"The concentrate will speed up his recovery time," Cindy says.

"It works on a flesh wound?" Hank asks.

"Yes, we never released the data on this beyond the lab," Cindy says.

"Why not? It's crazy not to," Hank says.

"We've only got the capabilities to make so much concentrate each year and can't waste it. We're talking about enough concentrate to revive the earth's population," Cindy says.

"I'm afraid we'll be using up the concentrate sooner than we're ready for. We'll never have enough," Bryan says.

"The freakin' concentrate is inactive without a willing participant, so technically we won't be using any of the concentrate," Leslie says.

"We have a willing participant." Jack looks at me.

Everyone looks at me.

"What?" I look behind me. Shoot, they're looking at me. "Where do I fall in this scenario?"

"You're the key to activating the antidote," Bryan says.

"Well, your blood is the key," Leslie says.

"Actually, the proteins in your blood are the secret weapon," Cindy says.

"Same thing," Jack says.

"False," Cindy says.

"I'd like to help Bryan. So I guess I'm your willing participant," I say.

"It'd require me to draw a small amount of blood. Would you be comfortable with this?" Cindy asks.

"If it'll help Bryan heal faster from what I did, then yeah, I don't mind," I say.

"You can trust me. I know what I'm doing with a needle. My MD-PhD credentials are in my bedroom safe—would you like me to run up and grab them?" Cindy asks.

"And I'm a doctor, too, but I left my credentials in the car. Do you trust me too, Anna?" Sam laughs.

"You're such a smart-ass." Leslie shakes her head.

"Sam, muzzle it." Cindy says.

"That just sounded weird is all. I wouldn't trust anyone I just met with a needle. Sorry, Cindy," Sam says.

"Look who finally woke up," Jack says.

"I've decided I prefer you half-awake when I'm around you." Cindy looks at Sam.

"Please just close your eyes. I'll wake you when I need you. Please close them," Bryan snarls at Sam.

"I trust you. No one's lied to me yet," I say.

"I've been waiting for the moment I get to do this again," Cindy says.

"When you worked in a lab, couldn't you reach out for volunteers? I'm sure people with this blood type would help," I say.

"We did years ago," Bryan says.

"We've had subjects over the years work with us during many case studies. But we had to stop. It was drawing too much attention to the blood type, unfortunately," Cindy says.

"How so?" I ask.

"The subjects we worked with questioned the case studies. They were informing friends and family of the tests we were performing," Cindy says.

"They signed documentation prior to participation, agreeing to nondisclosure," Bryan says.

"So, what went wrong?" I ask.

"Someone blabbed to the media about the lab and ruined everyth—"

"The week the story aired we had a record number of Interhybrid fatalities," Cindy interrupts Hank.

"We learned just how closely the Stags track the world. They don't want humans tapping into the bloodline capabilities," Bryan says.

"The number of attacks—well, they've been consistent ever since," Cindy says.

"The system at that lab was hacked that week too, remember?" Leslie asks.

"Did they get anything?" I ask.

"No, they were given their own code to use," Bryan says.

"What do you mean?" I ask.

"Everyone in the CIA communicates through a coding system. The LFP alone use three code variations due to the sensitivity of our operations," Bryan says.

"The lab they hacked was a satellite location, meaning all research completed was disconnected from primary lab locations," Cindy says.

"Are there other agencies out there studying people like me?" I ask.

"Yes, there are. It's another reason the Interhybrid fatalities have grown," Cindy says.

"Stags wipe out the labs too. There was a massive explosion in a lab in Fort Lauderdale. If there are other agencies, they're discrete like us," Bryan says.

"Do they know you're aware of their presence?" I ask.

"We've stopped many attacks, so they're aware of an opposing force. Stag attacks are staged to look like accidents—just like your car accident, for example," Bryan says.

"If they discretely come out of the woodwork, it's less likely to be linked to a homicide and less likely an opposing force can intercept. And let's face it, an accident in the news doesn't provoke fear in the population like a murder would," Leslie says.

"How many have you caught?" I ask.

Cindy walks to a large cabinet and lays down a tray. The room is quiet.

"None," Jack says.

"None?" I ask.

"The assholes burn into flames when they're threatened," Hank says.

"I thought I caught one, remember?" Jack turns to Hank.

"You weren't even close." Hank shakes his head.

"I was close," Jack says.

"You tried to karate kick the only Stag I've ever seen with a delayed fire trigger and failed. Plus, you almost shot yourself," Hank says.

"And you caught on fire. I ruined my jacket putting it out," Leslie says.

"Never mind," Jack says.

Cindy walks over to me. The side conversation stops. "You ready?"

I nod.

She slips on a pair of gloves, lays down a syringe, and opens a pack of alcohol wipes. "I never imagined I'd be working with you like this so soon," she says, searching my arm for a vein.

"I never imagined I'd be sitting in a lab, giving blood to an agent I stabbed," I say.

"He'll be fine. But before we start and just so you're aware—each protein in your blood can treat and cure a virus," Cindy says.

"That's amazing," I say.

"You're a walking miracle," Jack says.

"Make a fist for me really quick. I think I found the vein," Cindy says.

I grip my hand tight and feel my fingers tingle. The adrenaline's wearing off. I feel the nerve pain lingering around my shoulder blades as I hold a fist. I ignore the sting.

"I got it. Hold still. You'll feel a poke," Cindy says.

"Can you use my blood if I were to die?" I feel the needle pop through my skin.

"We've tried over and over to preserve the blood of a deceased Interhybrid. Once an Interhybrid passes, there's a matter of minutes before the blood's obsolete," Cindy says.

"It's like a computer shutting down. You must be working to donate the components we need," Bryan says.

"What about blood transfusions?" I ask.

"Your blood will aid in transfusions for a matching RH positive human, which is another mystery and another department in the LFP lab. Blood types and the RH factor were only discovered in 1937. We're still learning," Cindy says.

"Simply put, the components of your blood we need become dormant if you were to pass," Bryan says.

I feel the needle slide deeper. "I wonder how you'll do it."

"Do what?" Bryan asks.

"Bring everyone like me together and explain all this," I say.

"There'll be a lot of agent stabbings," Jack laughs.

"There has to be a way to relay your message to other Interhybrids," I say, disregarding Jack's comment. "Or what if you artificially produced the blood? Then you'd prevent changing one's life drastically."

"They agency continues to rule out every scenario—developing concentrates and serums, advancing technology at every degree," Bryan says.

"And?" I ask.

"Nothing. We have teams around the world duplicating the components in the blood, and we've got nothing. You can't be cloned either. There's a team dedicated solely to the cloning matter alone," Cindy says.

"Why can't I be cloned?"

"You're missing the D antigen. All RH negatives lack the D antigen in general. So, you can't be cloned," Cindy says.

"Whoever or whatever made you was really smart," Jack says.

"And why are you so quiet tonight, Hank?" Cindy asks.

Leslie and Jack look at Bryan and me. They burst into laughter.

"Tell you later," Leslie snorts.

Cindy pulls the needle from my arm.

"Thank you for being so gentle. It hurt when I had blood drawn in the past."

"That seems to be a common denominator between you guys. Your body makes it difficult to take blood. It's like you were created not only to be kept alive but to give out your resources willingly. Your veins will slide if you're not holding the needle right," Cindy says.

I look over at Sam. He's sleeping.

"Is that Sam guy sleeping while standing up?" I ask.

"Him? Yeah, he does that," Jack says.

"That's incredibly bizarre. I'd fall over," I say.

"Most people would. Sam's a rare breed—no pun intended," Leslie says.

Jack walks over to Sam and kicks him in the shin. "Wake up, man."

Cindy takes out a bandage. "Standard protocol," she says, laying a band aide over the needle mark. "Now for the fun part." She walks to the fridge and pulls out a small glass tube.

"The concentrate," Jack says.

"That's practically nothing," I say.

"The cells from your blood will do most of the work in this case. The concentrate activates the cells at the infected site," Cindy says.

"I have a question." Leslie looks at me. "Haven't you noticed that you've never been sick?"

"I just thought I took care of myself," I say.

"What was the largest wound before your accident? You know, falling off a bike or running into something as a kid," Jack says.

"I stubbed my toe on concrete a bunch of times, and I've lost a nail from running in bad shoes," I say.

"My point exac—"

"Oh, I got one," I interrupt Jack. "I nearly cut off the top of my finger in high school."

"And what happened? You didn't go to the hospital, because we would've known," Jack says.

"Which finger was it? Most of us would scar from something like that. I know I would," Leslie says.

"I don't remember."

"See—you can't find it, because you heal differently than a human," Jack says.

"Did you just put me in a nonhuman category again, Jack?"

"Sorry, I didn't mean it like that," he says.

"Hank's never this quiet, and you're never this chatty. You must be enjoying having a guest your age," Cindy says.

Jack looks at me then looks away.

Cindy sticks the needle in the test tube and presses down on the top of the syringe. She mixes the concoction with needle. "It takes about a minute of stirring the two together."

"That's hardly anything at all," Hank says.

"Like I said, that's all it takes, for this type of wound," Cindy says, concentrating on her serum.

Bryan adjusts himself on the table.

"Keep your head down." Hank pats Bryan's forehead. "You feel warm, buddy." He lets go of Bryan's shoulder and storms out of the room.

"Where's he going?" Bryan asks.

"I'm sorry about this Bryan. I feel awful. I've never physically harmed anyone before—ever," I say.

"We know," Jack and Leslie both laugh.

"Very funny. Will someone walk up and pinch me? Maybe then I'll wake up and realize I've been dreaming the entire time and the CIA hasn't been tracking my every move."

Sam walks up and pinches me.

"Ow."

"Ignore him, Anna. He thinks he's being cute," Bryan says.

I look at Sam. "Was that pinch caused by your condition?"

"Seriously, Sam? You already sprung that on Anna? I bet he used the word in the very first sentence," Hank says.

"I can imagine how this played out. Anna introduced herself again to another person who already knows her name, and Sam answered with one word. Inertia. Fast friends," Jack says.

Sam shrugs.

Cindy stops mixing the concentrate. "So, bringing us back to right now, watch close as I place this on the wound, and it'll—"

Hank hustles into the room with a wet towel and ice pack in hand. He lays the pack on Bryan's head.

"What the hell are you doing? I'm fine." Bryan swats at Hank.

"Let him help you," Leslie says.

"Sorry, you felt warm. Did I miss anything?" Hanks asks.

"Nope, we were waiting for you. Can you run and grab Bryan some water while you're up?" Leslie asks.

"I'm not thirsty," Bryan says.

"He must stay hydrated," Leslie says.

"Be right back. Just one?" Hank asks.

Leslie nods and waits for Hank to leave the room. She turns to Bryan. "Let him take care of you. It'll help the PTSD."

"Ah, gotcha," Bryan says.

Everyone is silent.

Hank runs back in the room and hands Bryan water.

"Thanks. You're right, I'm a little warm," Bryan says.

"Monitor the wound closely the next few days," Cindy says.

We watch Cindy dab the mixture against the wound. She blows on the liquid and applies a second layer. The liquid resembles a water spill on the edge of a table that stops before it trickles over. The substance forms into a jelly and hardens seconds later.

"Great, looks like it's working," Cindy says.

"I can't believe my blood hardened that quick."

"Bryan's wound won't risk infection after this application," Cindy says.

"I guess you can look at it this way—you filleted a man only to fix him," Leslie says.

Cindy covers the wound with a large bandage.

"How about we open up some wine? I could use a glass. Hell, we could all use a glass. Right? Hank, you in?" Bryan asks.

"Yeah, I could use a drink right now." Hank nods.

"I bet you do. We got you good," Jack says.

"You got a taste of your own medicine. From the years of being 'Hank pranked.' I felt—let me rephrase that—the group felt it was necessary," Leslie says.

"Yeah, not sure how I'll top that off," Hank says.

"Anna, how about a nice glass of red? I've been saving a bottle. It's a good one," Bryan says.

"Sounds nice."

I watch everyone trickle out of the room. Cindy grabs a disinfectant wipe and cleans the table.

"Need any help in here?" I ask Cindy.

"We're all set. I'll get the rest in the morning. Pretty neat stuff, huh?"

"Yeah, there's a lot to learn. I'm ready for that glass of wine," I say, following Cindy.

We walk across the living room. I see a shadow cross in my direction out of the corner of my eye.

"You okay?" Jack asks.

I jolt. "You scared me."

"I ran up to grab a sweatshirt. You scare easily. It's been comical to watch at moments, especially when I see it coming before you experience it."

"Not so sure I find that funny."

"I know. And I'm sorry. I'm a little desensitized to everything," Jack says.

"It does feel like I've been cast in a form of *The Truman Show*," I say.

"Yeah, I'd be a mess myself if I were in your shoes. I'm glad Bryan got you out of there. They would've come back for you."

"I saw something out my laundry room window when Bryan was in my house. A handprint—six fingers. What do they look like?"

"They're covered usually."

"I know you've seen one. Hank said you ran up to one."

"I did."

"And?" I ask.

"I couldn't really see it."

"You had to see something. Hank said there was a delay."

"I did, but it's hard to explain."

"What did you see?"

"I don't really remember now. But I remember I was afraid," Jack says.

"I like that you're able to admit that."

"What?"

"That you were afraid. Not many guys would admit something like that."

"I had been in training for years. Drill after drill. Over and over. Encountering one made everything so real. It scared the shit out of me."

"I bet. I only saw an imprint and that was scary enough. So, what do you remember?" I ask.

"They're humanlike, but bigger and stronger. I don't know, I was running at the thing."

"If they're able to blend in with society, they may be more humanlike than what you thought you saw."

CHAPTER 15

We enter the kitchen. Everyone's slumped around a large granite island. Jack grabs a chair for me. Bryan pours a glass of wine and hands it to me.

"I'd like to say something really quick," Bryan says.

We turn to Bryan.

"Anna, thank you for taking the news well—better than anyone I'd imagine. Stay positive, kid. We're all in this together now." Bryan pours Cindy a glass of wine.

"What the hell was that?" Hank asks.

"It's Bryan. What'd you expect—all facts, no emotion," Leslie says.

"That was—depressing. Like we're all going down in the Titanic together depressing," Jack says.

"Stop. I never had kids. Sorry, Anna, the sentimental stuff isn't my thing," Bryan says.

The room is silent. I drink my wine.

"Whatever. Just drink your wine—it's been a long day," Bryan says, handing Leslie a glass.

"I appreciate the words. Tonight could've been my last night, had I been home," I say.

"If not tonight, something major would've happened soon," Leslie says.

"I'm sad to say—they won't stop until you're all gone," Cindy says.

"Unless your ancestors pay a visit," Jack says.

"My ancestors? What are you talking about?" I ask.

"Too much, Jack. Way too much," Cindy says.

"Let her ask the questions. Otherwise let Cindy do the talking. Okay, buddy?" Bryan pours the rest of the bottle.

"I'm fine, I swear. Thanks for the curveball, though. Now you must tell me." I look at Jack. "Well? What about my ancestors?"

Jack looks at Cindy.

"It's really late," Leslie interrupts.

"I'm not tired. Maybe I'll sleep tonight if I'm able to make more sense of the situation," I say.

"I guess we got you through the hardest part," Bryan says.

"I don't think you guys can phase me at this point—can't be any weirder," I say.

"To be honest with you, the history is remarkable. Our team of scientists unraveled more this past year than ever before," Cindy says.

"I'll grab more wine." Jack paces to the wine rack and walks over with two bottles of wine. "The cab or the merlot next?"

"This guy." Bryan shakes his head and looks at Cindy. "I've never seen him talk so much."

"I think I know why," Leslie says.

"Yeah, I see it too," Hank says.

"I'm standing right here. I can hear you guys," Jack says.

I look at Bryan. He's rubbing his five-o'clock shadow and looking at Jack. There's a light beaming down on him from where he sits. The light unfolds a sleep deprived man. His eyes have shadowy circles around them, and his hair looks feathery, smashed over to one side from laying on the table.

I look around the kitchen island. Everyone has their elbows plopped up against the granite. Hank yawns, causing a chain reaction. I feel the yawn work through my system and gulp it down. Jack uncorks a bottle and walks over to Bryan. He tugs the empty wine glass from Bryan's hand.

"You take the next glass. You look like you could use one." Jack pours a glass and hands it to Bryan.

"I can, thanks." Bryan nods.

Jack sets a glass in front of Sam.

"Are you kidding, man?" Sam hands Jack the glass. "I didn't drag myself out of bed for a cocktail hour."

"You're the most pleasant person in the entire world." Leslie rolls her eyes at Sam.

"I can say the same about you," Hank says.

Leslie turns to Hank and smiles with her glass of wine.

Bryan clears his throat. "We're all tired and have stuff to process from tonight. Anna, you have every right to ask any questions and deserve to know the truth. I agree with what you said—you won't be able to go back to the life you had. So I feel you should know everything."

"I appreciate that," I say.

"Go ahead, Cindy, tell her," Bryan says.

"Okay." Cindy takes a sip of wine. "To be straightforward—we believe your ancestors were the opposing force during a past invasion," Cindy says.

"Which was here on Earth, during the ancient Egyptian era. They're known known as the Veraxum," Bryan says.

"Simply put, you inherited your rare blood from the Veraxum. And after testing old skeletal samples, our scientists concluded the Veraxum were visitors from another planet comparable to Earth," Cindy says.

"The name sounds like a type of insect," I say.

Jack sets his wine down and covers his mouth. He stares at the counter.

"I guess you're right—the name sounds a little buggy," Cindy says.

"So ancient aliens? My blood is from ancient aliens?" I ask.

"What if we change it to ancient ancestors instead? I feel it rolls off the tongue better," Cindy says.

"Why? They sound the same. Both words start with an *a*—they have the same number of syllables," Jack says.

"Thanks, Jackson. I was intentionally replacing the word alien before you added your two cents," Cindy says.

"Sorry, I really didn't get it," he says.

I take a large gulp of wine. And another.

"You okay?" Bryan asks.

"I'm working through it easier thanks to Jackson." I smile.

"His middle name's Herb," Leslie says.

"Jackson Herb, eh?" I ask.

"This is true," Jack says.

"And his last name's Garden," Hank says.

"Jackson Herb Garden?" I ask.

"They were a family of farmers, just ask h—"

"Gorden. My last name's Gorden," Jack interrupts Hank.

"Meerkat," Leslie says.

I look at Leslie. "Huh." I turn back to Jack. "I'll accept ancient alien if you'll let me use *Garden* as your last name," I say.

"Fine—if it makes you feel better," Jack says.

"I'd feel better if I knew why ancient aliens were hanging out on planet Earth with the Egyptians. And if they meant no harm, why not release this info to the rest of the world? They're living among us as we speak," I say.

"Our planet is at war with its own kind. Humans will never accept alien visitors if they're unable to fully establish a genuine equality among their own race," Bryan says.

"Can you imagine if we went public with our studies? It would create an uproar. Humans are finally getting to a point of accepting the possibility of life on other planets, so imagine what the population would do if we skipped from it's possible to—Stags and half-bred aliens walking among us," Leslie says.

"Well, as one of these so-called aliens, that's upsetting news," I say.

"Look, you're not ET. The word *alien* is, by definition, belonging to a foreign country or nation. You're not a little green man. You just have some of the little green man's blood," Jack says.

"Really? Was that supposed to help?" I ask.

Jack drinks his wine.

"I'm sorry, Jack. I know you're only trying to make light of the situation. If it wasn't happening to me right now, I'd find that funny," I say.

"It's okay, I get it," Jack says.

"I'd like to start from the beginning." I stop and look at Cindy. "If my blood's connected to the Veraxum species, where do humans come from?"

"They can trace it, and there's no mystery—human blood comes from a monkey," Cindy says.

"A monkey?" I ask.

"The rhesus monkey, hence the RH negative and RH positive factor. The RH factor was discovered in the 1930s, which isn't really that long ago, if you think about it," Cindy says.

"And what about the Veraxum? How were they discovered?" I ask.

"Scientists ran tests on a well-preserved Egyptian carcass in the seventies, finally linking the Rh negative bloodline to a possible source. The name came from piecing together ancient scripture inside the walls of pyramids. The art displays the Egyptians being of one group, reaching out to those of another population," Cindy says.

"Couldn't the other group just be a second tribe of some sort?" I ask.

"Not exactly. They were taller than the Egyptians in the scripture, with more profound features, though very humanlike in many ways. It was clear in the art—they were from different worlds. Alongside the mysterious group continued a story of aircraft drawings. The story shows the Veraxum arriving on Earth, making peace with the Egyptians, sharing resources, then leaving Earth. The drawings showed some of the Veraxum stayed on Earth with the Egyptians the day the Veraxum aircraft left," Cindy says.

"What if the drawings were created by an Egyptian nutjob?" I ask.

"Our scientists tested DNA from burial sites and found the Veraxum buried alongside Egyptians. Some of the remains we once thought as human were proven to be Veraxum. As for the art, every Veraxum had a black cube drawn close to the body. During the follow-up investigation, they found a black cube in close radius to each Veraxum burial site. The cubes won't budge from the site under any weather condition and serve as some sort of permanent marking. Plus, the cubes are made from a substance they're unable to identify," Cindy says.

"The findings were the first of many to support the Veraxum presence," Bryan says.

"And it was the first experiment validating some truth behind the ancient Egyptian art. That species from two planets coexisted, leaving behind their stories of unity. At one point humans welcomed visitors from other planets," Cindy says.

"I'm going to take a stab at it and guess—I'm the result of the two crossbreeding," I say.

"You're catching on quick. Identifying the DNA was the initial test that led the team to the second big discovery." Bryan points at me.

"Having the ability to distinguish the DNA was significant when families of infants and babies were buried together. The next step was proving the two species were capable of reproduction, and when resampling DNA of some of the baby remains, scientists found a third result." Cindy stops and sips her wine.

I point at myself.

"Yep, the DNA was a combination of both species—Veraxum being slightly more dominant. What we see over time is a genetically advanced superhuman, an Interhybrid," Cindy says.

"I find this all interesting. But I don't see where the Stags play into this," I say.

"The Stags are unrelated to your DNA," Bryan says.

"They're basically the storm troopers in your situation," Jack says.

I turn to Jack. "What?"

"Jack, please? Good analogy, though," Bryan says.

"Scientists believe an Interhybrid was created between the two species to save the Egyptian race and form an alliance between two planets. As you're learning, an Interhybrid can donate every aspect of themselves—blood, plasma, bone marrow, even the proteins in their blood to cure viruses. You with me so far?" Cindy asks.

I nod.

"In the same carvings, there's a third presence seen throughout. If we're finding truth to what the Egyptians left behind, they were sharing their stories to warn us. Pictures of a malicious third species, being the Stags, carved in the walls were displayed as attacking the Veraxum-human alliance. Graphic and violent scripture shows the alliance being captured and tortured. These are followed by the Stags in flames, signs of peace, and the Veraxum leaving Earth," Cindy says.

"This could mean there was a successful defeat. I've seen a lot of the photos from inside the pyramids, and it's incredible how well they replicate the Stag's fire trigger on the side of a pyramid wall," Bryan says.

"You'd think they'd leave behind instructions on how to handle the Stags." I shake my head.

"They did. Get it?" Bryan asks.

"The story they left was to make sure we find you," Cindy says.

"I understand. But you found me, so now what? Am I supposed to know what do? Because if I came face-to-face with a Stag, I wouldn't have a clue," I say.

"You won't be facing the Stags, ever. We'll have orders when the time comes, and you'll be safe, reviving the infected," Bryan says.

"The infected?" I ask.

Just like our mission to live on Mars, we believe the Stags have a mission to life on Earth. We feel they need our planet and our resources intact prior to take over. They've been using artificially made viruses. The plague, HIV, H1N1—each attempt getting stronger and stronger with potency," Cindy says.

"The research from studying Interhybrids has not only led the LFP in treating, but curing many of the artificially made viruses," Bryan says.

"What do you mean 'artificially' made?" I ask.

"Think about it—malaria, dengue fever, West Nile, yellow fever, and Zika—these are just five diseases spread through mosquitos, killing well over a million a year. These were engineered and implanted in animal carcasses. They're designing the viruses to enter the human blood stream in any possible way," Cindy says.

"Oh my God, I'm getting it," I say.

"It's only a matter of time before the next strain," Bryan says.

"How much?" I ask.

"We have a year, several at most. The potency will depend on how many of you there are left," Bryan says.

"You're immune to the artificial viruses and can revive an infected human by injecting the blood-concentrate serum into the bloodstream of the infected," Cindy says.

"I'll help in any way I can," I say.

"When we get you back to heathy and strong," Hank says.

"I've decided to call headquarters in the morning and explain everything," Bryan says.

"Are you sure?" Hank asks.

"Positive. And I'm going to suggest we begin an Interhybrid evacuation plan immediately," Bryan says.

"Lives will change indefinitely. You certain it's time?" Leslie asks.

"I'd rather be prepared," Bryan says.

"Well, whatever you decide, I'll back you up," Hank says.

"All of us will," Leslie says.

"I appreciate it. We should get some rest," Bryan says.

"We done then? Can I head up? I'm exhausted from watching Anna two days in a row." Sam rubs his eyes.

"Wait. You didn't work at all today. And you make it sound like you've been babysitting a toddler strung out on sugar for two days," Jack says.

"Sorry, Anna, I didn't mean it like that," Sam says.

"What's wrong with you, man? You had the day off and slept," Hank says.

"You should be rested by now from your two days on. I think you need to start taking more vitamins," Cindy says.

"I swear, if you weren't so good on the job, I'd request to transfer you," Bryan says.

"I second that," Hank says.

"Anyways, before we call it a night, I think we need a plan for tomorrow morning," Bryan says.

"Correction, sun's about to come up." Hank looks at his watch.

"Shit, the plan for today, then. I'd like you to continue with your schedule. I know Anna's safe with us, but I want to keep an eye on her home and any suspicious activity." Bryan turns and cups his side. He grits his teeth.

"You look like shit, man. You need to get some rest," Hank says.

"We'll go about our routines, and you can divide up the smaller tasks as they come up," Cindy says as she points to Bryan's side. "You need sleep. Let Hank take over."

"I agree with Cindy," Jack says.

"We've been working together a long time; you can trust us to help. Get some rest," Leslie says.

"I trust you, which is why I'm going to take your advice. Hank, you're in charge. Anna, they'll get a room set up for you. Take some time to yourself to get your mind right. No matter what, stay in the house," Bryan says.

"Of course," I say. I finish my wine and make eye contact with Jack.

"Here." Jack takes the rest of a bottle and slides it over to me with a wink.

We watch Bryan struggle as he walks out of the kitchen.

Hank puts his finger over his mouth, signaling to keep quiet. "Let's continue and not make a scene for Bryan's sake. It's the only way he'll rest," Hank whispers.

"If we're going about our schedules, I'm on shift again in a few hours," Sam says.

"I'll go with Sam tomorrow," Jack says.

"I can go in the morning with Sam. Jack needs rest," Cindy says.

"No, you should be here with Anna. Jack's a kid; he can handle it. I could go days without sleeping at his age." Hank looks at Jack.

"I'll do it," Jack says.

"I wish there's something I can do. You guys seem overwhelmed," I say.

"We've been a high-functioning skeleton crew lately, and it's slowly catching up." Bryan walks in the kitchen.

Hank looks at Bryan and clears his throat. "Since Anna's safe with us—Jack, I'd like you with Sam. You two can switch off napping, just keep an eye on the house. Leslie and I will help Bryan sort out shit with headquarters and then switch with you when we're done," Hank says.

"Won't headquarters think somethings up if we start switching up our schedules? We're normally consistent. They'll catch something at the gate," Jack says.

"I'll clear it all up once I'm on the call with them," Bryan says.

"When you're out tomorrow, let's just stick to common sense. Don't do anything stupid the next few days. How about that?" Hank looks over to Jack.

"Really?" Jack throws his arms in the air.

"Oh, sorry. My timing was off. Didn't mean to direct that at you. I was going to assign you another task for tomorrow," Hank says.

"Fine. Sure. What?" Jack asks.

"I'm putting you in charge of Anna's alibi for her family and friends. You'll be in a car all day, so think between naps," Hank says.

"I agree. Let's keep ourselves a few steps ahead. This is an important task," Bryan says.

"I can handle it," Jack says.

"You need a cover-up that works with every angle. Think of worst-case scenarios and how to react on the spot. You haven't had many your first year on the squad, so this will be good practice," Bryan says.

"No, I got it," Jack says.

"Okay then. I admire your confidence," Bryan says.

"This will be easy," Jack says.

"Oh really?" Hank looks at Jack. "Well, good, then. We're going to play a little game during dinner tomorrow night called stumping the new kid. You better have every possible scenario tied down."

Jack slouches in his seat and looks down at his hands.

"Anyone have anything to add?" Bryan asks.

"My side's hurting just looking at you," Leslie says.

"Bryan, please leave. We've got everything under control," Cindy says.

Hank stands up, towering over the group. "I agree. Get some rest, man. You've been stabbed. Go to the condo, sleep, and have some time to yourself."

"Wait. You guys have another place?" I ask.

"Yeah, there's a condo," Jack says.

"We all need our privacy sometimes," Leslie says.

"I'm out. Any last questions?" Bryan asks.

"Nope," Jack says.

"Grab a new burner phone tonight before you lay down. Call me if you need anything, otherwise Hank's in charge." Bryan walks to the elevator.

We wait for him to get in the elevator.

"Finally. I thought he'd never leave," Cindy says.

"He couldn't do the stairs. See that?" Leslie points to the elevator.

"Leslie and I will make sure we're at the condo first thing in the morning," Hank says.

Sam's head clunks onto the table, causing Jack to jump up in his seat.

"Oh shit, Sam, I'm sorry. You're free to go up to bed, buddy," Hank says.

Sam stands up and twists toward the living room, running into the doorframe.

"Jack, you and Sam take two cars and stick the monitoring devices from headquarters inside the trunks. Leslie and I will switch cars with you, so find decent spots for the cars to sit day and night. Study the house as though Anna's in it," Hank says.

"Okay, got it," Jack says.

Cindy looks at me. "I'll get a bed ready and some clothes for you."

"I'm not sure I'm ready for bed yet," I say.

"I understand. Go do your thing. There's an enclosed patio out back if you want some time to yourself, and there's plenty of food in the kitchen. Help yourself," Cindy says.

"The patio sounds nice. I'm going to top off my glass and think a few things through. Thanks for everything," I say.

"You'll be in the room directly at the top of the staircase. I'm in the room to the right if you need me." Cindy puts her wineglass in the sink and dims the kitchen lighting.

Everyone follows Cindy's lead.

"Wait, Jack," I say.

Jack turns.

"If I give you my house key, are you able to grab some stuff for me? I'm not sure when I'll be able to go back home."

"Hank?" Jack asks.

Hank turns. "I heard."

"You think it's okay if I run in?" Jack asks.

"If you see zero activity and make it quick. Otherwise leave the list on the dash of the car, and I'll grab everything when I get there," Hank says.

"Got it," Jack nods as he makes his way out of the kitchen. "Good night, Anna," he says, looking back at me.

"Thank you so much. I really appreciate it." I take a sip of wine.

I grab the wine bottle off the kitchen counter. I feel tipsy, and I don't care. I think I'll have another.

CHAPTER 16

Juggling the wine between my frail fingers, I carefully make my way through the living room of mismatching chandeliers and notice an enormous floor-to-ceiling sliding door leading to the back porch. I unlatch the glass barrier and slide the deadweight door enough to step through.

As I step inside a sooty-black room, I smell traces of cedar and evergreen sap. I feel a draft circle each nostril, igniting a sting. Whispers surround me as the winter wind slogs the windows. I fumble my hand against a ridged wooden wall for a light switch. I feel a sting as I brush my hand up the jagged wood.

"Shit," I shriek. I feel a splinter of wood slide inside the tip of my pointer finger. Patting the wall, I locate the switch and snap it down.

My finger throbs. A piece of old barnwood plowed underneath my nail bed and through the corner of my nail, where it's lodged into the cuticle. I put the wounded finger in my mouth in attempt to pop the sharp-edged wood chip back out.

I look up. The room's charisma distracts me. A low wattage twinkle across the ceiling reveals two contrasting strands of bulbs. A dim caramel color and a livelier sandstone hue drape loosely across the ceiling, forming an *X* as they cross in the middle.

The furniture is made of espresso-brown wicker wood. I like how the cushions align each couch ranging in size, material, and shade of blue. The room looks to be an add-on to the original structure, as the walls are made of refurbished wood. Structurally, it branches out independently from the rest of the house. Potted plants enrich the homey appeal. They stagger across one wall of the boxy room. I see the leaves quiver on one of the plants as a wisp of wind snakes through the window creases. I feel the heat kick on.

On the opposite side from the mini plant conservatory, three massive bookshelves line the wall, overflowing with literature. Little trinkets ranging from Buddha heads and candles to a mini cactus plant and other succulents separate the numerous stacks of books. A turquoise daybed sits between two shelves, and a mustard-yellow single seater with matching ottoman sits between the other two. A refinished wooden minibar sits along the end of the last bookshelf at an angle next to a mahogany-brown leather recliner. I see a brass-based standing light with a dangling old chain. The standing lamp separates the minibar and the old recliner. I get it—this is the room for clearing the mind. I feel at ease.

I make my way to the bookshelf, laying the wine bottle on top of the whiskey bar. I swig the wine in my glass and feel an immediate buzz. I need a timeout from the wine. There're pictures scattered throughout the shelves. I recognize each agent in the photos, smiling with what appears to be their family or friends. I wonder how each of them go about maintaining relationships. Do they take time off for family visits? I can imagine it's not very often.

As I brush my finger across one of the shelves, I come across a picture of Hank laughing with a beautiful woman. I pick up the picture and recognize the kitchen in its background. I squint at the picture and the woman's hand. What is that? A ring? Hank's married? How does that work?

I walk to the leather chair. I must sit on this snug looking thing. I lower my battered body onto the seat, shaking as I use my hand to lift each leg onto the ottoman. Oh, that's nice. I may sleep here. I turn to a standing lamp and tug the chain. I'd use this room everyday if I lived here with multiple people. I'm content.

I look out the window. There's nothing to observe but the pitch-black darkness of the midnight skies. No stars or city lights, only the sounds of the late-night wind charging at the windows. What a day. How did I end up here? Everything happened so fast. I feel like a computer overloaded with information. I've had too many files downloaded at once, resulting in a forced shutdown. I don't feel anything. Nothing. Maybe it's the wine.

I remember a few instances in life where I believed I was lucky. Most children bring home their germy little friend's flu bug, passing it on to their family members. Unlike my brother, I never had the chicken pox, flu, head lice, all the fluctuating viruses. I never received a flu shot. I didn't think this was an oddity, as we ate healthy and used hand sanitizer religiously. It makes sense. I felt bad for my little brother.

I shocked the hell out of my dad when we went camping for the first time. I was picking up sticks and other plant life to build a tiny cabin for my dolls while dad pitched our tents. I had the cabin halfway assembled, with landscaping and all, when my dad stood over me, shrieking at me to stop. Not only was I holding wads of poison ivy in both hands but I was holding a piece between my lips, as my hands were full. He still brings up this story, as he caught it from cleaning my skin and passed it to my little brother. I was perfectly fine. My poor brother.

I turn to the side table and see an edge of an album tucked under a blanket. I slide the book from the table and recognize my new acquaintances. I read the words "In Loving Memory" as I move the cover through the light. It must be the roommate who passed away, as Jack's missing from the photo. Her dark, exotic features and large brown eyes draw her from the rest of the group. It's same woman in the picture with Hank.

I flip through the album and see pages of memories with the striking woman. Hank and the beauty are laughing together in nearly every picture. It's bizarre to think this group has a social life outside their intense roles. I skim to the last page, where Hank is on one knee, proposing to the woman in the picture. She's holding her mouth, while the group cheers in the background. Her story ends here. Bryan's bit to Hank earlier now makes sense, as the poor guy lost his fiancé. A piece of paper falls into my lap, revealing the information from her funeral. Her name was Theresa Nicole Mills—born January 23, 1978; died June 25, 2016. What?

She died the day of my car accident. I hold my breath and rub my forehead, feeling my heart pound faster. Bryan said they lost one of their squad members on the day of my accident. It was Theresa. Was this because of me? Shit. I feel queasy, like the time I rode the spinning teacup ride two times in a row. I'm sitting still, but the room is violently spinning. Jack didn't say much about the situation, and I can only imagine what Hank thinks of me. Am I at fault?

A shadowy blob moves through the hazy light reflection in the window. What was that? The spinning in my head abruptly stops. I hold my breath and listen for sounds. The figure appears in the window and stops. I see blur. Is it coming from outside? No. No, it's behind me. It's inside the house. I turn my head, straining my eyes as I look over my shoulder. I feel a breeze on the back of my neck.

It feels like someone's hiding behind my chair. I feel it again. A tickle against my neck. What if they got in? They tracked my phone. This is it. I turn and face forward. I should scream. I look in the window. The figure is gone. *Come on, Anna. It's all in your head this time. You've been drinking, and now you're seeing things. Nothing's behind you. You're in a safe place.* I open and close my eyes and release some air. What was that? It's gone. I feel uneasy about the windows. I can't see out, but someone may be watching me inside. I squirm to the edge of the chair and stand up.

I wobble around and see the outline of a large person standing in the middle of the doorway. The shadow skulks my direction. With my weapon options limited to a succulent or paperback book, I look for an escape route. I have nowhere to run. My mouth quivers, and I bite my lip as the silhouette totters into the light. It's Hank.

"Was getting water and saw you reading that book. I couldn't help but stop," Hank mumbles.

"You must hate that I'm here in your home. If it wasn't for me, she'd still be here, wouldn't she?" I ask.

"I don't hate you. If you're talking about the prank from earlier, I was caught off guard. I didn't mean to come off as cruel," he says.

"So she died during my accident?"

"May I come in?"

"Yes, of course. Sorry, I didn't mean to go through your stuff."

"It's for everyone to enjoy. That's why its laying out in the middle of the room."

"I don't know what to say, but I'm truly sorry. You were going to marry her."

"You have nothing to apologize for." Hank walks over and grabs the book.

"Theresa loved watching over you, take my word on that. She lost her mom as a teenager to a drunk driver."

"A teenager?"

"Yeah, at fourteen. She took it hard, watching you and your mom in the accident. For her … well, it was like she was reliving her own nightmare."

"Watching someone take away your mom's life is heartbreaking."

"I had to tell her over and over not to approach you when we were initially dissolved from our assignment—that is, until we discovered you were flagged orange at the hospital that day."

"I bet you miss her very much. It must be hard to meet someone in your profession to begin with … and engaged."

"Theresa worked hard to get where she was. Most of us have family members in the CIA, which helps, having a legacy. She started her career in law enforcement and worked her ass off."

"Thank you for welcoming me into your home. I promise I won't disappoint you guys."

"If Theresa was here today and felt you were in danger, she'd gladly give her life a second time. Hell, all of us under this roof would. We see the bigger picture. Something's going to happen. It'll come on so sudden; we'll be gone before we had a chance."

"Aside from my mom and my health, what you just said is the most frightening thing I've ever heard someone say."

"Luckily, we have a strong operation and developed a reliable antidote. We're prepared on one end. It's a matter of bringing the rest of you together."

"Have you ever come face-to-face with a Stag?"

"No. Only on footage and from a distance. They nearly look—"

"Look what?"

"Human."

"Jack said the same."

"Stags may have similar body features, but they're the furthest from human. The first time I saw footage of a Stag's eyes, I felt sick. Their eyes are red in light. Basically, asshole demons wanting what's not theirs."

"The print I saw was enough for me to feel sick. There must be a way to catch one."

"When Theresa saw them annihilate your car, she drove into their vehicle. She jumped out of her car and ripped open the driver's door. They killed her right there."

"She was brave," I say.

"She did it without hesitation. If only she knew you made it out alive."

"I can't wait to fight back and make Theresa proud."

"You need to get healthy first. Let's start with the basics of walking, kiddo," Hank laughs.

"Good point."

"Sorry I startled you. I'm going to head back to bed, but I'm glad we had a chance to chat. You should get some rest." Hank turns and walks out of the room.

"I will. Thank you for everything."

"No problem," Hank says, disappearing back into the dark living room.

"Good night," I say quietly.

Tall Hank pops his head back into the room. "I just remembered—I short-sheeted the bed you're sleeping in."

"What? Why are you telling me?"

"I just remembered I did it to screw with one of the new guys coming in, so on second note, give me a few minutes to fix the bed."

"Just can't win today, huh, Hank?" I laugh.

I contemplate pouring more wine and decide to give it a rest. I choke down the last sip of wine and decide on a glass of water. I take one more look at Theresa and lay the book down where I found it.

Following the dim light from the kitchen, I maneuver around the obstacle course of living room furniture. I see a note on the kitchen table.

> Anna,
>
> Your bedroom door is open so you know which room is yours. I put pajamas on the bed with some other essentials for you. Whatever Jack forgets, I'll grab at the store. Coffee and breakfast will be ready in the morning. Looking forward to filling in some of the blanks for you.
>
> —Cindy
>
> PS Leave a list here for Jack. I told him to grab it on his way out. Make sure he has the keys ... we don't want to raise any flags at your residence.

I see Cindy left a notepad and pen out for me to create my list. I pull out a kitchen stool and look around the lonely kitchen. It's after five in the morning. I grab the pen and tap it against the table.

Jack,

Here's a list if you get the chance. I really appreciate it.

-My Bathroom stuff- I have a red travel bag with essentials and a blue bag next to it with my every day stuff.

-There's a suitcase in my closet- one should be directly to the right of the closet when you flip on the light.

-Grab a wad of things from each drawer of my dresser. -There are 5 drawers.

-Grab everything from the side table next to my bed that looks helpful for back pain.

-My neck pillow in my bed.

-All ice packs in fridge and my back brace that is in the laundry room.

-Vitamins in the cabinet over the coffeepot (Just take them all; they help boost my healing).

-Anything else you can stuff in that suitcase that seems realistic.

These are the things I can live without, so if you don't get them, no biggie.

See you later,

Anna

CHAPTER 17

I hear a muffled woman's voice vibrating from a distance. The pitch gradually intensifies like wind howling before a thunderstorm. I can't comprehend the words. The sweet, calm tone soothes me as I open my eyes. I'm lying on top of a snow-covered bench in the middle of a blizzard. Rolling off the bench, I brush a layer of the winter glaze off my chest and realize I'm wearing an emerald-green satin dress. When I pull up at the side of the dress, I notice a new pair of heels.

Large shimmery flakes mingle around my hair, melting upon contact. I walk around the accumulated snow, hearing a crunch below my steps. I rub the bare skin on my arms and feel content in the cold. A gust of wind coils through my hair, brushing a piece into my mouth. With every graceful step, I realize I feel nothing. It's as though someone poured my sensations down the drain and flipped on the garbage disposal. I'm desensitized to pain.

As the wind intensifies, the trees around me rattle. Every tree in sight is in full summer blossom and is saturated with snow. I hear the woman's voice through the rustle. She's calling my name. I twirl around and search for the woman. A large vacuum tube appears from the sky and lowers over my head. I feel a pulling force from above as the tube inches closer. The world goes blank as I'm sucked into the vacuum.

"Anna, it's ten in the morning," says a woman's voice.

"Huh?"

"It's me, Cindy," the voice says.

"Cindy?"

"I have breakfast ready for you and some potent coffee."

"Whoa, last night really happened?" I ask.

"Yes. Yes, it did," Cindy says.

I press myself up in bed and rub my eyes. "This room has no windows. I would've slept all day."

"Good. Your body's healing and needs it," she says, looking around the room. "But, for your safety, it's probably better to be in the room with no windows."

"Give me a few minutes and I'll be down to join you. Thanks for making breakfast."

"You can come down in your pajamas; it's just you and I here for the day. Sam and Jack started their shift, and Leslie and Hank drove to the condo to check on Bryan. I'll grab you a change of clothes and lay it on the bed."

"Okay, thanks."

I slide the sheets off me and turn to get out of bed. I feel shooting pain down my leg again. The adrenaline from yesterday's madness officially dissolved. I think of the knife. Crap, I stabbed a man last night. Poor Bryan—I bet he's feeling pain today.

I feel like I'm standing for the first time after a hip or leg surgery as I center the weight between my feet. It's like I'm walking for the first time without a walker post operation as I shuffle toward the bathroom door. The chilly room has an eerie appeal. It'd be pitch black had Cindy not turned on the dim setting of the one and only light in the room. Each wooden floor panel creeks as I add my body weight. The ground feels as though I'm walking on a cold cement cellar base. This room screams old industrial warehouse closet.

I flip on the bathroom light and look round, avoiding eye contact with myself in the mirror. The bathroom is set up for visitors, practical and hotel-like. A basket holds bathroom essentials collected from differing hotels. Various soaps, lotions, dental care, and other little samples fill the brown basket to the brim. What a smart idea.

I catch a glimpse in the mirror as I stick my hand in the basket. My auburn hair looks chestnut brown from the mangled mane accumulating grease. I take my long locks and twist the hair into a bun on the top of my head. I'm going to make it a point to shower today. Running the faucet, I splash water on my face and dab it with a neatly folded hand towel. I put my hands on the sides of the sink and pull my face closer to the mirror. *You look just like everyone else does; don't get in your own head about this.* Anna the Alien? Gross, the words go well together. Don't ever say it aloud; I'll never hear the end of it. Last night was weird. I turn my neck to one side and roll it around slowly. I tuck my chin in, stretching the muscles in a therapeutic motion.

I pull up my shirt and turn to one side in the mirror. Strange how so much pain can come from the spinal cord. It's deceiving, as there's no external bruising. I look like a normal female adult human on the outside. Internally, I'm confused. This will take some time to digest.

I make my way to the stairs and peer down. I see a nightmare combination—slick shiny wood and steep stairs. I'm curious as to how I made it up to the top last night. I grip onto the railing and begin the obstacle course. My head begins to pound from the wine as I propel down each step with my partially frozen feet. I contemplate turning around and sinking back into bed until I smell the coffee.

I follow the scent. Smells of fresh coffee combined with steamy water and lingering bacon traces rise through the staircase. I pass the halfway point of my struggling stair travel and see Cindy blow past the bottom of the staircase, carrying a stack of books. I hear the patter of her feet as she darts away from the kitchen, heading back toward my direction. She crosses the stairs so quickly that I couldn't grab her attention.

I get to the last step and hear Cindy coming toward the front of the staircase.

"Hey, Cindy, I've—"

"Holy crap," Cindy yelps. She drops a handful of books, nearly knocking me onto the stairs. She holds her hands out in front of her.

"I'm so sorry. I didn't mean to startle you."

"My goodness. It's okay—was grabbing a few things from my lab room. Thought the literature would help you," Cindy says as she hits the ground, picking up her book spill.

"You've got a lot of books there," I say.

"I figure we'd relax after breakfast, and I could go over some stuff with you. I don't want you to feel like a lab rat."

"Relaxing sounds nice." I smile at Cindy.

"How're you feeling today?"

"Think I had a little too much wine last night. I'm still wrapping my mind around things—this house, my mom's death, and my accident."

"I can only imagine the overload you're experiencing."

"I was almost healthy again. I can't believe I'm back to gripping staircase railings one step at a time. It's infuriating, and to learn it was intentional …"

"I think you're handling everything well and I'm proud of you." Cindy places her hand on my shoulder.

"Thanks. I'd help you with the books, but I'm worn out. You guys have a challenging set of stairs."

"Next time yell for me. I don't want you making your spine worse."

"I will—not sure I can do the stairs a second time."

"Follow me. How about we start the day with a nice breakfast?"

"You don't have to ask me twice. The coffee's intoxicating."

Cindy guides me toward the kitchen. I press my fingers against my temples, hoping to release the hangover. The kitchen is warm and inviting, even more so in the daylight. The morning sun bounces off the eggshell-white painted walls, enlarging each room as I pass by. The bold specs of contrasting colors riveting through cracks in the exposed brick pop well in the natural light. I feel okay with staying here if I need to.

"There are eggs, bacon, toast, and fresh fruit," Cindy says.

"I have to admit, you cooked my breakfast favorites. But I'm going to assume everyone knows this stuff from now on." I let out an awkward laugh.

"I can imagine this must feel bizarre."

"You've no idea. Do you know my least favorites too?"

"You hate lunch meat, zucchini, and leftovers. But, given your situation this year, you began eating leftovers," Cindy says.

"Wow, that's impressive. You've got me pegged."

Cindy lays a plate in front of me.

"What's your background? How does someone become an agent in such a discrete operation?"

"Most of my journey with the LFP I was a geneticist, as you already know, conducting research in a lab at main headquarters in Utah." Cindy grabs a plate and scoops a heaping pile of eggs onto the center.

"What was your specialty?"

"My colleagues and I were working on serums derived from the CCR5 Delta protein found in an Interhybrid's blood. My division specifically worked on a treatment and cure for the HIV virus. Individual departments are created at headquarters for virus-specific strains, and I was assigned to the HIV virus."

"There's a cure for the HIV virus?"

"Yes, it's in the middle stages of testing for approval." Cindy hands me a plate.

"How on earth did you link blood types to virus cures?"

"The RH negative factor was discovered in 1937 from research based on women experiencing miscarriages and other abnormalities post birth. After the initial discovery, and years of studying blood proteins in RH negative women, the CIA offered the team their own division. Things sort of evolved from there."

"Very fascinating. By the way, you make a great breakfast."

"Thank you. And to make things a little less weird, we monitor and report the food Interhybrids eat for studies associating nutrient intake and blood-protein potency factors—it's been me reporting your food intake."

"I guess that makes things a little less creepy." I shove a piece of bacon in my mouth.

"I should've made something for you to eat last night. Everything happened so abruptly; I didn't think to ask."

"Not sure I would've been able to stomach anything, so no worries." I watch Cindy take a bite of fruit. "What would happen to someone like me if I was injected with a virus? Would I be fine?"

"You'd initially feel off, like most would. Your white blood cells would quickly discover a crisis and go to work, forming fast-responding antibodies. Think of crumbs being dumped on the ground and a high-powered vacuum cleaning the majority up before they reach the surface—you should see it under a microscope."

"What was that liquid you mixed with my blood?"

"That's a formula we created in the lab for boosting and activating the attack mode response. Bryan's body will go to work faster, and he'll be less likely to develop an infection. The liquid activates the protein."

"So, in a way, my blood's like a flu shot for viruses?"

"Yeah, I guess you can look at it like that. There's a lot. But for Bryan—his situation, yes."

I plow through my fruit bowl. I hope she'll talk more. I'd like to shovel as much food in as I can. I'm starving and didn't realize it until the bacon touched my tongue. Maybe it's a hangover or quite possibly my new sense of security.

"You make a good cup of coffee," I say.

"I'm the house barista. My parents—it was their thing when I was a kid. They'd sit and have coffee together when they could."

"Where'd you grow up?"

"I was born here in Chicago, actually. Moved to New Jersey when I was a baby. Both parents were doctors."

"Wow, that's amazing. It must feel natural to you, then?"

"My dad was a neurosurgeon, and my mother was a psychiatrist. I guess the combo of brain and behavior was the norm I grew up with, though I felt an element missing in the puzzle—DNA and the history linked to varying blood types."

"You light up when you discuss your profession. I hope I can relate one day—if I ever work again, that is."

"What you're doing now, being here with a group of strangers, trying to understand and help at the same time—you'll be able to take on anything when you're well again." Cindy's phone rings. "It's Bryan." She grabs the phone and taps the speaker button.

"How're you feeling today?" Cindy asks. "I'm with Anna, wrapping up breakfast."

"Breakfast, huh? You're up late today. It's noon," Bryan's voice echoes.

"And ..." Cindy pauses.

"Ah, I'm doing okay. I'm a little sore. Feels like what I imagined being stabbed in the side would feel like. Leslie and Hank are here."

"I'm glad you're doing okay today," I say, forcing myself into the conversation.

"Reason why I'm calling, have you heard from Jack?" Bryan asks.

"Nope, not since last night. Why? He's probably napping," Cindy says.

"When I spoke to Sam earlier, he said he was setting his alarm for a two-hour nap, switching off with Jack," Bryan says.

"Was Jack sleeping in his own car or did he go to Sam's?"

"No, Jack hopped into Sam's vehicle to sleep—never went back to his own vehicle. When Jack woke up, he said he was going to grab Anna's suitcase." Bryan pauses. "That's the last we had any contact with him."

"When was that?" Cindy asks.

"Two hours and fifteen minutes ago. When Sam couldn't get Jack to respond, he waited to make sure there weren't any issues with the phone. He pulled up to Jack's car and saw he hadn't returned to his vehicle. Here's where we stand."

"We haven't heard from him on our end," Cindy says.

"Shit. I figured, but I thought I'd see if he called at all—maybe he had questions from Anna's list. Okay, Hank's heading over there now to see what's going on," Bryan says.

"Maybe he dozed off at my place. He said he hasn't slept in a few days," I add.

"Hang on," Bryan pauses. "I'm calling Sam on speaker."

"Yeah?" Sam's voice carries over speaker.

"It's not like Jack to go unresponsive, so I'm sending Hank and Leslie over to you now." "Good idea. I'm fairly certain he's in Anna's house," Sam says.

"Don't go up to the house until Hank and Leslie are with you. That's an order," Bryan says, ending the call.

"What's going on?" I ask.

"Bryan? You there?" Cindy asks.

"Yes, I'm still here. I'm concerned—if they're tracking your phone, they probably came back again.," Bryan says.

"Wait, no. My phone isn't there. I brought it with me," I say.

"Anna, where's your phone? I saw you leave it on the counter," Bryan says.

"No, I tucked it in my pants. I grabbed it when you weren't looking and I'm sorry. I only did it in case you planned on killing me. It's not here now."

"Where's your phone now? Specifics are crucial," Bryan says.

"We forgot to tell you, as there was so much commot—"

"Who's we?" Bryan interrupts.

"Me and Jack. Back in the garage, Jack saw my phone and took off on a bike. You guys were already inside the house. He said he hid the phone in a plastic bag in the back of the movie theater. He left my phone on if you want to track it yourself."

"He should've told us immediately," Cindy says. "They'll know where you went, including our home. They may already be watching us."

I feel a quiver inch up the back of my spine. Maybe I was being watched from the back window last night. While I was drinking wine and staring out the back window, something could've been standing up against the window, stalking my every move.

"That was smart thinking on the kid's part, but something he should've told us immediately. He should know by now—I don't take risks when it comes to our overall safety," Bryan says.

"Maybe they'll think I was heading to a movie or something and got stuck in traffic around the front of the house," I suggest.

"Nope. There's no traffic that time of the night to cause you to sit that long. And not sure how many midnight madness showings were playing at the theater," Cindy says.

"I can check showtimes," I offer. "You never know."

"No, we can't base anything off the possibilities—only reality. Reality is they're tracking her phone." Bryan stops me. "I want everyone at the condo this evening and you two out of there before dark. This location has been compromised."

"What can I do right now?" Cindy asks.

"Stay put until you hear from me. I want to find out what's going on with Jack." Bryan stops. "Hank and Leslie, head over to Sam now."

We hear voices in the background, ending with a snort. I realize it's Leslie.

"What was that, Hank?" We hear Bryan's voice trail off.

"I said the kid's probably just going through her underwear drawer," Hank says.

"Meerkat—come on, now you're being inappropriate," Leslie says in the background.

"I'll call you back in twenty," Bryan says and hangs up the phone.

Cindy and I stare at each other in confusion.

"Ignore Hank. He thinks he's funny," Cindy says.

"Why do you guys keeping saying meerkat? I'm confused," I say.

"We say meerkat when one of us thinks Hank is stepping over a comfort boundary," Cindy says.

"Makes sense now," I say. "Is this out of Jack's character?" I ask.

"Yes, it is. Let's wait for Hank and Leslie to get over there," Cindy says.

"I never should've asked him to go in my house. I feel awful."

"Don't assume the worst." Cindy maneuvers around the living room, propping the pillows for me to sit. "Come in here and sit down. We'll keep each other distracted for now. You can look through some of these books."

"I feel sick. Not sure I can look through books right now. What if they attacked him?"

"Let's give them some time to sort this out. He always knows what's best for everyone," Cindy says.

"How can you distract the mind with a situation like this?" I ask.

"It can be difficult when you have the time to worry. We're trained to react during immediate catastrophes—to remain calm and unemotional."

I sit down next to Cindy and grab one of the books.

"That book is filled with photography from inside the ancient pyramids. One of the recent studies came from a tomb located half a mile from the featured site."

I flip through the first few pages. "What's the study?"

"This study was truly remarkable and ties into what we brought up last night. Scientists took samples from the remains of several corpses, bringing a clean sample to a boil. When the sample reached seven hundred degrees, the microbe was still alive. They found matching results from boiling the blood at seven hundred degrees with liquid nitrogen from a deceased Interhybrid."

"What about human blood?"

"Not even a close match, though every blood type has a distinct microbe."

"How's it possible for something to go from dead to alive?"

"It's the polarity of the blood cells. The blood is electrically magnetic and chemical based. When the mummy dust was placed in a potential hydrogen perfect solution, the same as the live blood, it turned back to life."

"Maybe they can create a Jurassic Park with mummified humans," I say.

"That'll be the day I run for president," Cindy says.

"But where did the Veraxum go? You said there are pictures linking an existence from two other worlds." I browse through the pictures on one page.

"That is a mystery."

The phone rings, startling the two of us.

"Leslie and Hank are en route to Jack's location. Jack brought a burner phone with him, so we can't track him or Anna's phone." Bryan lets out a deep breath.

"My phone wasn't full on battery when you were in my kitchen. I remember that much. It's probably dead by now."

"Could be, though I'm going to assume they found it. Cindy, you may want to begin cleaning the basement bathroom."

"Will do." Cindy hangs up the phone.

"Huh? I'm lost from that conversation. We're searching for Jack, and he wants you to clean the basement bathroom?"

"No," Cindy laughs. "That's our house code for clearing the evidence connected to our existence."

"Good one. I never would've known."

CHAPTER 18

Hank peels out of the parking garage.

"All right, what's our plan?" Leslie asks, loading a gun. "Grabbed my new silencer. I'm shooting to kill today."

"Easy there, lady," Hank says, gaining speed as drives around a city block. Hank pulls up to a main street and darts onto the road. He steps on the gas and slams hard on the brakes.

"Hank, seriously? I just had lunch," Leslie says.

"Is the clock wrong or something?"

"No, why?"

"The traffic—it's a mess. I'm not dealing with a midday rush hour. Where I'm from, people know how to drive." Hank steers to the right shoulder and tailgates the car in front of him.

"Where you're from, people believe in horse and carriage. I'm not dealing with your driving lectures today, so stop."

"But you've got no id—"

"We've talked about this. It's just me with you—Jack only tolerates your mouth because the kid's new. Just put a muzzle on it. Want to see me angry?"

"No, el diablo can go back to her gates of hell, por favor." Hank drives on the shoulder, increases speed to a parked car, and veers back in the line of cars.

"You got ahead of two cars—good job," Leslie says.

"What wrong?" Hank asks.

"Nothing."

"I know something's wrong—can't fool me."

"I'm not in the mood for your reckless driving. Find a side street around this shit or let me drive."

"I get it," Hank says, pulling behind a car. He stops in line with traffic.

"Try me."

"You're genuinely worried, aren't you? About Jack? We'll be there soon, Les."

"I thought we'd hear from him by now. Last night he said he noticed a difference in one of the side windows—I didn't believe him."

"We'll know soon. Just hang on. I'm going to be an asshole driver."

"You're an asshole driving, that's for sure."

"And Leslie's back."

"Just get us there," Leslie snarls.

Hank speeds up, creating his own lane as he passes several city blocks of gridlocked Chicago traffic. He floors it to the front of line, angling the car in front of a pickup truck. The man driving the lifted pickup truck eases forward, nearly touching the bumper of Hank's vehicle. The driver holds down his horn. He rolls down his window and flips off Hank, keeping his hand on the horn. Hank rolls down his window.

"Don't."

"Fine." Hank sticks his hand out the window and waves back at the man and stomps on the gas as the light turns green. The man gains speed behind Hank, swerving over to one side of the merging lanes, trying to pull in front of Hank. The truck growls behind them.

"He's trying to run us off the road. Buckle your seat belt, devil woman."

"Careful."

Hank holds his foot down and veers into the man's lane, hauling over the middle of the two merging lanes. The man slows down before he crashes into the side of the on-ramp. Hank takes off, gaining distance. As the truck falls back, the driver rolls his window down, holding his hand out the window with a fist.

"That guy just gave me the fist. Chicago drivers—they're insane."

"If they only knew what we're really up to, they'd make way for us to pass," Leslie says, tossing her hands up.

"Come on—you're waving the damn gun in the air when you talk. Put it down. Speeding, reckless driving, bearing firearms ..." Hank lists, maneuvering onto the shoulder.

Leslie folds over and turns on the flashers.

"Thanks. Now quit playing with the gun and look out for cops. We don't have time to deal with police today."

"Sorry." Leslie puts the gun away and stares out the window. She rubs her nose.

Hank looks at Leslie and to the road. He looks back at Leslie. "It'd be funny if you shot a Stag in the ass with that thing. It's a nice-looking gun," Hank says.

"You're trying to make me feel better. I know you just as well," Leslie says.

"Forget it. I was only try—"

"What are you doing? Exit right and then get back on the expressway at the light. Pass these cars. There's a stall up ahead on the shoulder. See?"

"You know what? How about you go back to playing with that new toy of yours. You're the worst when you're nervous, Leslie Marie. I'm getting anxiety."

"I'm worried about Jack."

"I know. I'm worried too." Hank pulls off to the right, taking Leslie's advice. He catches a green light and merges back onto the highway. "It's not like the kid to go radio silent."

"Pothole—"

Hanks drives over the pothole.

"We should've taken the Tahoe," Hank says.

"We're almost there."

Hank exits the highway.

"Turn up the police radio. There's always accidents off this exit; you should've gone to the next one," Leslie says.

"Strike two, lady."

Leslie's phone rings. "Turn it down—it's Sam," Leslie says.

"You're lucky I like you, Leslie." Hank turns down the radio. "Next time hook up to Bluetooth. Put Sam on speaker."

"It's a burner phone, dummy," Leslie says. "Sam?"

Sounds of a muffled speaker.

"Sam, you read me? El diablo and I are pulling down the street right now," Hank says.

"Sam?" Leslie asks.

Hank pulls to a four-way stop and turns left. A tire blows.

"Crap, just keep going," Leslie says.

"Stop," Sam says.

"We're turning on the street," Hank says.

"Don't turn down here. Just pull over. Now. I see Jack," Sam says.

"We just turned. It's a one-way street," Leslie says.

"I'm pulling over. I see a spot back here. What's going on? Sam?" Hank veers to the side of the street. "Damn it—we're riding on the rim."

"What the f—"

"Firecracker?" Hank interrupts.

"I know," Sam says. "Pull over where you are."

CHAPTER 19

2 hours and 22 minutes earlier

Jack hears ringing in the distance. Chirping sounds of crickets infused with stifled wedding bells rumble. The mangled-up harmony intensifies between heartbeats. Louder and louder the vibrating sounds deepen until Jack pops open his eyes and chokes for air.

"Whoa, man. It's all good. Just dreaming, Jackie," Sam says.

Jack rubs his eyes and turns to Sam. "Was that a full two hours? You're screwing with me."

"No, man," Sam says.

"So that was two hours, huh? I need more sleep to function—this isn't going to fly."

"I know. I felt the same way. You're way more vocal about it though," Sam says.

"I haven't slept in days and all you do, is talk about inertia. Vocal about what?" Jack asks.

"I guess everything in life. I read it's a millennial thing."

"I told you—you're a millennial too. Google it. Stop with the millennial shit, man." Jack yawns.

"And I'll tell you again—millennials should be broken down into two categories."

"I'm going back to my car if you don't shut up," Jack says.

"You're right—who cares right now, you're half-awake anyways. We need to fill up with gas. It's cold today, and I had to turn the car on and let it run in a little. I'm not sure the car took a charge—it's using gas, not battery, for the first time."

"Now? We'll have to circle around for parking until the next church service gets out. Spots are full right now," Jack says.

"I think I can manage."

"Why don't we get in my car and fill yours up later?" Jack asks.

"Remember what I said? Two categories—and I'd rather fill up now and not be lazy, if that's okay with you." Sam turns on the car.

"When was the last time we filled this thing up?"

"Not sure. Don't worry, though. I'll make it quick. I'm ready to start my next two hours of nap time." Sam takes off down the street.

"You do realize if we switched to my car, you'd be sleeping by now?"

"And you do realize we're switching cars with Hank and Leslie later? Be considerate."

"Sorry, my inertia." Jack rolls his eyes.

"Geez, man, you're cranky as shit." Sam turns around the block and pulls into a corner gas station. "Two blocks. That's all we had to go. Do us both of a favor and buy yourself an energy drink."

"Yeah, fine," Jack says, slamming the car door.

Sam hops out of the car and looks for the gas tank. He gets in the car and backs it to another pump.

Jack walks out the door, holding energy drinks and a large bag of junk food. He shifts the bag to one arm and thrusts the other in the air. "I'm holding this one over you."

"It never needs gas. Go ahead—belittle the eco-friendly," Sam says.

"When you put it like that—"

"What did we discuss?" Sam interrupts.

"Uh, that you're getting old as shit, and your metabolism's slowing down." Jack hops in the car.

"Seriously, Jack, you're killing me today." Sam slides in the car. "Screw it, what did you buy?"

"I grabbed your favorites too," Jack pulls out a bag of pepperoni Combos and a second bag of gummy bears. "Splurge day—it's a special occasion."

"The only thing that's special about today is I get to sleep while working." Sam pulls out from the gas station and heads toward Anna's home.

"You get two hours; then we switch again," Jack says.

"Look at that, Jack. Spot's still there." Sam points.

"Well, good for you."

"Slam that energy drink and face-change. I'm going to eat those Combos and pass out," Sam says.

"Yeah, fine. I'm going to grab Anna's stuff. Check you in a bit." Jack slops on an oversized hat, a pair of thick-framed glasses, and imitation braces.

"Just to note, your face-change combo needs work. Stags would run from you, man. Now get out, jackass."

Jack looks at himself in the side mirror and shrieks. He shakes his head at Sam and slams the car door, taking off down the street. He circles around the block twice, staggering through alleys, keeping close to the buildings.

Looking over his shoulder, Jack slips inside a coffee shop and darts to the bathroom. He locks himself inside a stall and strips off his top layer of clothes. He reverses his jacket for color change and spits out the braces. Jack steps out from the bathroom, pulling out a winter ski hat and a pair of sunglasses. He storms out of the coffee shop.

"Stags would run from you …" Jack mimics Sam's words as he tosses the baseball cap and glasses into a box sitting next to an alley.

Jack sucks in a deep breath and slides out of the alley, skidding onto the pavement. He walks another block and reroutes toward Anna's home, pulling out the keys while searching over his shoulder. Jack glances over to Sam's car from the distance. The seats folded backward. Sam is fast asleep. "That didn't take long," Jack mutters. Making his path up the front-porch stairs, Jack jingles the key ring, loaded with keys of various sizes.

"Geez, Anna. I've got a car key and a house key. What is she, a locksmith?" Jack grumbles to himself. He starts with the first key and works his way through.

Reaching key number six, Jack dances in place as the wind attacks him from between the porch beams. "At least color code the damn keys." Jack looks around, struggling to protect his face. His hand trembles as he pops the next key in the lock. At a far angle, he spots an object scurrying behind him. Remaining still, Jack looks down and veers his head slightly to one side to get another look. He startles himself as the shadow gains speed from behind him. Someone or something is approaching the house. "Damn it, Samuel." Jack jingles the next key into the lock, feeling the key stick as he presses his frozen fingers toward the right.

"Excuse me. What do you think you're doing with those keys?" asks a high-pitched voice.

Jack unlocks the second dead bolt. He clenches his teeth and raises his eyebrows. He releases the keys, leaving them hanging in the door. Marching in place, he shuts his eyes and shifts around.

Jack turns to face Jessica.

She crosses her arms and glares at Jack. Her head cocks to one side as she bites her lip. The wind blows her hair sideways. She opens her mouth and her hair slaps her in the face. "I asked you a question—I know you heard me." She rips her hair away from her face.

Jack stares at Jessica.

"I'll ask one more time—what are you doing with Anna's keys?"

"She—"

"You know what, I'm calling the police—you can explain why to them." Jessica holds out a key chain of mace, threatening to pull the trigger. Keeping her eyes on Jack, she pulls out her phone with her free hand.

"Wait. You never gave me a chance to speak," Jack says.

Jessica raises the mace.

"You must be Anna's friend, Jessica." Jack raises both hands up and waves with one hand. "I'd go in for the hug, but I don't want mace in the face. This isn't how I envisioned meeting Anna's best friend."

"What on earth are you talking about?" Jessica demands.

"Anna's taking a nap at my place," Jack says.

"You're lying. I don't know who the hell you are. Never met you in my life—I'd remember you," Jessica says, stomping in place.

"How about you ask me a question about Anna, so I can prove I'm not a psycho killer? Ask a question that someone dating your friend a month should know."

"Wait. Dating Anna—you're dating Anna?" Jessica laughs and takes a step forward with mace.

"Yes, and she's sleeping at my place as we speak."

"She's never talked about you before. She would've said something to her best friend. You did something to her, didn't you? And you stole the keys to her house after you dumped her body," Jessica raises her voice, bending her knees simultaneously.

"What? No, I'm not crazy. Ask me any question."

"Fine then, get it wrong, I call the police, and you can explain this to them."

"Go ahead. Ask me anything."

"Where does she work?"

"You're trying to trick me. She's not working from her accident still—was a graphic designer," Jack says.

"You think you know about the accident? When was the accident?"

"June, out in the suburbs—on the way to her parents."

"Parents?"

"Well, to see her dad and brother. Her mom passed away."

"Thought I had you for a second. Not sure what to say—you may be real. She may be hiding you from me."

"Look, I'm a good guy trying to help your best friend. She had a really hard night last night," Jack says.

"Yes, she was very upset last night. That's why I'm here to check on her."

"What can I say to make you believe me?" Jack asks.

"Let me think—stop talking a second."

"You're nervous—I can tell. How about I hold my hands above me and sit on the ground?" Jack asks.

"Yes, do that." Jessica points with the mace.

Jack lowers himself to the ground with his hands by his head.

"How about we start with last night?" Jessica asks.

Jack lowers himself to the frozen surface. "She called me and said she was leaving her dinner with you early because of some woman at the bar."

"Go on."

"She called you because she didn't want to be alone and changed her mind. I told her I'd come pick her up. She didn't want to burden you—said she wanted you to stay out and have fun."

"Stop talking. I'm calling the police—something still feels off," Jessica says.

"But why? I'm telling you the truth," Jack says.

"I don't know why. But what you're saying—it's making sense. She couldn't have been less interested in meeting guys last night. But I feel I should know about you, you know?" Jessica asks.

"I agree, though the fact that I know every detail from last night—that she forgot her credit card with the guy from the bar, and you'd be bringing it back—doesn't that say something?" Jack asks.

"Yeah, I guess."

"I'm telling the truth. She gave me a list—it's in my pocket."

"Okay. Get up. You're either following her around or telling the truth," Jessica says, lowering the mace. "Either way, I can tell you're not a psycho. You know too much."

"Thank you. It's freezing out. I can't imagine Anna stuck out here a few weeks back."

"Oh, I know. I bet you're the sweetheart who salted her front porch, then?"

"You got me."

"You know, she was freaked out about that," Jessica says.

"Not sure why. I did the porch while she was waiting on tests in the hospital."

"Really? When did she find out it was you?" Jessica raises the mace.

"After that night. She was on a bunch of drugs in the hospital. Can we go inside? I have a list from Anna—here, look." Jack pulls out the list from his coat pocket.

"Handwritten?"

"Yeah, look yourself. She even used my name on the list," Jack holds the paper in the air.

Jessica yanks it out of his hand. "What's your name?" she asks, skimming over the list.

"I'm Jack. Sorry we had to meet like this. She wrote me this list before she took a nap."

"What the … that's a lot for a day. A suitcase? Really?"

"She's going to spend the week with me. She's in a lot of pain, and I think last night made her want to get out of the house."

"No, I get it. She's been through a lot of suffering this year. This is Anna's writing. Her phone's been off again, by the way. It was ringing earlier this morning, and now it's off."

"She was limping to the bathroom this morning and dropped it in the sink. It's in a bag of rice right now."

"Does that old trick still work with phones nowadays?"

"Not sure. It's worth a try, though," Jack says.

"Yeah, I guess." Jessica points at the door.

"Can we head in? It's pretty cold outside," Jack says.

"I guess—can't believe she hasn't mentioned you."

"Let's chat more inside," Jack says, opening the front door, signaling for Jessica to go ahead of him.

"Sorry if I'm coming off rude. I'm just in a bit of shock. She tells me everything. How long have you two been dating?"

"Over a month now. She hasn't had a boyfriend in a while, so I'm guessing she was waiting until she knew it was working before she said something."

Jack searches around the house. He makes his way to the staircase, with a nosy Jessica behind him.

"What are you looking around like that for?" she asks.

"She told me to make sure everything was in the clear—you know, the people she saw at the restaurant. She wanted to make sure they didn't follow her home."

"Yeah, I guess. You think they'd do that?" she asks.

"Nowadays you can never be too sure," Jack says.

"True. So, where'd you meet? You and Anna?" Jessica asks.

"At her last doctor's checkup before she slipped. We were both stuck waiting an hour, crammed next to each other and started talking."

"What happened to you?"

"Me? Nothing. Why?" Jack asks.

"You said you met in the waiting room. So, what happened to your spine?"

"Oh, I was waiting with my grandma—her appointment."

"Yeah, she hated those appointments. They'd take forever—she was by far the youngest there."

"I hate to cut things short, but I have to hurry. I didn't leave a note, and she can't call me without a phone, so—"

"Of course. Let me help you. I can speed this up, as I know where everything is," Jessica says.

"Thank you. I'd really appreciate the help, and it's nice to meet you too. She says she needs to get better about her cell phone, so I'll work on her."

"Oh, you're a blessing—nail that in her brain." Jessica gives Jack a hug in the middle of the stairs. "She worries me too much."

Jack turns around and races up the stairs. He smiles to himself and holds his chest.

"What do you do, Jack?" Jessica staggers up the stairs behind him.

"Huh?" Jack searches around the room. "Oh, I work for the government. I'm a case manager."

"Case manager? What do you specialize in?"

"I can't legally discuss exactly. But I can say I deal with crime before it's in the papers, and I know the victims' names before they're released to the public. I can't really go into too much detail, unfortunately."

"Interesting."

"Yeah, I guess."

"Maybe it'd be easier to enjoy this convo when we're able to meet under better circumstances." Jessica shrugs.

"Agree—with Anna around too. She's still getting to know me, you know?"

"Agree. Follow me this way. I'll get her suitcase."

"Thanks."

Jessica walks toward the closet and looks at the list. "So you got any cute single friends?"

"What? Me?" Jack asks.

"Yeah. But only if you're not a serial killer, and my friend Anna turns up soon."

"That's what I thought you said. Sorry. Uncertain how to respond—still shaking off the little mace incident," Jack laughs.

"You're right. Changing subjects now. This list she gave you?"

"What about it?"

"I see it's her handwriting, but why?"

Jack wipes the sweat off his forehead and gapes at the ceiling. "I'm not sure I understand. Why what?"

"Sorry, thinking aloud." Jessica grins. "I'll grab her big suitcase I guess. Is she moving in or something? There's just a lot written on here."

"What? No."

"Just curious, then, as to why so much freaking stuff?"

"I told her to stay for the week or so and let me help with lifting objects. She needs to relax so she can heal."

"Amen, Mister. She's stubborn."

"Also, unlike this place, I don't have stairs. She thinks she can do more than she can, so staying with me temporarily limits her."

"Yeah, you're right about the stairs." Jessica lugs a suitcase from the closet.

"Or maybe it's all in her plot to slowly move in with me?" Jack laughs.

"You're not that handsome."

"Well, she likes my charm—add some quality time with me, I doubt she'll ever come home."

"I admire your confidence, and I'll give you this—she's never hid a guy from me. Take that for whatever it's worth."

"I'll take the compliment." Jack helps Jessica with the suitcase.

"I swear—if I'm here next week helping you pack up her dishes …"

"Same time next week, then?" Jack laughs.

"But in all honestly, jokes aside, even when she's in pain, she's the sweetest, most caring friend in the world. Just wait until she's healthy again. You won't be able to keep up with her."

"I'm pretty quick," Jack says, taking handfuls of clothing from each drawer. He stuffs them inside the suitcase. "She's amazing, and I enjoy spending time with her. So far, so good."

"Good to hear."

"Wow, I didn't realize how organized she is. Has she always been like this?" Jack asks, pointing to the closet.

"Oh, you have no idea. She would come over as a teenager and help me organize my closets and yell at me when they were messy again a week later."

"Her clothes are color coordinated. Unbelievable. I'm teasing her for this." Jack shakes his head.

"I think this all started after the accident—the actual color coordinating. There are days she's bored out of her mind."

"Reading a book could be a solution."

"Reading is her evening fix." Jessica opens a drawer. "Here, these are her favorite pajamas. She'll be happy you packed these."

"I'll make sure she calls you when I get back."

"Thank you. I'd really appreciate that. She needs to get better with calling me back. I know I treat her like a child lately, but after she lost her mom, and I almost lost her … well, I guess I fear something will happen again."

Jack pulls out his phone. "What's your number in case we can't get her phone working?" He flips open the phone.

"What the hell is that?" Jessica laughs. "Don't they give you updated phones at work?"

"Yeah, this one's an oldie. I brought it with me to set up in case her phone won't turn back on. It's so old I'm not sure it even works, but I'm able to turn it on." Jack opens the phone.

"I'm not sure they're able to set up an old phone like that. I'm just kidding. That's very thoughtful of you. Anna knows my number by heart, so have her call me when she gets up." Jessica darts out the door toward the bathroom.

The phone lights up in his hands. It's Sam. Jack shoves the phone in his back pocket.

Jessica runs in with a handful of bathroom essentials. "This should do for a week of packing," she says as she lays the items into the suitcase.

"Thank you. I appreciate your help. I'm going to do a quick walk around and make sure everything's locked up, if you don't mind." Jack zips the suitcase and carries it down the stairs.

"No, not at all. That's nice of you, and I'm glad we bumped into each other."

"I'd say you scared the daylights out of me—wouldn't call it a bump," Jack laughs. "I'll be right back if you want to meet me at the front door."

Jack leaves the suitcase at the bottom of the stairs and courses around the living room toward the kitchen. He steps up to the back door and tugs at the handle. He presses against the latch, affirming the lock is tight. As he treads around the kitchen, he sees goosebumps on his arms. The draft leads to the laundry room. Rummaging through the kitchen drawers, Jack grabs a marker and a pad of paper, and stuffs them in his jacket. He lurks toward the laundry room.

The roar of the winter wind funnels out of the laundry room. Jack reaches down and unfastens a gun from his ankle. Between each step, Jack pauses and looks around. Slipping one leg into the laundry room, he lunges his body behind, stretching himself to the entranceway of the little room. He points his gun.

The window latch is laying on the ground. The smashed pieces validate a forced entry. Jack turns around and faces the bathroom between the living room and kitchen. He aims his gun at the closed bathroom door, bracing to open fire, and squints at the bottom crack of the bathroom door. The glow of the afternoon sun bars at the front of the door. Jack squints a second time. Two vague objects resembling feet stand close to the edge of the opposing door. Jack rubs his forehead and grips both hands around the gun.

The two feet shift back from the doorway. Jack slides across the wood floors and inhales. Holding his breath, he approaches the bathroom door and wraps his hand around handle.

"I drove here. I can give you a ride if you need it," Jessica's voice rumbles down the stairs. The steps creak as she prances downward.

Jack releases the door. He steps back and wedges his gun inside the holster.

"Did you hear me? I can give you a ride," Jessica repeats, appearing from the stairway.

"Huh? Oh, sorry. I was getting a wood chip out of my shoe. It felt like it went through my foot." Jack jiggles the gun tight and stands up.

"A woodchip?"

"Yeah. You know, it'd be wonderful if you could drop me off at the mall area by the big movie theater, if it's not out of the way. I'd like to check on phone options in case her phone's deceased."

Jessica walks toward the bathroom, facing Jack. She leans against the door and takes out her phone. "It's not a problem at all. I held mace to your face and made you sit on the cold cement—the least I can do is give you a ride."

Jack stares at the crack in the door and squirms.

"I'm checking the best route." Jessica picks up one foot, itching her other ankle. She misses her ankle and taps the door. "You know—I can call her dad really quick and see what he knows about her phone plan."

The two shadows step to and from the door. Jack drops his jaw and bends to his gun. "Her dad knows nothing about me. I don't want to alarm him," Jack says, grinding his teeth and bending his knees. "Come on, I'll lock up so I can get back to Anna. I'm going to check on the flip phone and make it a quick trip."

"I understand. I should use the bathroom before we get on the road. Not sure what traffic's like right now." Jessica reaches over and grabs the handle.

"No traffic," Jack blurts, startling her.

Jessica pulls down on the handle and shakes it up and down. "It's locked. That's odd." She jiggles the door handle, applying weight.

"The pump was broken a few days ago. I bet she did that to save someone the embarrassment of clogging the toilet."

"Strange—you think she'd just get it fixed and be done with it," Jessica says, stepping away from the door. "Eh, I can hold it."

Jack exhales and watches Jessica walk ahead. He stretches his arms and thrusts them in circles behind her. He grabs the suitcase and walks backward, leaving a free hand for the gun.

"Now you can tell Anna a good story when you get home," Jessica says. She stands in the doorway and checks her phone.

Jack turns to Jessica and rolls his eyes.

"I can't believe how late it's getting. We were here way longer than I needed to be," Jessica says, typing on her phone.

Jack glares at Jessica's phone and walks into her. "Whoops! Sorry, I wasn't looking. Thought you had the door." He brushes past her and rips the door open. "After you."

"Ow, sorry," she blurts.

"No, I'm sorry. I should've been watching. You okay?" Jack asks.

"Fine." Jessica walks out the door.

Jack turns and faces the inside of the house. He reaches for the handle and pulls the door. As he pulls the door shut, he hears a lock pop from inside the house. He pulls the door tight and fumbles with the keys. "Too many keys."

"It's the white one with the Chicago flag imprint. I had that problem too—so frustrating when I was carrying her heavy groceries."

"Thanks." Jack locks the door and takes off running down the stairs.

"What on earth?" Jessica asks.

"It's so cold out. I needed to run." Jack strides to the sidewalk.

"You look like one of those Olympic power walkers," Jessica laughs. "And you're walking the wrong direction. My car's this way."

"Got it," Jack says, passing her from behind.

Halfway down the block, he slows alongside Jessica, lugging the suitcase behind.

"Thank you again for driving me. I promise you'll hear from her in a few hours."

"Not a problem at all. Here's my car. The next one."

Jack walks past Sam's car, catching a glimpse of Sam through a sunbeam in the front windshield. He locks eyes with Sam.

****

Present

CHAPTER 20

Hank drives down the street. The tire flaps as he pulls behind Sam's vehicle. Hank slams on the brakes.

"Park the car right here. There's a spot." Leslie points.

Hank grabs Leslie's head and tips it upright. "Hang on, Les."

"What the hell?" Leslie grabs her phone. She stares at Jessica and Jack, laughing together on the sidewalk. Without blinking, she lifts her phone and snaps a picture. "Jack's lugging a suitcase."

"They leaving for vacation?" Hank asks.

"No jokes right now," Leslie snaps.

"I wonder what he's told her. Look at her—she's smiling," Hank says. He backs alongside a car parked under a large tree.

"This can't be good," Leslie says.

Bangs and cracks against one of the windows cause Leslie and Hank to jump. Hank looks in his side mirror and sees Sam cowering along the bottom of the car.

Sam pounds again and yanks at the door handle. "Let me in—hurry."

"Geez, man." Hank holds his chest and unlocks the door. "He scared the shit out of me."

Sam slides in the car, slamming the door behind him. He catches his breath. "Bad day?" Sam points to the flat tire.

"Something like that," Hank says. "Mind telling me what the hell's going on?"

"I was resting when Jack went in the house for Anna's crap. Looks like she was at the house too. I'm confused."

"Why would he be walking with Jessica to her car? What if he spilled the truth—brings her to the house?" Leslie asks.

"What else do you know?" Hank asks.

"That's it. I called you as soon as I saw him."

Jessica hops in her car. Jacks turns to Sam's car and points at the suitcase. He opens the back trunk and lifts the suitcase inside. Grabbing the notepad from his pocket, Jack scribbles on the paper and tucks it in the bag. He removes the suitcase from the trunk and slides it on the sidewalk, waving his arm before he slams the trunk.

"See that?" Leslie asks.

"He thinks you're in your vehicle. He left the suitcase for you," Hank says.

Sam presses his face against the car window. "What the hell? "He's not going to—"

"Yeah, he's getting in her car." Hank scratches his head. "Go back out there and grab the suitcase, please. Les, send Bryan that pic."

"What if she sees me—with the suitcase?" Sam asks

"You sneaked over here fine—scared the shit out of us. Do it now before she sees the bag sitting on the sidewalk," Hank says.

"Now—she's about to pull away. I'm sure he's distracting her," Leslie says.

"Fine." Sam takes off down the side of the car, slinking across the sidewalk. He tucks behind the trunk of the big tree and pops his head out at Hank and Leslie.

Leslie glares at him through the window and signals for him to go.

"I wonder how this will play out," Hank says.

"Picture sent," Leslie says.

"Look, he's already on the way back with the bag," Hank says.

Sam jerks open the door, throwing the suitcase across the seat. "Boy, that was a rush."

"Wait a minute—look over there." Hank points to a car driving through an alley.

"Shit, it's unmarked," Leslie says.

"Hey, guys—the note. Jack's note," Sam says.

Hank shifts the car in drive mode. "Make sure your seat belts are on."

"What did Jack say?" Leslie asks.

"He said there's Stags inside the house right now, and he's getting her out," Sam says.

"That's it?" Leslie asks.

"Yep."

"Look, the car—Hank, do something." Leslie points at the alley. "It's driving over to them."

The car pulls alongside Jessica's car and stops, boxing them in. The brake lights go off.

"Damn it. With three wheels, this one's going to hurt, guys. Leslie, grab your gun," Hank says, tugging at his seat belt.

"I'm ready." Sam braces himself in his seat.

"I'll drive into the back of the car. Sam, get your keys ready. The moment we make impact, you grab your car. Leslie and I will attack through the front windows. If you have a chance to follow, leave us here. Questions?" Hanks grabs his gun from his ankle holster.

"Got it," Leslie says.

"Wait. Stop. The Stag car's moving—they're only checking them out," Sam says.

"What if this is a setup?" Hank lets go of the steering wheel. "Jack says they're in the house," Hank says.

"Maybe they're seeing how many people we have. Who knows what went on in that house and what information they have," Leslie says.

Jessica's taillights beam on.

"Bryans calling," Leslie says.

"Just stay still. Don't use the phone. Lean back and put your heads down—faces covered," Hank says.

"Shit, what if they saw me grab the suitcase?" Sam asks.

The unmarked car coasts to the end of the street. Jessica pulls out of her spot and drives away.

Leslie's phone lights up. "It's Bryan again."

"Go ahead, answer it," Hank says.

"I … ah, I'm at a loss of words," Bryan says.

"There's more; we'll fill you in. Right now, what do we do with Jack?" Hanks asks.

"He went with Jessica," Leslie adds.

"I'm looking at the picture you sent—he's carrying the bag with Anna's things, and Jessica looks fine with this, so let's wait for him to call," Bryan says.

"You need to clean the downstairs bathroom right now and fix the toilet immediately, before it overflows," Hank says.

"On it. Come to me," Bryan says.

"Last thing—we have a flat, and I fear we're in midst of a sting. Not sure if they've marked the cars on the street," Hank says.

"Shit. Stay right where you are." Bryan hangs up.

"I guess we wait here," Hank says.

Sam's phone lights up. "Hey." Sam puts the phone on speaker mode.

"I switched burner phones, sorry about that," Bryan pauses. "When you feel it's clear, call a cab—get dropped off on Michigan Avenue, walk a few blocks, and get into another cab. Everyone besides Hank—destroy your burner phone. Questions so far?" Bryan asks.

"No, go on," Hank says.

"Maneuver around until you get to our emergency spot. Can't believe I'm saying this—go to the spot Hank named 'dog poop.'"

"Over and out." Hank smiles.

"Dog poop," Sam laughs.

"God, you're such a man-child." Leslie rolls her eyes.

CHAPTER 21

I hear Cindy rustling around the kitchen. She's opening and closing cabinets. The racketing thuds of wood cabinets colliding transforms to sounds of dishes rattling and crinkling plastics. A dish shatters on the ground.

"Are you okay in there?" I call out.

"Me? Yes, I'm okay," Cindy says.

"How long has it been?"

"Little over thirty minutes."

"Should we call Bryan?"

"No."

I stand up and hobble to the kitchen doorway. Cindy is on her knees in front of the broken dish, both hands cupping the sides of her head. Her eyes are closed.

"Are you okay?" I ask.

"Jesus, child, you startled me again." She looks at me.

"I'm sorry. Here, let me help." I walk to her.

"Don't step on glass. I got it, Anna. Thank you."

"Are you worried?"

"I'm okay. Just having a moment."

"Has anything like this happened before?"

"No."

"No? So … just a no?"

"Sorry. You know what—yes, I'm worried. I hate to admit it, but you're clearly reading me. I'm running all the possible scenarios through my mind," she says.

"About Jack?"

"Yeah." Cindy stands up. "Everything's spiraling fast. I know what to do and am ready to pull the trigger—didn't think we'd be discussing an evacuation this soon."

"I feel like this is all my fault."

"You must change your mind-set. It's not you causing their aggression—the Stags. Their planet may be depleted, and they're desperate to relocate. And Jack, I bet he's okay. He's smart."

Cindy's phone rings. "It's Bryan." She walks through the glass and grabs her phone.

"Your feet," I say, looking away.

"Yeah?" Cindy flips the speaker on.

"Jack's okay," Bryan says.

"Thank God," I say.

"They found him. I'm sending you a photo," Bryan says.

"Hang on a sec." Cindy presses a button and stares at the low-quality burner phone image.

"What?" Cindy hands me the phone.

"What the hell? Jessica?" I blurt out.

Cindy grabs the phone. "Explain."

"We don't know what happened, but he has a suitcase from your home. I'm thinking there was some sort of run-in at the house."

"I can't wait to hear this one. You think he told her—about you guys?" I ask.

"Don't know what was exchanged. I'm waiting for Jack's call," Bryan says.

"In the meantime, clean the downstairs bathroom and fix the toilet—that's an order," Bryan says.

"Fix the toilet?" Cindy asks.

"Yep, sorry you're alone on this—I'll be there as soon as I can." Bryan ends the call.

Cindy stands up and pulls glass from both feet. Droplets of blood smear on the ground with each step. She walks to the kitchen sink and pours a glass of water, takes a sip, and then drops her phone in the water.

"I wasn't expecting that," I say.

"We're getting out of here," she says.

"When?"

"Right now."

"What did Bryan say?"

"We must evacuate immediately and destroy everything—you'll see yourself." Cindy takes off running.

"What?"

She stops, turns, and sprints toward me. "I don't have time to explain. You need to go back to the living room and wait for my instructions. Don't move or go anywhere—it's an emergency."

"Okay."

Cindy sprints to the stairs.

CHAPTER 22

Jack points out the window. "The store should be right up here to the left."

"You want me to wait? I can drive you back to Anna," Jessica says.

"What's your record time in and out of a cell phone store?" Jacks asks.

"Ouch, is there such thing? Forty minutes maybe, depending on how much they're trying to sell me."

"My point exactly. I'll grab a cab," Jack says.

"I don't mind helping."

"I know you'd stay—you're a good friend. If it's okay, I'd like to help a little," Jack says.

"Of course. It makes me happy to hear you say that. Please call me when you get home. I'd like to talk to her."

"Thanks for driving me. She'll call you as soon as I get back."

"I appreciate it." Jessica steers around the circle drive entrance of the shopping center.

"I wouldn't go back to Anna's. I'm going to tell her about that creepy car with the tinted windows. Could be her stalker. Just keep away until you talk to her, okay?"

"Yeah. I'm still a little freaked out. It was hard to see, but I swear he had a stocking mask on."

"And looked eight feet tall—I'll tell Anna what happened."

"So creepy. I think she should file a report."

Jack opens the door and hops out. "Pop the trunk?"

"I almost forgot."

Jack walks to the trunk and waits for a line of cars to form behind Jessica. He runs up to her window. "Last thing—I'm sure Anna's dad and brother are worried. Will you let them know she's all right and will have a working phone soon? Maybe put in a good word for me?" Jack smiles.

"Of course, I'll call him now. You better introduce me to one of your single friends."

"Deal."

Jack walks behind the open trunk and leans inside. A driver, blocked by Jessica's vehicle, glares at Jack through his windshield. Jack squats and makes eye contact with the driver. He takes his finger and moves it around in circles next to his head. "She's insane," he mouths to the driver.

The driver gestures back.

Jack signals for the man to lay on his horn and closes the trunk. A car horn echoes through the parking lot. Jack slides behind a parked car and waves at Jessica with one hand, using the other to hold the imaginary suitcase. "Thank you," he mouths to the man and watches him drive off.

Jack walks inside the closest store.

"Can I help you?" an employee asks.

"Oh, sorry—was dropped off at the wrong store. I'm ordering a ride, and I'll be on my way." Jack exhales and grabs his phone.

Jack: *I'm okay. Couldn't use phone. Need to talk to you. Call you in a few.*

Bryan: *I'll be waiting for the call.*

Jack leans against the door and looks around the shopping center. He opens the door and runs toward the movie theater. Spinning his back to the entrance, he gaits backward into one of the doors, clearing himself. Elevator music blares inside the double glass doors. The entrance is empty.

Wiping sweat from his forehead, Jack sways to the nearest wall and looks around. He presses himself against the glass door and scams up and down the circle drive. All cars parked around the circle have Illinois plates and appear empty. The stores are quiet. The only people in sight are a woman holding her child's hand and a bundled-up couple, strolling down the sidewalk of the stores.

Jack unzips his jacket, reversing the colors back to the original look.

"Bad day," he mutters and walks through the elongated entrance of the theater. A slick power walk turns into a light jog as he races toward the large sign leading to the lobby. Halfway down the echoing hall, he notices a bathroom and slides in. The elevator music carries on.

He walks to the sink and stares in the mirror. Both hands quiver as he turns on the faucet. The water sprays sideways from a leak, splattering all over the mirror. Jack holds his hands in front of the leak and cups the droplets. Steam rises as the water warms. He fills his hands with water and drenches his hair.

"Seriously? You idiot—what are you going to do now?" he snarls to himself, lowering his half-soaked head toward the faucet. "I'm screwed." He slaps water on his face. Watching the water run down his cheeks, he forms a bowl with his hands, taking small sips.

A man walks in the bathroom and uses the urinal. Jack parts his hair down the middle and slops some more water into the center part, forming a perfect line down the middle of his head.

"Gross," he barks, combing out the sides with his fingers. "All I need is a bowtie and a stogie."

The man stares at Jack. "You look like one of them stooges."

"Thanks. That's what I'm going for." Jack lowers himself toward the running water and drinks from the faucet. He thrusts open the door and continues down the hall. Approaching the lobby and ticket sales, Jack squirms past the staff and walks to several floor-to-ceiling windows. He presses his damp forehead against the window and looks for the emergency exits.

The wind spits squalls of dirty snow against the glass. Tall city buildings form an imperfect circle around the exposed theater property. The open space catches the channels of wind rumbling among the giant city structures and launches it toward the wall of the theater. High-pitch whistles screech through the window creases from the airstream power.

"Can I help you?" A woman's voice echoes through the empty lobby.

"Not again," Jack murmurs.

"You here to purchase a ticket?" The woman's voice grows louder.

"Uh, yeah."

"We don't have another movie starting for forty-five minutes. Theater's all in use."

"Oh, I'm running late." Jack turns and faces the employee.

"Which movie?" she asks.

"The new one with the superhero. In … in theater eleven, I believe." Jack looks over her head and stares at the movie times.

"That show's halfway done and is a documentary about a blind man."

"I consider the blind superheroes, ma'am."

"Good point. Why do you want to see if halfway through?"

"Oh, I had an emergency when I was here last and wanted to finish the flick." Jack smiles.

"I see. Just go ahead, then, quickly. My manager's on a smoke break."

"You sure? I can pay."

"Go ahead. Enjoy." The woman smiles.

Jack paces past the woman down one of the wings. He runs to the exit and cracks open the door. The wind loops at the door, pulling it shut. He kicks the door open and steps outside, using his other foot as a doorstopper. As he stretches from the door, his foot slides across ice. The door slams and locks.

"Frigid firecracker," Jack growls.

The exit doors align around the curved building structure. Jack drags his shoulder against the building as he counts the exit numbers marked on every door. He stops at theater eleven, spotting his dirty mound of snow.

Ice wedges underneath his nails as he claws halfway through the winter frost. He stops to heat his hands. "I know I put it here," he says, lowering himself over the mound of snow. Ripping through the rest of the heap, a frozen piece of cement lodges under his nails as he strikes the pavement. Jack falls backward. The phone's gone.

"No." Jack sits upright and kicks through the rest of the snow. He walks to the other side of his mess and kicks again. "No. No. No."

He stands up and leans against the wall, breathing into his hands. He sinks toward the ground and slows his breathing, applying pressure to his chest as he gasps for air. The wind blows the snow particles across the cement. The snow around the exit is clear of footprints.

Jack pries himself from the ground, placing both hands behind his head. "Focus. Breathe. Focus. Breathe. Think." Pressing his body against the brick wall, he skims the surface of the theater, looking in every direction. The snow crunches with each step as he scrapes his back against the wall. He holds a hand behind him, rattling the door handles of each emergency exit. Each door is locked tight.

Jack sprints through knee-length snow toward the front of the shopping center. The sun beams, revealing black ice on the pavement ahead. He massages a side cramp as he hurdles onto the sidewalk, staggering through the patches of black ice. Ripping open the theater entrance door, he slides in and sits against the wall. Elevator music blares. Jack covers his ears.

The man from the bathroom walks out of the theater. "See ya later, Moe," he says, stepping into the cold.

Jack holds a hand to his forehead and stares out the window. He dials Bryan.

"On a burner?" Bryan asks.

"Yes, they've got Anna's phone," Jack says.

"Who has Anna's phone?"

"Stags." Jack Pauses. "I burie—"

"I already know. You forgot to mention her cell pho—" Bryan pauses. "You know what, that's not important any longer. Where are you?"

"Where I buried her phone. They took it." Jack breathes into the phone. "Oh God. They know."

"Take a deep breath," Bryan says.

"They—"

"Jack, regroup your thoughts."

"They were here. They saw me today. I may have walked into a trap."

"Calm down, Jackie."

"They're watching me. I bet they tracked her phone and were waiting to see who came back for it."

"Stop. Deep breaths. Can you take a deep breath for me?" Bryan asks.

"I can't move. I know they're watching me."

"Breathe, Jack. You're going to get out. It's broad daylight. We're on burner phones."

"What if they can track burner phones?" Jack shrieks.

"They may be."

"Jesus, Bryan."

"Calm down—think clearly for a second. I make you change phones daily, sometimes more. You with me?" Bryan asks.

"Yeah."

"We speak in code most of the time—"

"I know. But they were in the same room as me, listening. They drove up and stared me down. I wasn't in disguise."

"Snap out of it. I have a plan," Bryan says.

"What?" Jack asks.

"You need to make your way over to an e-spot. Hang tight." Bryan drops the call.

Jack's phone lights up.

"I have thirty seconds—listen up," Bryan says.

"I'm listening."

"You're going to get the hell out of there and go to Hank's e-spot. You with me, kid?"

"Yes. Bird poop?"

"Dog poop—Hank's an idiot. The others are on their way as we speak, so leave now."

"All the way over there?"

"Yes, get going. They'll be waiting in a cab for you outside of Hank's spot."

"Did they get Anna's bag?"

"I don't give a shit about a bag. Start running—now."

"Is Anna with you?"

"No."

"Is she okay?"

"Okay, I'm sensing you've got a little crush, so you better run if you'd like to see her later."

"I need to think."

"What's there to think about? Run, kid. You did this over and over in training."

"The simulations? Those were way different than the real deal."

"You run through the city all the time."

"Yeah, I know, bu—"

"Jack, did I stutter? Five seconds. Get your ass out there and run. That's an or—"

"Bryan?" Jack asks, looking at his phone.

Jack's phone lights up.

"Jack, thirty seconds. I'm wasting burner phones," Bryan says.

"I know," Jack says.

"Why don't I hear you running?" Bryan asks.

Jack stands up. "I can't run long distance while talking on a phone."

"If I don't hear you running by the end of this call, I'll track you down and shoot you myself," Bryan says.

Jack hangs up on Bryan. He bursts through the door and runs out of the shopping center. He sprints across four lanes of traffic and continues down the bicycle lane. His phone vibrates.

"What do you want?" Jack asks.

"Thirty seconds," Bryan says.

"I get it with the thirty seconds—you're wasting a burner," Jack snaps.

"Good, you're on your way. Run into a market soon. You need to face-change. You okay? You get your head straight?" Bryan asks.

"I'm fine, stop."

"Well, you had me worried, you little shit. Destroy your phone—you know your orders." Bryan drops the call.

Jack sprints a half mile and finds a grocery store. He limps into the parking lot and checks for pedestrians. "Fu—"

A child gallops out of the store with his mom.

"Fudge brownies," Jack yells and bends over to rub his leg. He runs his hand against his pant leg and jolts. Lifting the pant leg to the base of the gun holster, Jack sees a blister. He limps inside the store.

A woman stares at the top of Jack's head as he enters the store. Jack pats the center of his hair and treads down an aisle toward the back of the store. The aisle dead-ends at the refrigerated section. He wanders over to a jar of pickles, breaks open the top, and drops his phone inside.

Holding on to the pickle jar, he totters backward and closes his eyes.

"Can I help you find something?" a young woman asks.

"Uh, sorry. Didn't mean to block the aisle. You carry any sort of clothing in this store?" Jack clears his throat.

"We've got several items in the organic section," she says with a warm smile. "Do you need me to sh—"

"I got it, thanks." Jack turns and trips over a toy a child dropped from the top of a shopping cart. He scoops up the toy and tosses it back to the little boy. The stuffed animal hits the little kid in the side of the face and lands back in the cart.

"I'm so sorry," Jack apologizes, looking around for the mother.

The little boy claps. "Again, again." He drools and drops the toy on the ground.

Jack twirls around and looks at the little boy.

The mother releases a refrigerator door and leaps over to her child. "I'm really sorry. I'm having a hard time reaching the top shelf right here." She grabs the cart and pushes her son away from Jack.

Jack starts in the other direction and stops.

"Here, I can get that for you." Jack turns around and walks over to the fridge.

"Thank you." The woman tears up. "I'm sorry."

"There's nothing to apologize for. Your son was playing."

"My husband's usually with us to reach the high-shelf items," the woman says, looking down at the floor.

"I don't mind," Jack says, pulling open the fridge. "They need to restock the juice soon, or they'll be out." He hands the woman the carton and reaches for the boy's stuffed animal. "Here you go, kiddo," he says, shaking the stuffed animal from side to side.

"Can you grab one more?" she asks, tearing up.

"Of course. Are you okay?"

"Just having a hard time. My husband was supposed to be back from a quick work trip in Bangkok and came down with the flu. They're keeping him in a hospital."

"I'm sorry to hear that."

"It's okay. I'm just worried. We're stocking up with juices and vitamins for his return." The little boy releases his toy from the cart.

"One more time," Jack says to the little boy, fetching the toy. "What's your name, little man?"

"This is Trent—named after his father. Say hi, Trent." The woman forces a smile at her son.

"Nice to meet you, Trent. I'm Jack."

The little boy buries his head inside his shirt.

"Don't be shy, Trent," she says. "I'm Lilly."

"Nice to meet you both. I hope your husband makes it back safe. Do you need my height for anything else?"

"No. Thank you again for your help."

"No problem." Jack turns in the other direction and struts off with the jar of pickles. A vigorous walk grows to a moderate trot as he cuts across the store aisles. He knocks into several grocery carts as he reads the floating signs. Entering an open area at the center of the store, he finds a multicolored pastel organics sign. A swiveling rack holds several picked-over accessories. Jack races over to the display and fumbles around.

"Wow, this stuff's pricey," Jack says to himself as he flips through price tags. He rummages through the limited options of pink and orange colored hats, scarves, and shirts. Scanning up and down the rack, he snags a hat and scarf and strides to checkout.

"Would you like a gift receipt?" the cashier asks.

"Nah, I'm good. Oh, and the jar of pickles," Jack says, releasing the jar from his arm. "I'll take a bag for the pickles, please." Jack pulls out a wad of cash.

"Sure thing."

Jack grabs the clothing articles, sliding the pink-and-orange flowered stocking hat over his head. He wraps the bright orange scarf around his neck. "One more thing," Jack pauses as he reaches for a copy of the monthly featured best seller. He turns to the man next in line. The man takes one look at him and looks away.

"It's a good one, the book. I just finished it," the cashier says. He scans the book and hands it over to Jack.

"Thanks." Jack smiles.

"You have yourself a good day."

Jack lowers the stocking cap past his eyebrows. He wraps the scarf a second time, covering his mouth and nose, and pulls the plastic bag handles up his forearm. He bows his head and flips open the book.

"Here we go. Try not to get yourself killed," Jack whispers to himself inside the scarf. He presses himself against the door, looking left and right. Shoving open the door, he scrambles down the sidewalk, dropping his head back into the book. The late afternoon sun vanishes behind the skyline, causing the air temperature to dip. Jack cowers close to each building as he walks through masses of chilled Chicagoans. Clouds of hazy smoke from the bitter winter air filters from his mouth into his eyes with every attempt to peek upward.

"Who does that?" a woman's voice rambles in passing.

"I'd run into a pole reading like that," a man responds to the voice.

"If only you knew," Jack mutters.

Crossing the street, Jack notices the first building. A fire-engine-red high-rise stands alone from the other city buildings. Remaining to the right of the crowd crossing the street, he slips close to the bright structure. He brushes a hand against the surface of the building and holds the book in the other, forcing his gaze back down. His arm flops as he comes to the end of the monstrous architecture. A narrow alley divides the space before the next glass high-rise. He slips into the alley, adding speed to each step. The whirling wind tunnel leads to a side entrance of a parking garage. Jack closes the book and hustles to the possible escape route.

"Please be public access," Jack utters as he grabs the door handle and cranks it down. The door opens. "Yes," Jack shrieks, pushing the door open.

He lunges inside the garage and turns to close to the door. The handles on the plastic bag rip, causing the bag to drop on the cement floor. The pickle jar strikes on the hard surface, instantly shattering inside the bag. Pickle juice sprigs out from the opening, spraying all over Jack.

"Are you shitting me?" Jack snaps. "I should've left it on a store shelf, but no, you can't break the damn rules." Jack wipes pickle juice from his pants. "Now you're just rubbing it in your clothes, you idiot." Jack rages, catching movement from the corner of his eyes. A woman stops walking and pauses. The woman takes a few steps back, turns, and runs away.

"Great, you just scared someone away," Jack mouths. He grabs the broken corners of the sopping glass-filled bag and cautiously carries it to a garbage. He lays the bag open onto a half-filled trash can and carefully picks his phone from the rubble. The salty, garlic brine smell wafts into the air from the bag as Jack holds his burner phone. He flips open the phone and snaps it in half.

"This is what you should've done," he grumbles, tossing the phone into the garbage as he runs to an exit.

Bursting open the back door, he releases a deep breath and inspects the scene. The dreary, slate-colored skies surround the city as the last flicker of daylight emerges between buildings. Streetlights shudder on as the sun vanishes in the distance. People continue to pour in and out of the high-rise shopping malls. Sounds of shoes pattering on pavement and pedestrian side chatter echo in the wind.

Jack watches a streetlamp highlight a group of laughing tourists as they cross under the warm lit hue. He waits for enough distance between passing crowds and takes off through the shivery introduction of night. The temperature plummets in the sunless city as the dark swallows the day. Pulling his scarf tightly around his face, he jogs around each walker, gaining speed as he turns down a less chaotic street.

The breeze blows sideways through the fibers of his stocking hat, trickling into his ears. Jack gains momentum as he angles up a ramp leading to a flight of icy stairs. His feet brush sideways with every step up the slick route.

He reaches the top of the stairs and sprints toward a single-standing luxury apartment complex. The complex dead-ends upon reaching the entrance, and the surrounding buildings require a reversal from his position. Jack notices a drop from the top of the building to an alley where trash is collected. The alley links back to a main road.

Jack creeps up to the ledge. A security guard stands up from the window of the building.

"Shit," Jack says, watching the guard from a pocket in his peripheral. He turns toward the other direction and walks until he sees the guard sit back in his seat. Without hesitation, Jack twists back the other direction into a full sprint toward the edge of the property. He pulls both arms back and wails them forward as he lunges over the edge, thrusting them around for balance. Spotting ice on the pavement halfway down, from a glare in a low-lit streetlamp, Jack holds his arms out to brace his landing.

Both feet plummet to the frozen surface as he flails his arms to hold balance. The overcompensation from his upper limbs overshoot the landing, placing him on the arches of his feet. Immediately upon ground contact, he catapults forward. Embracing the fall, Jack tucks and rolls with the pull of his body. He lands alongside one of the dumpsters.

"I thought yer gonna to land on yer back," a man shouts from the other side of the dumpster.

"Ah," Jack groans, grabbing ahold of the paint-chipped garbage collector.

The man on the other side of the dumpster slow claps.

"Why are you clapping?" Jack asks.

"Want some booze?" the man asks.

"No. No, I don't want booze. I want to get out of this cold," Jack yells.

"Me too," the man shouts.

"I'm sorry. You must be cold, sir."

"Want some booze?" the man repeats himself.

"I gotta go," Jack says.

"Need a place to hide from the cops?" the man hiccups.

"No, aliens are following me," Jack says to the man and takes off down the street.

"Well, me too," the man howls. "And one's my ex-wife," he snorts.

Jack races to the end of the alley leading to a main road and halts for pedestrians. One of the streetlamps flicker in the moonless sky. With a clear path in sight, he darts across the four-lane street and veers down a slanted sidewalk leading to the river walk. Dim lighting aligns the pathway around the water that faintly reflects off the ice. Tears run down the corners of his eyes from the wind hurling off the frozen river. He bolts through the crowdless path of grim bleakness, watching for strangers in the darkness.

The city is noiseless below the congested streets. Tattering sounds of raspy wind ricochets against the river walls, swallowing the noise pollution. Gasping for air, Jack forces both hands to the edges of his abdomen. He massages the side cramps and maintains speed.

The beating noise from Jack's shoes striking the pavement transform into a chorus of pitter-patters in the distance. He lifts his arms above his head, clasps his hands behind his neck, and scans for the source of sound. The sounds grow louder.

A crack echoing in the ice startles Jack as he steers around a sharp corner and under an industrial bridge. A bundled-up group of runners stagger by from the opposite lane. Several group members hoist an arm at Jack in encouragement as they flood by. He nods and picks up the pace, rubbing his snotty nose. The sounds of teeth-chattering wind overpower him once more.

The pavement straightens beyond the bridge, revealing a staircase opportunity to hide from the torturous cold. Jack fidgets with his scarf and glares at the staircase. He passes the upward exit, immediately striding backward for a decision alteration. Taking a deep breath, he stomps up the rusty metal winding stairs. The echoing from the river disintegrates as he makes his way to the top. He stops and looks around.

Bright blood-red colored lights of a pharmacy storefront sign blare from the other side of the bridge. Jack walks over to the bridge and looks for an opening between groups. People move like huddled penguins across the rusty red metal bridge. The cold forces clouds of white smoke to funnel out of each person's mouth and across the bridge lights. The illumination from inside the pharmacy streaks onto the pavement as people move in and out of the store from a distance. He slides in-between walkers and jogs outside the crowd across the old industrial bridge.

Jack uses the scarf to wipe sweat from his face as he approaches the entrance. He yanks open the pharmacy door and maneuvers to the back of the store. Shivering from the cold, he raises his fiery red knuckles and tugs the scarf from his mouth. He hisses warm air on his fingers and palms as he searches around for a new disguise. Tugging off his jacket, he reverses it.

Sounds of side babble and phone chimes grab his attention. People fill the narrow aisles of the pharmacy store. The checkout line at the entrance wraps around the front of the store and streams down one of the aisles with impatient customers. Jack walks over to an aisle filled with antsy Chicagoans bearing baskets of items. In the middle of the chaos, he spots a small section of souvenirs and clothing.

"You've got to be kidding me," he burbles and looks down at his watch.

A woman's voice rumbles through the loudspeaker. "Help needed up front for a return." Jack looks down the aisle once more.

"Help needed up front for a return." The voice grows louder.

Making his way toward the front of the store, Jack searches for a form of camouflage. He discovers stacks of free savings magazines next to the door and yanks one from the pile. People brush against him as they walk into the entrance. A breeze swirls inside the store as a woman texting on her phone enters. The woman runs into Jack as the door slowly closes.

"Excuse you," the woman says looking downward on her phone.

Jack ignores the woman and rips open the magazine. He balances the center of the booklet over his head and prepares to dart back into the crowded sidewalk. Masses of people scurry past the glass door.

Jack waits for space between people on the crosswalk and pops open the door. Bracing the magazine over his head, he breaks away from the mass of people into an alley. A staircase leading back to the riverfront is visible from halfway down the alley. Jack yanks at each side of the magazine, holding it firmly over his head. He stomps down the staircase and steers back onto the lakefront path.

"One more mile," Jack says. He jumps up and down in place, kicking his knees high, and takes off into the darkness. A quarter of a mile in, he finds a garbage can under one of the bridges and tosses the magazine. Balling his hands into fists, he tucks his hands inside the jacket sleeves.

With tears freezing out from the corners of his eyes, Jack flutters his eyelids, forcing the salty substance to drip. The path leads to the edge of the lakefront and multiplies to the option of continuing alongside the lake or spiraling up a ramp back to a city street. He angles forward and begins the upward challenge. The nasty Lake Michigan wind whips at his core, causing him to sway as he runs at an incline.

Reaching the top, Jack limps across the street toward a grocery store lot. He notices a line of taxis parked in the waiting zone. People enter and exit the high-end dog groomer next door. He backs inside the revolving doors of the grocery store.

"Where's your souvenir stuff?" Jack asks the first employee he sees.

"You okay, sir?" the employee asks.

"I'm good. Just cold." Jack wipes his nose.

"Your lips are purple. Can I get you a warm beverage?" she asks.

"No. No, I'm fine. Where are your souvenirs?" Jack trembles.

He follows the woman to a stand next to the checkout.

"This is what we have—sure you don't want a warm drink?"

"Nah," he says, grabbing a baseball cap and a scarf.

"I can check you out," she says.

"Thank you. Can I please have a large bag?"

"There's a bag tax."

"It's fine."

Jack rips the tags off the hat and scarf and puts them on. He removes his jacket and places it in the shopping bag.

"Have a nice day," Jack says.

"And you should put that jacket back on ..." The woman's voice trails off.

Jack steps outside, and a yellow van pulls up.

The side door pops open. Hank tugs Jack in the van and slams the door.

"Thanks for waiting, sir. You can head to our location now," Hank says to the cab driver.

The group is silent.

"Bad day, Jack?" Hank asks. He slides over for Jack and angles the rear-air ceiling vents on him. "Can you crank the heat up a notch?" he asks the driver.

"You've got no idea," Jack says.

"We can talk about it when we get to Aunt Jane's," Leslie says.

"Your lips are blue, man," Sam says.

"Shut it." Jack grits his teeth and stares blankly out the window.

"Is your hair frozen?" Leslie asks. She reaches over the seat from the back row, touching a piece. "It is—a piece just broke off." Leslie removes her jacket and throws it over his lap.

Hank and Sam remove their coats and tuck them around Jack. Sam reaches out to touch Jack's hair. His mouth quivers as he swats at Sam.

"I put water on my hair at the movie theater, stop. Did your fucking inertia prevent you from noticing Jessica in front of your face?" Jack asks.

"Jack—"

"Leslie, stop," Jack snaps. "Where the hell were you? I was standing at the door like a fucking idiot. She parked a few cars in front of you—moments after I got out. Now they've seen me. I was standing in front of the house with fucking mace in my face, in broad daylight, while the Stags watched, man."

"We should figu—"

"I said stop, Leslie."

"Why'd you agree to go in her house in the first place? You asked for it—clouding your mind with feelings," Sam snaps back.

"I asked for it? Good to know you're watching my back." Jack hurls the layers off him and lunges at Sam.

Hank intervenes, forcing his long arms between the two rows of seating. He slaps Jack in the forehead, moving him back. Jack jumps over the seat.

"No fighting in my cab," the driver yells.

Sam holds Jack with both hands by the throat. "Get off me."

"Stop it, you idiots," Leslie shouts, smearing her hand against Jack's face, forcing him back.

Hank knocks Jack backward into the back of the driver's seat.

"Enough," the driver says, slamming on the brakes.

"They're fine. They're brothers," Leslie says.

"I won't tolerate that kind of behavior in my cab," the driver says.

"Sorry," Jack says.

"I see why your parents have to follow you around. You two act younger than my twelve-year-old," the driver says.

"What? I'm not their mom. How old do y—"

Hank covers Leslie's mouth. He glares at Sam and Jack. "I'm sorry again for the frustration."

"Do these two live with you guys?" the driver asks.

"What?" Hank asks.

"Do they live under the same roof as you?" the driver asks.

"We all live together, yes," Hank says.

"There's the problem—the millennials feel entitled. Kick them out," the driver says.

"Great idea." Hanks looks at Leslie and tightens his grip around her mouth.

CHAPTER 23

I rub my eyes and watch Cindy. She runs up and down the stairs, flying past me in a full sprint as she retrieves everyone's belongings inside the house. If they did house drills, she clearly practiced on her own time. I see the determination in her steps as she hauls bag after bag into a pile on the ground.

"I'd like to offer my help, but I'd never keep up with you," I say.

"Stay put," she says, lugging a duffel bag from her shoulder. She's upstairs by the time she finishes her sentence.

I hear Cindy stomping around upstairs. I turn and stare through the glass of the back-porch door. The little room turns dark as the evening takes over. I think of Hank's album and walk to the porch. If they plan on leaving everything behind, Hank would be happy to have the album.

I touch the door handle and the lights inside the house go out. The thudding sounds from upstairs stop. I turn around and press my back against the door. I can't see; the house is pitch-black.

"Cindy?" I whisper.

There's no sound. I wait for a creak in the floor. Nothing. I slide against the door, feeling the handle graze my back. Where is she? I sit on the ground and listen. My heart flutters.

"Cindy?" I whisper again.

I try to remember the placement of the furniture. What's my course? I'll crawl and find Cindy. My knees crack as I flip on all fours. I feel my nerves fire from the abrupt shift to my spinal cord. I feel a force on my shoulder. I touch someone's leg.

"Who's th—"

"It's okay. It's me; didn't mean to scare you," Cindy says.

"What's going on?" I ask.

"I flushed all the systems holding confidential information. Somehow the power went out."

"Could that cause a power outage?"

"Didn't think so. The timing was odd though. As soon as the computer was wiped clean and the screen went black, so did everything else."

"What should we do?"

"Stand up. Follow me." Cindy helps me up. "We have a panic room."

"What if they got in? The Stags? They'll find us," I whisper.

"The panic room will give us enough time to wait for Bryan and the others," Cindy says.

"Let's go. I'm nervous." I grab ahold of Cindy's arm as she leads me through the room.

"We'll have power in the safe room, and I can check our security cameras."

"How's that possible?" I ask.

"The cameras operate on a separate platform—all but the front gate. That flushed with the main system and secured the gate."

"How's Bryan going to get in?"

"There's a side entrance. A code will activate a backup generator. It's a pain in the butt going through the side, but he'll have no choice. It'll alert headquar—"

"Wait." I stop her.

There's an inconsistent thump. The thumps echo as they get closer.

"Get down." She knocks into an ottoman and thrusts it in front of me.

I shield myself with the ottoman and hold my breath. The sound stops.

"Don't move," Cindy whispers, unsnapping her holster.

There's a scratch at the door. Cindy cocks her gun.

The power comes on. I peek over the ottoman and stare at the door. The door handle rattles up and down. The door pops open. Bryan walks in and gasps.

"Jesus, you almost gave me a heart attack." Bryan staggers backward, catching himself at the edge of the stairs.

"Seriously? Almost gave you a heart attack?" Cindy shakes her head and uncocks her gun. "I almost shot you."

"Sorry, I said I was coming to you," he says.

"The power outage? Was that you?" Cindy asks.

"Yeah, sorry about that. You locked the gate," Bryan says,

"You never mentioned the possibility of a power outage," Cindy says.

"My bad. I came in through the side and was trying to power down the garage—don't want a fire before phase three," Bryan says.

"I'm almost done if you want to get the vehicle," Cindy says.

"I'll get the rest of the bags; you get the vehicle," Bryan says.

"You're injured. Stop." Cindy snaps her gun back in the holster and runs to the stairs. "Pull the vehicle up," she shouts.

"She's normally not this bossy." Bryan looks at me.

"I'd listen to the lady. We need you healthy too," I say.

"I'll bring a load with me. I want us out of here—as close to ten minutes as possible," Bryan says.

"No lifting," Cindy shouts from the top of the stairs.

"Yeah, okay." Bryan lifts two large bags and walks out the door.

I sit on the ground and use my feet to push the bags toward the door.

"Nope." Cindy stops me.

"Bryan wants us out in ten. I'll give more blood if it helps him heal faster," I say.

"You're not a walking blood bank and I'm not wasting all our concentrate for his inability to listen." Cindy grabs a bag and storms out the door.

Bryan walks inside. His cheeks are flushed. "The elevator will no longer work. You should start the stairs," he says, grabbing two more bags.

I step out the door. The garage is dark. I see the red taillights from a GMC Yukon and smell exhaust. Cindy flips on the headlights, adding light to the narrow staircase. I grip the wood railing and step down. I watch the two of them lap me three times before I reach the last few stairs.

"We got everything?" Bryan asks, standing at the trunk.

"Yeah, we're good," Cindy says.

"Just a few more stairs, sorry," I say.

"Stay still," Bryan says, signaling for Cindy to follow. "Wrap your arms around our necks like crutches."

They lift me down the stairs and into the car.

"What'll happen to this place?" I ask.

"Headquarters will send a team on premise to clear house. They'll be here just after midnight. They want to talk to you too," Bryan says.

"Headquarters—the house, we've got pictures all over the porch," Cindy says.

"Forget it, we're never coming back. It'll be wiped clean in hours. Besides, she's with us," Bryan says.

"What's wrong with pictures?" I ask.

"It's a rule, though I'm sure there are other squads like us who put some up for a sense of normalcy," Bryan says, walking to the driver's side door.

"You sure you want to drive? I'm worried about you twisting around," Cindy says.

"I'm fine." Bryan uses the side handle and pulls himself onto the driver's seat. He jolts, his eyes widen.

"What was that?" Cindy asks.

"Nothing," he says.

"I saw it in your eyes. You just ripped a stitch, didn't you?" she asks.

"Maybe. Doesn't matter—I need to drive so you can do the vehicle changes," he says.

"Vehicle changes?" I ask.

"It's like a pit stop for vehicle appearance—helps confuse any possible tailers," Cindy says.

"It's for precaution." Bryan reaches underneath his seat and pulls out a compartment. He slips on a baseball cap and hands me one. "Cindy, I saved this one for you." He hands her a cap.

"I'm not putting that thing on my head," she says, searching under her seat.

"You've got no choice. I packed the rest for the condo," he says.

"You're such a shit," she says, turning the cap inside out.

"That's a true Eagles fan right there—hating on the Patriots, even in a time of crisis," Bryan laughs.

"What happened to the stereo?"

"All the wires have been cut in this vehicle, so we remain off-grid through GPS tracking," Bryan says.

"The radio works, though," Cindy says.

"We ready? Once we leave this garage, we can never come back." Bryan drives up to the door.

Cindy hops out of the car and dials a code into a device on the ground. She waits for the door to open and yanks the device from a cable on the floor.

"Keep your eyes peeled—she activated the main gate too," Bryan says.

"Hand me the chip," Cindy says, jumping back in the car.

Bryan hands her a small chip. "Say goodbye."

"Goodbye, home. You want to press the button?" she asks, locking the chip in the device.

"Give it to Anna," Bryan says, approaching the main gate.

"What will it do?" I ask.

"That garage was constructed as an add-on after one of our crews tore down the original. The wooden stairs were designed to catch fire, melting a component they installed along the base of the stairs. That'll activate self-destruction mode," Cindy says.

"I cut the power, so we didn't have issues during phase one," Bryan says.

"Sounds like that mouse game. The one with the trap. I used to pl—"

"Mousetrap," Cindy says.

"I guess." Bryan pauses. "Self-destruction mode will activate a floor-to-ceiling shield. Seconds later, the giant steel lockbox will fill with acid and begin phase three. A team will come in, detach the garage, and take it away in two pieces. They'll clear the rest of the home—you'd never know we existed."

I grab the device from Cindy and tap the red button.

"You're brave," Bryan says. He looks through the rearview mirror. "What we didn't tell you, is there's a fifty percent chance that the driveway and gate will face explosion with the garage."

"What? Drive," I demand.

"I'm just kidding."

"Your sense of humor alarms me," Cindy says.

"I'm going with Theresa's escape route. You know where to look," Bryan says.

"What can I do?" I ask.

"Look for unmarked cars," he says.

Bryan turns behind a line of cars, following the flow of traffic to the nearest highway. We drive into slow moving traffic from a left-lane highway merge, leading us onto the Kennedy Expressway. He speeds to the front of traffic and merges right. We come to a complete stop.

"Is there ever a moment without traffic in this city?" Cindy asks.

Traffic flow increases to five miles per hour. "Hang on." Bryan steers the car through five lanes of traffic, toward the next exit.

We exit and pull to a four way stop, under the 'L' tracks. He turns so that we're driving underneath the 'L' track. I look up and watch a train pass from the opposite direction. Bryan steers to the right, where two trains connect, forming a cross from up above. He makes a sharp turn into the garage of a local car wash.

"This won't take long," Bryan says.

"I'm confused. There's an emergency and we're washing the car?" I ask.

"It's part of the route," Bryan laughs.

"This is where we stop and check for tailing. It's a good spot too—there's an open view around us," Cindy says.

"We're making good time. The others should be arriving just after us," Bryan says, handing cash to the attendant. He pulls into the car wash.

"You're holding your side." Cindy points at Bryan's hand.

"Cindy, for Pete's sake, I can dr—"

"You're stubborn," Cindy says.

I watch the two of them bicker like a married couple as soap splatters across the windshield. We reach the dryer and Bryan is calm. He slides his hand across the seat. Cindy moves her arm and holds his hand under the center armrest. I smile and pretend I'm looking out the window.

"You can drive when we get to the next spot," Bryan says.

The car wash exit opens. They search the premise in silence. Bryan turns down a side street and circles the block. Backtracking a half mile, he steers away from the tracks and pulls into a local parking garage. He takes an electronic ticket and drives to the basement level.

"You've got exactly five minutes," Bryan says.

Cindy rips a screwdriver from the glove box and thrusts open the door. "Switch seats now."

"What's she doing?" I ask.

"Giving the car a quick makeover. We can exit for free within six minutes of entering the garage," Bryan says, sliding out of the driver's seat. "It's actually seven minutes, but they've never questioned me."

Cindy runs around the truck with a can of spray and a stack of trim pieces.

"Those things are custom magnets," Bryan says.

Cindy leans over the hood and lays a red thick-stripped magnet across the center. It aligns perfectly with the length of the hood. She pops off the front emblem, replacing it with a new one.

"Four minutes," Bryan calls out the window.

Cindy runs to the back of the car and pulls more accessories. I hear a popping sound from the back of the vehicle. The truck moves.

"Now what is she doing?" I ask.

"She's snapping on replacement wheel caps. They'll look like black rims unless you get up close—fits right over the chrome rim." Bryan looks at his watch. "You need to be back in the car in one minute."

Cindy pops mirror covers over the chrome on both sides and slaps the rest of the magnets around the car.

"This isn't the Chicago Auto Show. Swap plates and let's go. Time's up," Bryan says.

Cindy hops in the driver's seat. She tosses the old plate onto Bryan's lap.

"Just enough time," Bryan says.

"Just so you're aware, I know it's seven minutes," she says, turning into a neighborhood filled with large brick condos.

"This neighborhood's my favorite. You guys live here?" I ask.

"Nope, the next block," Bryan says.

We pull up to the garage of a modern-looking condominium complex.

"Whew. We made it," Cindy says.

"We in the clear?" I ask.

"Yeah, for now," Bryan says.

CHAPTER 24

I walk around the two-bedroom condo. It looks like a prefurnished corporate apartment. There are three windows between the living room and kitchen. Two of the windows are sealed shut.

"We're going to be crammed in close corridors for the time being," Bryan says.

"What happened when you spoke to the guys at headquarters?" Cindy asks.

"I've got a follow-up call with the higher-ups in an hour." Bryan walks to a kitchen cabinet and reaches for a glass. He drops his arm and grabs his side.

"Let me see what you did?" Cindy asks.

"It's not that bad," he says.

Cindy walks over to Bryan and grabs his shirt.

"Maybe one stitch, if any," he says.

"Three stitches—you ripped three. I'd scold you, but I know you'll do it again," she says, strutting toward the master bedroom.

The kitchen is silent.

"Don't look at me. I agree with her," I say.

Cindy storms in the kitchen with a first aid kit. "Sir Raggedy Andy, you'll have to ask Leslie to stitch you up next time."

The phone rings. A live security screen powers on next to the phone. I see tall Hank standing in front of the group. The air from his breath brushes across the bottom of the screen. Jack stands behind the others, both arms crossed.

"Good, they made it." Cindy looks at the screen and taps a code.

"That's a clear camera. Do all the units come with these?" I ask.

"Not exactly," Cindy says.

"Sam hacked into the system and reprogramed it with new technology," Bryan says.

"Not hacked. He rewired it, giving us full control of the building cameras," Cindy says.

"I'm actually shocked property management hasn't said anything. I was pissed about this," Bryan says.

"Why?" I ask.

"He got lazy with some of the wires," Cindy says.

"When he saw the wires wouldn't fit inside, he glued them to the sides," Bryan says.

"Why would he glue them?" I ask.

"Because he thinks people are too naive to notice or care," Bryan says.

"That's a nice way of putting it," Cindy laughs.

"He's got an engineering background and is a good agent—lazy when it comes to the simple stuff," Bryan says.

"No, Bryan, it's called intellectual arrogance, and it's your faul—"

"Our fault," Bryan interrupts.

"You're right. It's our fault for not speaking up when he's sloppy. Look how he left the navi screen in the truck," Cindy says.

"That was him?" I ask.

"Doesn't matter anymore. The radio works. I let him do his thing," Bryan says.

"Over and over again," Cindy says.

The dead bolt cracks. Sam kicks the door open. We stop talking.

"Thought the ride would never end." Sam steps out of his shoes.

Hank turns his head to Leslie as he walks in the door and trips over Sam's shoes. He grabs the shoes and chucks them into the hallway. "What's going on in here?"

Jack strolls in last. His face is pale.

"You all right?" Leslie stares at Bryan.

"He make you mad again?" Hank pokes me.

"What? No. He ripped his stitches," I say.

"What's your take on everything, Hank?" Bryan asks.

"I think the Stags know enough—that Anna didn't leave on a whim for vacation, and we're interfering with their operation." Hank grabs a water from the fridge. "Jack might as well be walking around with a target on his back. He needs to stay off-grid."

"Did they see you?" Bryan asks.

"We never stepped out of the car. I think we're okay." Hank nods.

"I did. I stepped out of the car to grab the stupid bag," Sam says.

"You had a hat on and creeped around like a ninja. Scared the shit out of me and Leslie. I think you're okay. But this guy—" Hank points at Jack and shakes his head.

"Jack, grab some water. You look like you've seen a ghost," Cindy says.

"You think he's capable of holding himself together?" Bryan asks.

"Who, Jack? Yeah, he'll be fine. He just needs a beer and a hot shower." Hank cracks his neck.

"I'm standing right here. I'm fine and can answer for myself," Jack says.

"He finally speaks," Leslie says.

"Good. Start the oven, Jackie. We're refueling with frozen pizzas tonight," Bryan says.

Hank grabs a beer from the fridge and hands it to Jack. "I'm putting myself in charge of the food."

"Fine. You three go change. I'd like to speak with Hank," Bryan says, waiting for the room to clear. "How bad is it?"

"Honestly, I think we need to get the hell out of here as soon as possible," Hanks says.

"And how do you feel about Jack and Jessica?" Bryan asks.

"They'd make a cute couple—love at first sight." Hank guzzles water.

"Quit dicking around," Bryan says.

"Honestly, pull Jack out for now. He's a risk," Hank says.

"Okay, the kid's out," Bryan says.

"As for Jessica—she's a concern. She's the only possible link to Anna, and I think we should keep an eye on her," Hank says.

"Got it, thanks," Bryan says.

The bedroom door slides open. Sam, Leslie, and Jack come out of the bedroom, bickering with one another.

"I'll have a talk with Jack later on," Bryan whispers.

"You guys hungry?" Cindy asks.

"You're an idiot," Leslie says, walking ahead of Jack.

"You would've done the same thing," Jack says.

"How about some food?" Cindy asks.

"I wouldn't have, and I'm dying to watch this one play out," Leslie laughs.

"Cindy's asking you guys a question," Bryan says.

"What the hell are you two squabbling about?" Hank asks.

"Just wait; you'll laugh." Sam brushes past Jack and Leslie.

"How you feeling?" Leslie asks.

"Fine, is there something you want to tell us?" Bryan asks.

"No," Jack says.

"Sam has a stupid smile on his face. What's so funny?" Hank asks.

"Nothing." Sam smiles at me.

"What? Why're you looking at me like that?" I ask him.

"Not sure what you're talking about," Sam says, turning his head to Jack.

"You have a weird look on your face is all," I say.

"He definitely has a weird look on his face," Cindy says.

"I don't have time for this shit, we've got a lot to discuss," Bryan says.

"Last stitch, and then you can stand back up," Cindy says.

"How about we eat a meal today," Hank says.

"Good idea. I could eat," Sam says.

"Throw some frozen pizzas in the oven. We'll discuss our next move over a quick bite," Bryan says.

"Grab what you need to sit comfortably and head to the dining room table." Bryan pats his shirt down. "Plans changed since earlier."

CHAPTER 25

I walk over to the table, pull out a chair, and look down at the wooden surface. The restored wood looks jagged enough to splinter a finger. I hear the wind blowing against the window. It sounds like someone's outside, whistling from the window ledge. The lighting above the table is dim and adds to the spooky effect. Traces of garlic and baked cheese snip my attention.

I look up and see a full table. I'm sitting across from Leslie and Hank, who are talking among themselves. Leslie looks to be doing most of the talking as Hank nods. She could be babbling on about nail polish colors, and Hank would continue to nod. Sam sits to the right of Leslie. He's thudding his finger to a consistent rhythm.

"Stop beating on the table; you're giving me anxiety." Jack whacks at Sam's hand.

"I always tap my hand, and it's never bothered you before. Dude, drink a beer or something," Sam says.

"I can't wait to hear about Jessica. Was she nice to you? What did you tell her?" I ask.

"Yeah, Jack, what'd you tell her?" Leslie laughs and continues with her side conversation.

"Shouldn't you be sitting next to your girlf—"

"Had a great conversation with headquarters," Bryan interrupts Sam, carrying a stack of papers to the table.

Cindy follows Bryan with pizzas. "Good, can't wait to hear."

"Everyone needs to eat something; we'll be working tonight," Bryan says, pulling a beer from his jacket and rolling is across the table to Jack.

Bryan tugs the open chair and slides in next to Cindy. His face is expressionless as he slaps the papers in front of him. He lays a burner phone next to his notes. Both of his eyes are bloodshot. The dark and puffy bags below look as though they're about to sink inward, devouring both eyeballs. His five-o'clock shadow from yesterday has another twenty-four hours added to the salt-and-pepper scruff. He looks around the table, clears his throat, and adjusts his posture.

The tapping sound stops along with Leslie's anxious side chatter. I look at Hank and see him sighing in relief. I hear a clean snap and the crisp pop from the aluminum as Jack opens the beer. He takes a large gulp.

"You're making that beer look tempting," Leslie says.

"Jack and Anna can have a few beers. The only way they'll be leaving this place is in a vehicle bound for headquarters," Bryan says.

"I guess I know where I stand with this squad," Jack hops out of his seat and walks to the fridge. He grabs a few beers and sets one in front of me.

"It's only for the remainder of the time here, which is only hours," Bryan says.

"That fast, huh?" Hank asks.

"Agent P said so. He's personally taking on this case and wants Anna out of here as soon as possible," Bryan says.

"Agent P? No shit," Hank says.

"Who's that?" I ask.

"One of the big guys at headquarters," Jack says.

"He says he knows exactly how to get her family out safe—"

"Cyanide?" Sam interrupts Bryan.

"Eat your pizza," Bryan yanks a slice of pizza and tosses it on Sam's plate. "We'll get your family out along with Jessica—she'll need to come too," Bryan says.

"Jessica?" I ask.

"Yeah, and she'll be given the opportunity to get her family out. They'll be safe and can stay together in Tin City Place," Bryan says.

"Where's Tin City Place?" I ask.

"It's the name of the underground community built below headquarters—in Utah," Bryan says.

"It taken over twenty years to construct, but there's underground housing available all over the world," Leslie says.

"It's where the infected will go after Interhybrid revival," Cindy says, pointing at the pizzas.

"Dig in," Bryan says, grabbing a slice of pizza. "You okay going to headquarters tomorrow, Anna?"

"If that's the plan, though, I'd like to be able to talk to my family once they're all together," I say.

"Of course, we'll make that happen," Bryan says.

"What's the general plan, then?" Hank asks.

"Very simple, actually. Keep Anna here, an eye on the warehouse, and an eye on Jessica. Agents will be here before sunrise," Bryan says.

"I have to tell you something that may add a hurdle to the game plan," Jack says.

"I figured that much after our little phone conversation earlier. Go ahead—take the reins." Bryan leans back in his chair and crosses him arms.

"I'd feel more comfortable if I told you in private," Jack says.

"We don't have time and I'll have to tell them anyways. Spit it out," Bryan says.

"Fine. Then I guess the best way to explain earlier—remember when you guys assigned me to Anna's alibi? Well, I nailed it." Jack looks around the table.

"What did you do?" I ask, chewing my pizza.

"Go ahead, Jack. We're all ears," Leslie smiles at Sam.

Sam shakes his head.

"I'm not sure how to say this, but—"

"Forget the alibi right now; we're getting out of here. What'd you see in the house?" Bryan interrupts.

"Stags came in through the laundry room and were hiding in the bathroom," Jack says.

"Did you say anything linking you to our operation?" Bryan asks.

"Nothing. Jessica has no idea," Jack says.

"Good," Bryan says.

"Wait. I need this all to make sense. I'm sorry, I need more than this. I know you're trained to talk quick and relay the life-altering stuff, but I'm not," I say.

"It's okay, just ask. I can imagine it'd be hard listening to people communicate like this all the time," Bryan says.

"Thank you. I'd like to rewind a sec. You're saying my best friend let a stranger walk into my home?" I ask.

"She didn't let the Stags in; they broke in," Jack says.

"Very cute. And you're right—you're a quick thinker. I also think you know exactly what I'm asking," I say.

"She wasn't easy to convince. Caught me off guard while I was working through your janitor keys," Jack says.

"And?" I ask.

"She bought my story. The big hurdle I was getting at—I told Jessica you'd call her as soon as I got back. You'll have to call her, or she'll call the police."

"What?" I ask.

"Well, she didn't actually say she'd call the police, but I know she'll call your dad. There's no doubt in my mind that your dad will call the police," Jack says.

"Yeah, I'd say that's a hurdle," Hank says.

"It's a hurdle, but we can make it happen," Bryan says.

"I had no choice; I'm sorry," Jack says.

"We'll have to post up around Jessica's residence before you make the call, but we'll make it happen. You did what you had to do," Bryan says.

"May I intervene a second?" I ask.

"Anna, go ahead," Bryan says.

"Why won't you answer my question? What did you say to the most cautious person in my life? What's my alibi? Why does she trust you?" I ask.

"Screw it, I'm uncomfortable watching him squirm." Leslie sets her pizza down. "He told Jessica you two have been dating for a bit, and you sent him to grab a few things. That's why Sam and I were laughing earlier."

I spit my pizza on my plate. "What? Why?"

"It was the quickest way I could get her off the patio and inside the house," Jack says.

"She's going to be upset. All she does is take care of me, and now she thinks I'm a liar," I say.

"It wasn't like that. Please trust me. We had a good conversation, and she even asked if I'd set her up with a single friend," Jack says.

"I guess you did what you had to do," I say.

"I'd like to think I created a strong alibi for you. What would you do better? She approached me from behind with mace while I was using your keys," Jack says.

"No, I get it.," I say.

"I told her you were waiting to see where things went before you tell her," Jack says.

"We've been friends since we were little. I've never kept a thing from her, but if she bought it, great," I say.

"I think that's a pretty good cover. As people get older, they learn to take their time before announcing their relationship," Bryan says, grabbing a slice of pizza for Cindy.

"Honestly, I'm okay. I just needed to know what I was getting myself into. I'm supposed to call her after all," I say.

"Looks like I've eaten too much and need to put on my fat pants," Sam says.

"Nope, sit down. You're going on the road," Bryan says.

"Where to?" Sam asks.

"We only have two cars in this garage to work with. I'd like you and Hank to post up in front of Jessica's place. Take the Chevy Impala," Bryan says.

"I'll leave now," Sam says.

"Wait. I think Hank should stay here with you. You're injured, Anna's injured, and Jack's been compromised. Cindy and I will go with Sam," Leslie says.

"I agree. Hank should stay back. There's that hotel across the street from Jessica's apartment. We can place two people down below and one up top," Cindy says.

"You sure?" Bryan asks.

"Incase they're able to trace the new burner—I'd feel most comfortable with Hank and Jack getting you guys out of here," Cindy says.

"I agree," Sam says.

"Me too," Jack says.

"Okay then. Take the car and decide among yourselves—who's posting up where. Just let me know when you get there—"

"Me and Sam will stay in the car, and Cindy will post up in the hotel. Done," Leslie says.

"Thank you. Cindy, grab cash from the safe for the hotel room," Bryan says.

"Will do. If everyone's done eating, let's go," Cindy says.

"Oh, and here's my phone number." Bryan hands Leslie a piece of paper. "It's a different type of phone. I was told only to use it if we were ever compromised. Do not call me unless there's an emergency. I'll call you in fifteen-minute increments."

"Got it," Leslie says, tossing Sam a set of car keys.

CHAPTER 26

"Would you like another beer?" Jack asks.

"Sure," I say, walking to the couch.

"Don't overdo it. I need you to be reactive if there's an emergency," Bryan says.

"I'm fine," Jack says.

"Are you okay?" I ask.

"Just a bad day. I saw things I wish I hadn't." Jack drinks his beer.

"At least Jessica didn't blow your cover. She's a great friend," I say.

"I realized that when I was laying facedown on a sheet of ice," Jack says.

"What?" I ask.

"Never mind," Jack says, sitting next to me.

"Can you two help me with something?" Bryan asks.

"Of course. What can I do?" I ask.

"I'd like you guys to keep an eye on the camera monitors." Bryan hands us laptops.

"Sure, which cameras?" I crack open a beer.

"The warehouse. The cameras are live," Bryan says.

Hank walks in the room and stretches. "I can take a ride over there."

"Absolutely not," Bryan says.

"I hate to say it—"

"What?" Bryan interrupts Hank.

"The warehouse cameras are obvious. The Stags will find them and trace them to your laptops," Hank says.

"I get that. But they must find the warehouse first," Bryan says.

"I guess," Hank says.

"They never found the one at Anna's," Jack says.

"Wait. You have cameras set up in my home?" I ask.

"Not in your home, no. We installed one after you returned home from your car accident. Strictly precaution," Bryan says.

"It's a small mount. Sam installed it on the tree in your backyard," Hank says.

"It looks like a piece of bark. That may be the best install Sam's ever done," Bryan says.

"It only monitored the back view. You could see the sides at times, but it depended on the time of day with lighting," Bryan says.

"Your light sensors are supersensitive back there, by the way," Jack says.

"Oh, I know. But now I know why," I laugh.

"Well, I had no choice but to kill the camera. I've got all the footage leading up to Jack's compromise, and I think there was enough lighting to see when the Stags got in," Bryan says.

"Please do. I'd like to know myself. I'll show her how to use the program," Jack says.

"Perfect." Bryan opens a laptop and sets it in my lap. "Anna, I'm setting you up on camera two. Jack, you watch camera one. Hank, I'd like you on camera's three and four."

"Got it." Hank grabs a laptop and sits in a chair.

"Play with the camera settings. You see the anything off, let me know. The slightest thing can make a difference," Bryan says.

I look at the screen and see the abandoned warehouse. "How can we defeat something we know so little about?"

"We continue to learn in moments like these." Bryan grabs a stack of notes and a laptop and sits next to me.

"Our role is to protect you and keep you alive. That's another division entirely," Hank says.

"The hunters. They could be hunting right now," Jack says.

"They're actually snipers, but we call them hunters. We've been living in the Midwest for too long," Hank says.

"I hope we've got a sniper with us," Jack says.

"Can't you call headquarters and find out?" I ask.

"I wish it worked that way. We're not allowed to interact with the other divisions. We're all one big team, but there's a strategy involved," Bryan says.

"I guess that makes sense," I say.

"It's about time I check in the with the others." Bryan grabs his phone and dials a number.

"Yeah?" Sam's voice echoes through the speaker.

"What time's the next train?" Bryan asks.

"Five minutes. The cab had to drop someone off, and now we're looking for a place to pull over," Sam says.

"Okay. How long is the train ride?" Bryan asks.

"Twenty minutes," Sam says.

"Bye." Bryan hangs up the phone.

CHAPTER 27

Leslie points out the window. "There's a spot. Stop."

"I don't like that angle," Sam says.

"You idiot—now we have to drive all the way around the block again."

"One more time around. I'd prefer to park somewhere I wouldn't have to bend my neck all the way back," Sam says.

"You're going to miss Cindy's signal," Leslie says.

"She said fifteen minutes. I'm right on time," Sam says.

"She said she was going to ask for a room with a lake view, so try to park on the left side of the street," Leslie says.

"Which means I should park on the right side of the street. You can only see the lakefront from the hotel rooms on the far left. She'll be able to see inside Jessica's place if she gets any of those rooms. So, if we park on the right, we'll have a different angle," Sam says.

"You should listen to yourself. Cindy will be up high, and we'll be down low. No matter what, we're at different angles to begin with."

"I don't know how the hell Hank partners up with you all the time. You're the worst copilot," Sam says. He backs into a parking spot and turns off the lights.

"Look, she's home. Lights are on, and I saw movement in between the cracks in the window blinds," Leslie says.

"Cool. Keep an eye on her place. I'll watch for Cindy's signal. I've got a minute left," Sam says.

"Hopefully the rooms aren't sold out. We didn't think of that," Leslie says.

"Nah, we should be good. There wasn't much going on in this neighborhood over the weekend. More people are checking out than in during this time of the week," Sam says.

"I hope."

"There she is." Sam points up. "One, two, three, four, five, and off."

Leslie's phone rings. "Everyone made the train," Leslie says and hangs up.

CHAPTER 28

"They okay?" I ask

"They're all set. Now let's get you set up." He grabs a phone and plugs it into a small device.

"What's that for?" I ask.

"It's new, but I only have five minutes to work with. This gadget supposedly adds an additional shield if we're calling a phone that's using location services. It's just precaution," Bryan says.

"That's more of our emergency stuff," Hank says.

"And what would you call our current situation?" Jack asks.

"Unlucky. I'd say we've reached a dry spell with luck," Hank says.

"Forget them right now. You ready to call her?" Bryan asks.

"I'm actually nervous to call her. I've never felt like this before."

"That's because you're lying to her," Jack says.

"Thanks. You just made me even more nervous."

"Don't look at it that way. You're lying to her, so you can keep her safe." Hank looks up from his computer.

"I guess you're right," I say.

"I'd like you to keep the call as short as possible. If she asks you questions regarding your location, lie," Bryan says.

"Where should I say?" I ask.

"Close your eyes and think of a home you like in the city and describe that," Hank says.

"That won't get us very far," I say.

"Why not?" Jack asks.

"Because it's down the street from here," I say.

"Yeah, I wouldn't do that if I were you," Jack laughs.

"I got a place in mind," I say.

"Good. Now imagine we're sitting inside that home. What would it look like outside the windows?" Hank asks.

"Thanks. That was actually really helpful," I say, opening my eyes.

"The phone will read as a foreign number. Just brush it off," Bryan says.

"I did say you broke your phone," Jack says.

"Well, thanks, Jack. You're finally giving me some useful information. Anything else I need to know? You should probably tell me now," I say.

"Nah, if I'm right here, you'll be fine." Jack stretches and scratches his messy hair.

"Fine. I'm ready." I reach for the phone.

"One more thing," Jack says.

I drop my arm.

"Your friend thinks I'm handsome. Maybe when all of this is over, I'll ask her on a date."

"Your chance with her is up now that you're dating me. We'll never date each other's exes," I say.

"I get what you're saying, but you're forgetting one thing—we're not really dating." Jack smiles.

"I forgot you're a comedian on the side," I say.

"Jack, let her make the damn call," Hank says.

"All you need to know is I was helping you with your phone, you're staying with me, and you were waiting to tell her about me." Jack smiles.

"All right, good talk." I grab my beer and take a large sip.

Bryan hands me the phone. His computer slides from his lap and into my leg. I turn and look at his computer screen, and I drop my jaw. The screen is frozen and zoomed in as far as it can go. I pull my head back and squint at the fuzzy pixilation. Inside my back-kitchen window are two elongated shadows of bodies hiding around the corner from the staircase. I feel every hair on my body raise as if someone had rubbed a helium balloon up and down my skin.

"Oh my God." I jolt back into the couch, forcing a shock down my spinal cord. My laptop falls off me as I lift my hands to cup my mouth. I feel as I've lost control as tears pour out of my eyes. "What the hell it that?" I start crying.

"It's okay, Anna. Breathe," Bryan says, pulling the laptop away.

Jack slips off the couch and kneels in front of me.

"Those things are in my house. They're in my h—"

"Were. They were in your home. This is older footage, remember?" Bryan asks.

"Why are they doing this?" I ask.

"Let's try not to go back to round one. We made it this far," Bryan says.

"Let me get you glass of water." Hank gets out if his chair and walks toward the kitchen.

Jack hands me a beer.

"Jack, stop. She needs to take it in, not numb herself," Bryan says.

"I'm okay. I just need a minute. It's a horrifying reality to witness," I say.

Jack puts his hand on my leg. "I know. I felt the same way just earlier today."

"I don't even know what I'd do if I was in the same room as one." I take a few deep breaths. "Make them go away."

"I had a mild panic attack over it today. Ask Bryan," Jack says.

"No, you had an actual panic attack. Thought I was going to have to come grab you." Bryan says.

"And he's a trained agent. This is why we shouldn't take them in this young," Hank says, walking in the room with water.

"I'm fine," Jack snarls. "Anna, I just want you to know you're not alone. We've all seen it too."

"Says the guy who ne—"

"Stop throwing fuel," Bryan interrupts Hank.

"When was this?" I point at Bryan's screen.

"This was during the time Jack and Jessica went up the stairs," Bryan says.

"So they were lurking around watching them?" I look over to Jack.

"I'm really glad you didn't get out of that car," Bryan says.

"Why wouldn't they just kill them?" I ask.

"Who? You mean me? Kill me?" Jack asks.

"Intact resources. The less commotion the easie—"

"She knows that," Bryan interrupts Hank.

"Don't put that vibe out there," Jack says.

"But what would two people matter?" I ask.

"Thanks again," Jack says, sitting back on the couch.

"If they were killed, they couldn't get to you," Hank adds.

"I disagree. I'm not sure about that. They could've killed Jack and Jessica and waited for Anna to return. They could kill her and leave, and no one would ever trace them." Bryan grabs his laptop.

"Have they been known to kill innocent bystanders?" I ask.

"It's uncommon." Bryan rewinds the footage.

"Maybe they're trying to learn about us in the process. They could be unsure of human capabilities and our response to their presence," Hank says.

"They've clearly determined they're being hunted back," Jack says.

"Which has made them aggressive," Bryan says.

"It's just pathetic, you know?" I shake my head.

"What?" Jack asks.

"We're wasting energy and lives fighting a war within our own world while we're slowly being ambushed. It's just sad."

"Humans are selfish." Jack drinks his beer.

"How're you feeling? Drink more water," Bryan says.

"I'm feeling a little less anxious," I say.

"Let me show you something really quick. Watch here." Bryan clicks on the image and holds down the mouse. "I want to teach you how to change the live camera settings." He opens a list of options. "Watch here. This'll be the best way to track them in the dark." Bryan clicks and changes the image.

"Infrared technology. Pretty cool, huh? Show her on the pictures from earlier," Jack says.

"Now look here." Bryan clicks on Jack and Jessica. "See? They're all reds and oranges."

"Warm-blooded. Body heat—"

"In technical terms, these cameras specifically detect the infrared energy of objects," Bryan says.

"Got it so far."

"Now, look at this shot of the Stags from the kitchen," Bryan says as he clicks and zooms in on the picture.

"What the hell?" I lower myself as far as I can toward the screen until the pain forces me to stop.

"Stags record differently than humans. The cameras are intended to convert the infrared data into an electronic image, which displays the surface temperature of the object being measured." Bryan looks over to me.

"Very bizarre," I say.

"You can see an orange outline around the body like a shell," Bryan says, clicking on the image.

"It's not even the same color orange," I say.

"It's more of a tangerine orange, with some yellow to it. The rest of them scan all blue and black. They're almost incognito," Jack says.

"Would I look different under an infrared camera?" I ask.

"You naturally have a lower body temperature. You show shades of oranges mainly, not as many reds. But it all varies. If you had a fever, you may have some reds. If a human was walking around without a jacket on in the winter, the colors would be lighter," Bryan says.

"You're a mutt," Hank says.

"You ready to make that call?" Bryan asks.

"Yeah, I'm relaxed and ready," I say.

"I'm going to make some coffee." Hank walks to the kitchen.

Bryan opens the phone and turns on the speaker. "Dial her number."

"Okay," I say, dialing the keypad.

"Jack, grab a notepad and marker for yourself," Bryan says, handing me a notepad and pen.

"What's this for?" I ask.

"If Jack confuses you in any way, write it down as you're talking to your friend," Bryan says.

"We'll be fine," Jack says

"Fine then. I don't want your lack in detail to interfere with this call," Bryan says.

"You may want to slow down the alcohol intake," Hank shouts from the kitchen.

"I'm not an idiot," Jack says.

I hand my beer off to Bryan. "I'm okay."

The phone rings.

"Just say you're using a temp phone of mine, not sure why it's coming up unknown, and change the subject," Jack says.

"Yeah, okay."

I close my eyes and imagine myself home on my couch, bundled up in my favorite fleece blanket, wearing my Christmas slippers. I picture the outside of a home in Lincoln park that I love. I'm looking out the window. I see narrow streets and the old streetlamps. Yes, I'm in Lincoln Park.

The phone rings.

"You got this. You can't screw this up." Jack pats the top of my leg and leaves his hand rested on the edge of my leg for comfort.

"Thanks," I say.

The phone rings.

"What if she doesn't pick up?" I ask.

The phones rings.

"Come on. Answer," Jack says.

Voicemail.

"No," I look at Bryan.

"Hang up and dial again," Bryan instructs.

"Calling twice. She'll hopefully know it's me, then." I close the burner phone and dial again. "It's ringing." I close my eyes. "Come on, Jess."

"I'm feeling nervous again," I say.

"Give me the phone. I'll start the conversation," Jack says.

"No," Bryan says.

"Trust me for once. Damn it, everyone." Jack raises his voice. He twists himself to the edge of the couch and signals for me to give up the phone. "Let me lead. Please."

"Stop," Bryan says.

"Here, I'll follow your lead." I hand Jack the phone.

"Shit," Bryan says.

"Hello?" Jessica answers.

"Is this the Chicago Department of Mace Training?" Jack asks.

Hank walks backward into the room and shakes his head.

"Mace training?" Jessica asks.

I close my eyes and wish the moment will stop.

"Is this Jack?" she asks.

"Yeah, it's me," Jack says.

"Can Anna hear me?"

"Not now. She just tried to call you and hobbled to the bathroom really quick. Or slow. I'm trying not to offend her."

"Did you tell her about the mace situation?" she asks.

"Nah, that's our little secret." Jack turns and smiles at me.

"I was getting worried there, Mister Jack."

"My apologies. As I predicted, the cell phone provider took half a day helping me resolve the situation. Good thing I didn't make you wait."

"Is this Anna's phone? It's coming up as some weird number."

"They weren't able to activate the old phone I had."

"I told you that," she laughs.

Jack turns to me and widens his eyes. He covers the mouthpiece. "What are you waiting for—say something," he whispers.

"So for now, she has a lovely prepaid phone with low minutes. She should be—"

"Is that Jess?" I ask, cupping my hands over my mouth.

"Oh good, I can't wait to talk to her," she says.

"You still going to put in a good word with her pops for me, right?" Jack asks.

"Don't worry, I'll hold up to my end of the deal as long as you hold up your end and set me up with one of your hot friends."

"I've already messaged a buddy I had in mind."

"Give me the phone, Jack." I say.

"You'd really like my frien—"

"Give me the phone now, please," I interrupt and grab ahold of the phone.

Jack pulls away from my grip and switches to the opposite ear. "Sorry about that, Jess."

"Is that Anna? I hear her voice," Jessica laughs.

"Jack, right now. Give me the stupid phone," I say, cowering over him on the couch.

"Jess, I've got to let you go. Anna's literally wrestling me for the phone right now. Look forward to seeing you again soon." Jack releases the phone.

"Hey, Jess, sorry about him."

"Why the hell were you keeping him a secret?"

"I wasn't keeping … I mean, I wasn't ready to tell you just yet. He was a little weird at first. You know how guys are."

Hank walks over and hands Bryan a cup of coffee. He turns to Jack and yanks the beer from Jack's grip, giving it to me. He shakes his head as he walks back to the kitchen.

"Well, things make a little bit more sense now after I met your hot boyfriend today. No wonder why you turned down that cute bartender. You had me fooled."

"Yeah, that's why," I say.

"I almost called the police on him."

Jack frantically starts writing on the notepad. *Make sure you tell her how much she helped me today … and you're thankful for her.*

I glance down at Jack's chicken scratch and swat at him to leave me alone. "Yeah, he said he was caught off guard."

"He had that list you wrote him. That was his saving grace," she says.

Hank trips and spills his coffee all over himself. "Ow. Ow. Hot."

Jack laughs.

"What was that?" Jessica asks.

"What was what?" I ask.

"That sound in the background. Turn down your TV or something. It sounds like a sick sheep bahing."

Bryan spits his coffee back into the mug midsip. Jack and Hank to plant their hands over their mouths as they burst into laughter. Hank walks from the kitchen and leaves the apartment.

"Anna?"

"I'm sorry, Jess. We forgot to pause the movie."

"What are you two watching?"

"What movie are we watching?"

"Yeah," she says.

"Oh, we're watching *Silence of the Lambs.*"

Jack smacks his hand across his forehead and runs into the bedroom. He closes the bedroom door and chokes out laughter. Bryan's coffee mug shatters on the hardwood floor.

"Isn't that movie about a serial killer?" Jessica asks.

"The movie? Yes, I'm only kidding," I say, looking toward the bedroom Jack decided to shut himself in. "Jack actually laughs like a lamb. It's pretty funny."

Bryan stares at me and shakes his head.

"Eh, I guess the man has to have flaws," Jessica says.

"I'm sorry I haven't told you about Jack yet. I didn't want to add more to my current situation. I've been more than enough to handle this year. Why add a guy to the mix?"

"No, it's fine. I understand. I'm just glad you're having some fun. Definitely a curveball, but a good one. And it's new; I get it."

I hear jack open the door and walk back into the room.

"I appreciate you and everything you've done. I just want you to know that."

"Did something else happen?" she asks.

"No, why?"

"Your tone."

"No, I'm fine. Jack's distracting me," I laugh.

"What's his place like?" she asks.

"It's nice. He's in Lincoln Park."

"I wonder if his friends are like him. I'm taking a break from those dating apps for a while. The way you two met just shows it can still happen traditionally."

"He told you?" I glower at Jack and point to the notepad, holding the pen in the air.

Jack shakes his head at me and gestures for me to keep the conversation going.

"Yeah, I was definitely caught off guard and wasn't expecting to meet Jack. But it's working so far. I hope I don't become a burden to him too."

Bryan signals for me to wrap up the call.

"I'll say it once more—you need to let go of the burden stuff, Anna. Don't talk about it over and over to Jack either. I don't know how to knock sense into you when you need it lately."

"I'll take the advice, thank you. I must get going, though. I'm not sure how many minutes I have on this phone," I say.

Jack points to his pad.

"Get that new phone as soon as you can," she says.

"I will, I promise. And before I let you go, Jack says you were beyond helpful today, and he'd be happy to set you up with one of his friends. He really likes you a lot," I say.

"That's really sweet of him. Tell him thanks," she says.

"I will. I'll talk to you soon," I say.

Bryan points to his watch.

"By the way, what's Jack's last name?" she asks.

"Fifteen seconds left," Bryan whispers.

"Jack's last name is …" I search around the room for an answer. Anything at all to end the awkwardness of this call. I look over to Jack and watch him drink his beer. "Beers. His name is Jack Beers."

"Beers, Huh? Jack Beers," Jessica laughs. "That actually has a nice sound to it."

"Sure, I guess," I say.

"Anna Beers. It rolls right off the tongue."

"Yeah, I'm sorry. Dinner just got here, and I must let you go. Love you and will try to call you tomorrow."

"Please do. I need more juicy details," Jessica says.

"Okay. Bye." I hang up the phone.

"Wow, women are crazy," Jack laughs. "Anna Beers?"

"Quiet, Herb Garden," I laugh. "How'll I reach my dad now?"

"Through her. Trust me on this one. She didn't bring him up, so let's not get him involved tonight," Bryan says.

"Did I do okay? I feel so bad lying," I say.

"I was a little concerned at first, but you both made a believable story. Jack, walk out and grab Hank."

"There's no way you've seen *Silence of the Lambs*; glad you recovered from that one," Bryan laughs as he lowers himself off the couch to clean up the broken glass.

"I've never seen the movie," I say.

"I figured, and I'd be pretty concerned if you told me you had."

Jack and Hank walk inside.

"Sorry about that—burned myself with coffee," Hank says.

"Yeah we noticed, Lambchop," Bryan says.

"That went better than I thought," I say.

"I was concerned for second, but you recovered," Bryan says.

Jack grabs a towel and walks over to assist Bryan. He squats and wipes up the spilled coffee.

"I should check in with the others," Bryan says, turning on the speakerphone. He lays the broken glass into the towel and lifts himself back up to the couch.

"Hi," Cindy answers.

"All done. You watch your show tonight?" Bryan asks.

"Yeah, the picture was so clear on the new TV," Cindy says.

"All right. Sleep in tomorrow and go with her to the train station if she decides to head out. Four of us have an early class," Bryan says and hangs up.

"Can you please translate?" I ask.

Jack holds his palm to his ear and looks at Hank. "Ring Ring. Ring Ring."

"Hi," Hank says, in a high-pitched voice.

"We called Jessica, and everything's good. What's going on with you?" Jack says.

"Not much action. We're in the clear," Hank says.

"Never would've guessed. What was the last thing you said?" I ask Bryan.

"I told her stay put until I give orders and to tail Jessica if she decides to leave." Bryan dials a number on a phone. "And then I said I'll have the next plan at four in the morning."

"Thought you guys had a yoga class or something," I laugh.

"You think we're in the clear?" Hank asks.

"It's hard to say. I'd rather be safe than sorry," Bryan says.

"What would you like us to do?" Jack asks.

"I want you and Hank out here with me for the night," Bryan says.

"You got it. You mind if I hop in the shower for a minute?" Hank asks.

"Go ahead. But first, call Leslie and fill her in." Bryan hands Hank a phone. "I put her number in here."

"What about me? I'd like to help," I say.

"You need to rest and get strong. I want you to take the guest room tonight. You can shower and get a few hours of rest. The girls have clothes in that room, so take whatever you like," Bryan says.

"Can I bring the computer in with me? I'd like to help until I fall asleep." I grab the computer and walk toward the room.

"Speaking of shower, can I take one really quick?" Jack asks.

"Ask Anna if you can use the shower. I need you and Hank back out here as soon as possible."

Jack looks over to me.

"You think I wouldn't let you shower? Go ahead." I shake my head.

"Thanks." Jack follows me into the room.

CHAPTER 29

I overhear Jack in the shower as I sift through the bedroom dressers. I hear the snaps and pops from the shampoo and soap bottles. At this point, I'm too tired to shower. I look at the warm and inviting bed. *Must sleep now.* The shower can wait until morning. I grab sweatpants and a shirt from the drawer and look around the room. If I move quick enough, I can change before he gets out.

I carry the mismatched clothes over to a chair just as the shower faucet turns off. By the time he dries off and changes, I'd like to be in bed. I lift my arms above my head and inhale the pain as I attempt to change shirts. Using my sturdier arm, I pull my shirt over my head and drop it on the ground as quick as I can.

Hurry up. Don't let him see you like this. He likes your friend Jessica. I hear the shower curtain rings collide and see his shadow appear under the door. Grasping the clean shirt, I try to open the tight fold and lose my grip.

"Shit," I mutter as the shirt falls to the ground.

I hear the bathroom faucet turn on and take a deep breath. I leave my sports bra on, deciding to come back to my upper half. I lower myself halfway onto the chair and begin the painful process of pulling my pants off.

Come on, you idiot. "Come on," I whimper, leaning onto my back. I use one leg to slide my pants down to my ankle. Using my foot, I force it off the rest of the way. I inhale and look around the room for a better option before I start the next pant leg. I'm stumped. The faucet shuts off.

I stand up straight and stare at the bathroom door. *You'll be mortified, if you don't hurry up.* I pray for Jack to stay in the bathroom a little longer as I thrust through the pain and kick my loose leg at my pants. I use my foot to slide the pants to my ankle and pry my toe against the fabric with force, hoping to slide it off my leg.

"Ow," I grunt. *Shit. Please, tell me he didn't hear me?*

I freeze and listen. The faucet turns on, and I hear an electric toothbrush. I hope his parents taught him to do the alphabet in his head twice while he brushed as a kid. My parents told me to recite the alphabet while I brushed. *I never did. Please be like that.*

I grab the pants I took from the drawer. They smell like summer breeze detergent—my favorite. *Focus Anna.* The faucet shuts off. I hear Jack spit in the sink. *Gross.* He powers off the electric toothbrush and gulps mouth wash. Gurgles echo from the bathroom. *Yep, he wins in the clean mouth department.*

I fumble around with the change of clothes. How do I do this? *Put the stupid pants on ... before he sees you like this.* I start by holding the very corner of the pants in my right hand and attempt to toss the opening far enough where I can catch my right leg into the pants first. The fabric slips out of my fingers, falling onto the floor in front of the chair. The faucet shuts off.

I plant my arms on the edges of the chair and squat down to my knees. I maintain my grip as I cower down to the ground, landing directly on my bottom. Pain radiates up my spine. I hear the bathroom door lock pop, and I shimmy to the side of the chair. In attempt to hide completely, I scoot around toward the back of the reading chair.

I hear the door slide open and close my eyes, wishing I could make this moment go away.

"Anna? You okay?" Jack asks.

I freeze and lean backward behind the chair.

"Anna?"

I close my eyes.

"I can see your legs."

"I was trying to get changed for bed and ... well, failed miserably. Don't look or come over here." I feel as though someone lit a match to my face. Lying flat on my back, I turn my head at my legs and notice my socks were still on. An epic fail.

"Did you fall?"

"Nope."

"You miss the bed and fall?" he asks.

"Nope."

"Missed the chair and fell?"

"No again."

"I'm out of questions. That just doesn't look normal. Do what you want, but you're wedged between the chair and wall and bed in a way."

I close my eyes, mortified. "If you must know, I was trying to get changed for bed and, well, now I'm here. I'll be fine once you leave the room."

"Can I help you get up? he asks.

"Nope."

"Why not? You in the nude over there?"

"In the nude? What? You from the early nineteen hundreds?" I ask.

"Geez, asking if you're in the nude sounds better than asking you if you're naked and stuck on the ground with your socks on."

"Good point."

"Good point, what?" he asks.

"In the nude sounds way better."

"Anna, I can help you much faster than you can help yourself right now."

"Fine. And I'm not naked, by the way."

"Seriously? I'm a gentleman."

"Fine," I say.

"Fine. What does that mean? I'm not stepping from this bathroom unless you give me the okay," Jack says.

"Will you please help me?"

"Okay, I'm walking over to you. Just letting you know."

"Just so you know, I normally don't rock the granny panties you're about to see."

Jack walks into my view, leaning over to lift me. "I'm helping you get up. What do I care about your shorts?"

"These aren't shorts. They're underwear."

"Those?"

"You know what, never mind. Yes, they're shorts." I stare up at Jack.

Jack's wearing a pair of basketball shorts with a shirt that's been washed so many times there are holes throughout. I can see parts of his muscular frame through the opening of the sleeves. He's even more handsome in his old shirt with his olive complexion peering out from the long winter dryness. His healthy mop of hair is messy from his shower.

Jack walks around the reading chair so that he's standing behind me and squats. "I'm going to hook my forearms underneath your arms and pull you up. Are you okay with that?"

"Yeah, just try not to look at me."

Pressing his body against mine, he slowly lifts me up. "Hang on."

Feeling my feet sturdy on the ground. I stand up and cover my waistline. I shake my head. "Thank you."

"I'm going to lift you to the bed and we'll put your clothes on from an angle. Is that okay with you?"

"You mean dress me?" I ask.

"It's not a big deal. You're in shorts and a sports bra."

"Whatever, fine."

"So … it's okay then if I carry you to the bed? It's easier to help you from up higher than bending over at the chair," he says.

"Jack, I said it's fine. I know you're not a creep."

He circles around my half-naked body, trying to find an angle to lift me.

"Please hurry, I'm feeling self-conscious." I glare.

"Seriously? For someone whose been limited in movement a year, you hold your muscle tone well," he says.

"Thanks?"

Jack squats down and slides his left arm between my knees, hooking his grip around my right leg. Pressing me at an angle, he stands up and clutches my right shoulder into the right part of his chest. "Is this okay if I lift you like this and carry you over to the bed?'

"Quit asking my permission. I said you can lift me," I laugh. "I'll tell you if you're hurting me."

Jack lifts me up, slides me across the room, and drapes me across the bed. He walks back to the corner chair and gathers my clothing from the ground. I wish I'm able to jump up and dash to the bathroom, check my hair and face, and possibly brush my teeth.

"I'm going to start with your right leg."

"I don't need a play by play. I can see what you're doing," I say.

Jack laughs.

"What's so funny? Is it me?" I ask.

"No, I've never dressed a woman before."

"I'm sure you're used to the very opposite. Will you hurry up please?"

"You're delicate, and I'm trying not to break you," Jack says, lifting my leg and sliding it into the first pant leg. "Very boring jammies—looks like something Leslie would wear."

"They're probably Leslie's and please don't call them jammies ever again," I laugh.

"What's wrong with jammies?"

"It reminds me of when I was a child and my parents would change me for bed, which is exactly what you're doing."

"Sorry, was trying to make light of the situation," he says.

"No, I'm sorry. I'm overtired and should be thanking you for helping me."

"You don't have to thank me," Jack says.

"I'm not talking about right now. I was talking about earlier. I'm really sorry, I never should've asked you to go in my home."

"You did nothing wrong."

"I had a feeling you'd say that." I shake my head.

"Honestly, I'm fine."

"Good. I'm happy you're good, then."

Jack bites his lip as he prepares the other pant leg.

"It seems like you took a liking to Jessica?" I ask.

"Left leg, please." Jack takes my other leg and forces it through the other side of my pants. He grabs both sides of my pants and slips them up to my waistline. I arch my back up to help.

"She's gorgeous, isn't she?" I pry.

"Sure."

"I can make it happen," I say.

"Make what happen?" he asks.

"Set you two up." I look for a reaction. "I mean, when all this is over."

"Jessica's pretty, but she isn't my type." Jack unfolds the shirt I dropped on the ground. He takes both of my hands and pulls me up to the edge of the bed. "Arms up."

I try hard to steer away from his face and find myself directing my eyes at his arms. His muscular arms force my eyes to his face. There's nowhere else to look. I realize I've jumped off the edge, a feeling I haven't had since before my accident. I'm interested in Jack. I'm smitten.

"Then what's your type? It must be hard to date in your profession?" I ask.

He slides my shirt over my head. I feel his gentle hands pull my messy hair out from the shirt. He brushes my hair to one side. "There you go. Much better than being stuck between the wall and a chair."

"Thanks," I say.

"If I were to read what's going on right now, by your question spree, I'd say you were a little jealous of my interaction with Jessica," he says.

"Me?" I feel as though I stole something from store, signaling alarms to sound. Spotlights are shining on me to confess. I feel nauseated and sweaty. He just called me out.

"You," he says.

"What do you mean?" I ask, trying to turn the conversation around.

Jack takes a step back and stares at me. "I feel like I know you pretty well, given the circumstances we're in and, well, my job."

"And?"

"I feel you're a little jealous."

"Me? Why on earth would I be jealous?"

"Because I teased you about Jessica and asking her on a date and becau—"

"I'm not jealo—"

"And because you're asking me right now," Jack interrupts.

"I'm trying to do something nice. She's perfect and I can tell by her tone, she's intrigued by you too," I say.

"So, why would you ask me what my type was?" he asks.

"Wow, you're enjoying putting me on the spot like this."

"Yeah, I am." Jack crosses his arms.

"I'm done talking tonight. I need sleep." I scoot back and yawn.

"No."

"What do you mean, no?" I ask.

"Sorry, I meant you can't bring up a subject and dance around it like this. Just say what you mean," he says.

"I'm too embarrassed," I say.

"Embarrassed?"

"I'm sure you can figure it out." I turn to the pillow.

"I don't like guessing games. I play guessing games when I'm deciding whether or not a Stag set off your light sensors."

"Are you always this serious?" I look back.

"No," he says.

"I bet you are."

"No, definitely not. Why're you turning this around on me? I asked you a simple question," Jack laughs.

"Just teasing you a little."

"I don't understand … why can't you just ask what you meant to ask?" he asks.

"Because now I'm enjoying watching you squirm a little. All you ever hear are facts, so this must be irritating," I say.

"Extremely."

"Now we both feel the same way about this conversation."

"Anna, why'd you ask about my type?" he asks.

"Because, I find you interesting."

"Interesting?" he asks.

"Yes, you're interesting. One of a kind. So how about you answer my initial question," I say.

"Which one? I'll play your little game this one time." Jack stares at me.

"What's your type?" I ask.

"Tall, auburn hair, and significantly injured. Want me to keep going?"

"Me?" I point to myself.

"Jack? You done?" Bryan knocks.

"Be right out." Jack stands up straight.

"Wait," I say.

Jack walks toward the door. "You put me on the spot, so—"

"I was extremely jealous," I say.

"Thought so. Guess we're on the same page then," Jack smiles and walks out the door.

I slip under the covers and grab the laptop. My face feels stiff from smiling to myself. I'm trying to wrap my mind around what had just happened. I can't help but replay the last fifteen minutes over and over in my mind, wishing I was well enough to dance around the room.

Opening the computer, I decide to occupy my mind by watching the surveillance videos. I click on the warehouse camera and zoom in. This may be the equivalent to watching paint dry. I watch the same thing over and over, playing around with the different settings Bryan taught me earlier. I turn all the live cameras to infrared and stare at the hazy screen.

Weight mounts heavier on my eyelids as I yawn. I pull the covers up high and rest the laptop on my chest. I'm fighting to stay awake. I grab the computer and force my hand on the screen, ready to close it for the night, when I notice movement on the warehouse cameras. The rash movements from the back of the warehouse looks like garbage bags dropping over a fence. I click and zoom in on the image. Three or four shadows with sunlit-orange outlines creep onto the property. I rub my eyes, pull myself upward, and watch the strangers lurk in the darkness toward the back door.

"Bryan. Jack. Get in here now," I shriek.

"What is it?" Jack bursts open the door. He flips the light on. He must have been drinking coffee when I began yelling, as he's wearing half of it on his shirt.

Bryan steps in behind him and looks around my room.

"I see them. Many of them. They're at the warehouse," I say.

Jack runs to the bed and grabs my computer from me. "Bryan, look at this." Jack signals for Bryan.

"I know. I was notified. Movement by the back-door sensors," Bryan says.

"You think this is from her phone?" Jack asks.

"Could be. They have possession of her phone. Possibly retracing her steps before you buried her phone." Bryan takes the computer from Jack.

"They'll get in," Jack says.

"Everything's been wiped at the house. They won't find anything," Bryan says.

Hank walks into the room. "You seeing all this?"

"Yes. Alert Leslie. I'll call Cindy," Bryans says.

"Got it." Hank walks out of the room.

"How many of them?" Jack asks, pacing around Bryan.

"Four, maybe five," Bryan says, taking out his phone.

"What'll they do?" I ask, searching Bryan's face for answers. He is expressionless.

"What's up?" I hear Cindy through the speaker.

"Four on home video," Bryan says.

"Does my voice sound crystal clear?" Cindy asks.

"Sure does," Bryan says.

"I'm getting ready for bed and will talk to you later," Cindy says.

"Night." Bryan hangs up the phone.

I look at Bryan and scratch my head. I don't understand. "What was that all about?" I ask.

"She was confirming that we're in the clear. The warehouse is clear," Bryan says.

"I'm scared," I say, pulling myself out of the bed. "What if they find us?"

"We'll be fine here until headquarters arrives," Bryan says. He stares at the wall and bites his lip.

"We're going to let the Stags plow through the house, then?" Jack asks.

"What if they find something?" I ask.

"Nah, I'm going to keep them out." Bryan hands me back the computer and scratches his chin stubble.

"You got any ideas?" Jack asks.

"I've got several. Stop asking so many questions ... let me think," Bryan says.

"What can I do?" Jack asks.

"You forget what I just asked you not to do? Put a lid on it," Bryan says.

Jack sits next to me on the bed. He points to my computer screen. The orange hues move as the Stags lurk alongside the back-porch windows. I cover my mouth and watch Bryan pace back and forth. Jack taps his foot against the ground. I put my hand on Jack's thigh and stop the tapping.

"Be quiet and listen. My idea's simple, but I'll need you both," Bryan says.

"Sure, whatever you need." I scoot toward the edge of the bed and let Jack help me on my feet. We stare at the computer screen. Jack bites at his nails, tapping his other hand on the keyboard. I yank at the computer and swat his finger from his mouth.

"Whatever it is, we should do it now. They'll be in soon," Jack says.

"I'm going to set off the burglar alarms and the fire alarms. The sprinklers will go off. Both the police station and fire department will show up." Bryan walks over to the desk and pulls out a tablet.

"Wait," Jack says. "Can they track us from the GPS system signal? You know, back to the device you're about to use?" Jack follows Bryan.

"No, they'll never make it that far. The system monitor is in the garage inside a steel lockbox. This'll scare the shit out of them," Bryan says.

I watch the vibrant color move across the screen as the Stags circle the back of the house. I see a blob of orange spring upward. One of the Stags clings to a window ledge "They're grouping around the door," I say.

"Hang on." Bryan holds his chin.

"What? Why're you stopping?" Jack asks.

"I'm wondering if it's best to let them break in, see nothing, and leave?" Bryan holds the tablet.

"What does it matter?" Jack asks. "Just sound off the alarms."

"I think they're prying the door open. Another went to the window," I say.

"I'm thinking this through. Authorities will show up if I do this. Give me a moment," Bryan says.

Jack paces behind Bryan. I sit on the couch and prop the laptop on my lap. I cover my eyes and peek at the screen through my fingers.

"Yeah, we're doing this," Bryan says. He walks over and sits next to me.

"Do it now. We're out of time. One just pried the door open." Jack points to the computer screen. "They're in."

"A second one's in. Look, it dropped on the ground from the window," I say, squirming in my seat.

Bryan grabs the tablet. Using his thumb, he inserts a fingerprint and swipes through a list of red switches, one after another.

"I hope this works," Jack says.

I look at my computer screen and see lights blaring colors of reds and yellows. The house lights up with the sirens. Water sprays underneath the lights with each light flash. It looks like it's raining inside the warehouse. My computer screen blurs from the mist. "What if they don't leave?"

"They will. I set off every siren inside and around the property. The alarms sounding right now are ear-wrenching. People will be able to hear them from the next neighborhood over," Bryan says.

"I still see them in the house," I say, watching the lightshow.

"Unless they're deaf, they won't be able to think, let alone get back out without some hearing loss," Bryan says.

"Look." Jack points at my computer screen. He switches camera views.

A Stag releases the window and falls to the ground. The two inside back into the windows. One of them kicks the door open and the other one follows it outside. They retract toward the fence. I drop my hands from my eyes and look at Bryan. My gums hurt from grinding my teeth.

"There we go," Bryan mutters. "Get the hell out of my home."

"It's working … so far," I say.

"Now I need you both to concentrate. We'll have authorities pulling up in moments," Bryan says.

"Isn't that what you wanted?" Jack asks.

"Yes, but we must stay out of the spotlight. The house is listed in ownership of David Jones. This has to look like an incident where the owner's temporarily unreachable," Bryan says.

"Why?" Jack asks.

"So authorities back off and we have one less thing to worry about," Bryan says.

"Done," I say.

"Fine. What's your plan?" Jack asks.

"When I say go, I'm changing our main phone line to a family voice recording," Bryan says.

Jack sits next to me. "What does this have to do with—"

"Enough. Listen, when I point to you, say a made-up name, and let me do the rest," Bryan snaps.

"What the—"

"Just shut it and do what I ask," Bryan interrupts Jack. "We're about to become the epitome of what not to do when you go out of town," Bryan says, dialing a number.

"To check your home messages, press one. To erase and record a new greeting, press two—"

Bryan presses a button. He holds up his finger.

"Please start your greeting after the tone and press pound to save your new greeting . . ." Beep.

Bryan holds his finger in the air. "Hey, you've reached David . . ." Bryan points to me.

"Samantha," I say. Bryan points to Jack.

"Aaaaaannnd Burger," Jack says.

Bryan rolls his eyes at Jack. "At the Jones residence. We're out of the country on a kayaking journey, and we'll be back on the twenty-third. Please leave a message, and we'll get back to you after our big journey comes to an end." Bryan saves the message.

"Burger? Really?" I shake my head.

"I'm not sure what that was all for," Jack says.

"I did that so we're not only unreachable, but our stupidity caused the intruder. It may or may not help, but it's better than an empty home with no contact," Bryan says.

"Look, they're already over the fence." I point to the computer screen.

"Three of them are," Bryan says.

"Where's the fourth one?" Jack asks.

"Give it another minute . . . Nope, there it goes," Bryan says.

"There's the first squad car." I point at a window reflection. Jack changes cameras and zooms in on the front gate. The officer hops out of the car and approaches the gate.

"Quick thinking." Jack nods at Bryan. "How'll they get past the gate?"

"They'll have to go over," Bryan says.

Hank appears from the hallway. "Just watched a good show from the toilet."

"What the hell are you talking about?" Bryan asks.

"It ended up being a short film called *Hosing Down the Aliens.* How'd you know the alarms would work?" Hank asks.

"I didn't. Sam and I made some adjustments around the house while you guys were out last year. I had him enhance the alarms to execute havoc on an intruder. We couldn't even test them when he was done because he said the add-ons would cause permanent hearing loss." Bryan smiles.

"What if they didn't work?" Hank asks.

"Or if any of us were in the house when they went off?" Jack asks.

"I guess that's a risk I was willing to take," Bryan says.

"Pretty shitty risk, if you ask me," Jack says.

"Quit complaining," Bryan says.

"Guys, look." I point to the computer screen. "See that orange around the fence?"

Bryan grabs the computer and zooms in on the fence. "What the hell is that?"

"Judging by the length of the fence, there's at least a dozen Stags back there. Never seen that many at once," Hank says.

There's an orange hue glowing between each fence panel. A half a dozen police cars swarm the property and a firetruck backs against the gate. The Stags vanish as the police swarm the property.

"They're gone," Jack says.

"What now?" Hank asks.

"We wait it out. We've only got a few hours left," Bryan says.

"Okay, we wait it out, then," Hank says.

Bryan points to the computers. "I want you guys to stay on the cameras. Monitor the authorities. Anna, try to get some rest. We've got another long day ahead."

I nod and grab the laptop. "I'm going to watch the rest of the police sweep from the bedroom then. See you guys in a few hours."

CHAPTER 30

I open my eyes and see a mellow-gray smog glowing through the cracks of the uneven blinds. I lift my head and look through a tiny slit in the window. The light is coming from a nearby streetlight. It's still dark out.

The lamplight gleams through one of the gaps in the blinds highlighting the lock on the window frame. There's a claylike substance molded over the latch and the rest of the lock. Specs of silver from the original bolt shine through the gluey matter. The window is sealed shut. I remember where I am now. Another day in a different location with my new reality.

I rub the sleep from my eyes and scratch my face. My skin is dry and leathery. I wish I had lotion and a glass of cold water. My eyelids feel heavy, and my throat feels like I ate a roll of paper towels after smoking pack of Marlboro Red 100s. I swallow a few times and adjust my head on the pillow. I shut my eyes.

"Would anyone like a cup of coffee?" a man asks.

Who's that? I hear a conversation carrying from the other room. I scoot my pillow to the edge of the bed and listen.

"Jack, go ahead and see if you can wake her up," someone says.

I comb my hair with my fingers and part my hair down the middle. Adjusting my head on the pillow, I pull the covers to my chin and close my eyes.

"Sure, be right back," Jack says.

I hear his bare feet slapping against the wood floors as he walks. The steps grow louder. Oh no, he's coming. *Don't let him see you like this. You haven't showered in days*. I pull the covers over my head.

The door creaks.

"Anna?" Jack whispers.

There's a light knock at the door. "Yeah?" I turn over. There's a silhouette of a man with messy hair, standing in the doorway.

"Hey, sorry to wake you," Jack whispers.

"How long was I sleeping?" I ask.

"Just over three hours," he says.

"That much, huh?"

"Yeah, sorry. Rest of the night, post warehouse drama was uneventful … in a good way." Jack walks toward the bed.

"Good. They here? Headquarters?" I ask.

"Yeah, they're here. They got here a few minutes ago," Jack says.

"How many people are here?" I ask.

"There are six people here from headquarters. Four add-on agents and two high authorities." Jack sits on the edge of the bed.

"They don't mess around when they say first thing in the morning. The sun's not even up yet. You sleep?" I ask.

"No."

"Bryan?"

"Of course not." Jack stretches out on the bed.

"Should I go out there?"

"Bryan asked me to wake you."

"If I go out there, will you lay down for a minute and take a nap? You haven't slept in days. I'll wake you."

"Fine. Yeah—wake me up in twenty?" Jack asks.

"I will." I roll to the edge of the bed. "What are they talking about out there?"

"I don't think we're the only team evacuating right now," Jack says.

"Really? There's more?"

"Yeah, apparently. I don't think we're the only ones cornered." Jack closes his eyes.

"Thanks for the heads-up. Did you overhear anything else?" I wait for a response. "I guess I should go out and meet them." I look at Jack. "Jack? You sleeping?" I lean to the edge of the bed and bend my arms.

"Wait." Jack grabs my arm before I push off.

"Yeah?" I ask.

"You trying to ask me on a date?" Jack asks.

"Huh?"

"You are; I knew it," he says.

"You're something else. Especially when you haven't slept," I laugh, patting him on the head.

"My answer is yes. I say yes to the date," Jack mumbles.

"That's great Jackson Herb Garden, though I never asked you out," I say, hiding my smile as I walk toward the door. I hold my hands in front of me and feel around for the knob.

I press my ear against the door and hear a muffled conversation. A man with a raspy voice interrupts the chatter. I brush the door open and slip out of the bedroom. The man stops talking. I turn and face a silent group of strangers staring at me from the kitchen.

"Bryan?" I ask.

Two gigantic men step away from the island, and I see Bryan and Hank sitting alongside a man in a suit. Bryan looks at me and stands up. Hank and the suit guy swivel around on their stools. They stop what they're doing and stand.

"There she is," Bryan says. "Come on in. I'll pour you some coffee."

"Sure. Thanks." I walk in the kitchen, staring up at the giants.

"Here's a seat for you," Bryan says, pulling out a stool.

"Hey, Anna." One of the giants nods at me.

"How're you healing?" a woman asks.

"Fine," I say.

"Lots of action around Chicago, huh?" A younger gentleman smirks.

"Uh?" I stare at Bryan and Hank.

"Indeed, there's been a lot of action around Chicago." Hanks sips his coffee.

"Hank," Bryan snaps.

"What? Can't I add to the awkward small talk?" Hank laughs.

"No," Bryan says.

"Everyone shut up," an older man says. "I agree with Hank. You guys just shit on the word awkward." He tosses a hand in the air. "Sorry, Anna, I'm sure you're already upset enough about everything."

"Don't worry about that—she's doing fine." Bryan puts his arm around my shoulder. "That was pretty bad, though," he laughs.

Hank blinks and shakes his head. "I can't even—you guys leave headquarters much?" Hank walks between the giants.

"Meerkat," Bryan coughs.

"Sorry, I haven't slept much," Hank says.

Bryan hands me a cup of coffee. "Anna, this is—"

"It's nice to see you." The man uncrosses his arms and walks toward me. "My apologies. I told these guys to be sensitive to your feelings."

"Sensitive, huh? Is that what that was?" Hank asks.

"Meerkat, Hank," I say.

"I can imagine you're experiencing a lot of emotions right now." The man reaches out for a handshake. "I've got a lot to discuss. But before I make our lives more chaotic, I'd like to ask—you holding up okay?"

The man's smile is inviting and decorated with a salt-and-pepper beard. He's wearing a pair of thick black-framed glasses and adjusts them as he grabs my hand.

"I'm doing fine." I shake his hand.

"She's handling the news great," Bryan says.

"I see that," the man says. "Look at you—all grown up."

"Have we met?" I ask.

"Once," he says.

"Are you Bryan's boss?" I ask.

"These guys were in my squad a long time ago," he says, nodding to Bryan and Hank.

"He's one of the directors of National Intelligence of LFP Operations," Bryan says.

"Forget the fancy title. For the time being, I'm an agent back in the field," the man says.

"I'm sorry I stabbed your leading agent," I say.

The man looks at Bryan.

"We haven't got to the stabbing stuff yet," Bryan says.

"Oh." I sip my coffee.

"There was a stabbing? What happened?" the man asks.

"Nothing. I'll tell you later," Bryan says.

"It's bizarre—the more I look at you, the more I feel like I've met you before," I say.

"Remember what I said about the day you were born?" Bryan asks.

"Yeah."

"This is Phillip, the leading agent from your mother's squad," Bryan says.

"Agent P's his nickname," Hank says.

"We're you the man who helped deliver me in the cab?"

"This is him," Bryan says.

I let go of Phillip's hand and hug him. "You're in an article with my parents. My mom always put the article on the fridge each year for my birthday month. Bryan told me that you lost your job after that. I'm sorry you had to transfer, but I'm thankful you were there," I say.

"It was hard to leaving Chicago, as I love this city—everything worked out in the long run," Phillip says. "I'm really sorry about your mom. I took the news hard."

"I appreciate it." I release my arms from Phillip. "It was devastating to say the least. But after learning the truth, I'm ready to help you guys out before this gets worse and more people die."

Bryan clears his throat. "After you heal a—"

"I know, I know. I have to heal some more first," I say.

"You're a lot like your mother—stubborn," Phillip laughs.

"Phillip came out here because he wants to take on your case personally," Bryan says.

"I left your family hanging for obvious reasons, and I felt awful about it. It makes the most sense if I explain everything to your father. I really hope he'll remember me—it's been years," Phillip says.

"I'm sure he'll remember the man who helped deliver me. They searched everywhere for you, so they could thank you."

"Well, I had dark hair then—no grays. No wrinkles back then, either, but I'll be able to make sense of everything once I get him to remember me. We've got a limited amount of time to make this happen, which I feel I'll be able to get him on board quick." He sips his coffee. "Which brings me to my next point—getting you out of here. You're no longer safe here."

"I realize, after watching some recent footage," I say.

"You'll have to come with us to headquarters. We can treat you—make sure you're safe and rested. You okay with this?" Phillip asks.

"When would I have to leave?" I ask.

"Now—before sunrise. Agent Donavan will drive you in one of our vehicles—flying's too risky," Phillip says.

"He'll get you to Utah safe and sound," Bryan says.

"Hi, nice to meet you." Agent Donavan steps forward and shakes my hand.

"You as well," I say. "I'm fine with leaving here—already discussed this with Bryan and his squad. I just want to be sure my family and Jessica will be safe."

"Of course, I understand. Once we have your father on board, we'll use him to help us go down the line of family members and friends. They'll be invited to stay in Tin City Place," Phillip says.

"I told her about Tin City Place," Bryan says.

"Good. We need to move quickly here. You have any questions so far?" Phillip asks.

"How long until I see them?" I ask.

"We should be close twenty-four hours behind you—give or take a half a day. I'd like to be thorough during this process with your family, as we won't be able to go back. We believe this is it," Phillip says.

"What do you mean—this is it?" Bryan asks.

"You sure about that?" Hank asks.

"Everything's amplifying at once, especially the Stag attacks. As of yesterday, we may have the first country clear of Interhybrids and any ties to their RH negative bloodline," Phillip says.

Bryan scratches his chin. "Fine, but some countries had a lower RH negative presence to begin with. One country wouldn't be enough with all the living Interhyb—"

"The Stags left behind a message in zone thirty-two," Phillip says.

"What are you talking about? We're dealing with another specie—what do you mean they left a message?" Bryan asks.

"It was directed at us, and it was vulgar," Phillip says.

"Try me," Bryan says.

"They mutilated an Interhybrid and slaughtered her team of agents—our investigators found trails of skin. I don't find it necessary to go into details—ladies present," Phillip says.

"Did you say her?" I ask.

"Her name was Pensri. She was a medical student and young, like you. The squad was with her in zone thirty-two since the day she was born," he says.

"We've heard stories about that squad. *Elite Three Two*, the agency calls them. The girl's been rescued more than anyone on record, and she's lived a healthy and normal life," Bryan says.

"I've heard that LFP snipers can't even trail that squad they're so discrete. They've burned up more Stags than anyone in the field," Hank says.

"We're not taking this lightly and refuse to take any more risks. We implemented an evacuation strategy for zone thirty-two, and the Stags killed off every Interhybrid in record time, which is why evacuations will only be discussed in person right now. We were only in week two of evacuations—that's how fast things turned," Phillip says.

"We already knew the Stags would initiate by wiping the countries with a scarce Interhybrid presence." Bryan says.

"Not this fast. We had a thorough plan intact," Phillip says. "It's our technology—they're able to hack faster than we're able to improve and advance our devices."

I pull out a stool and sit down. I want to run away and hide. "This is really bad."

"Let's get moving, then," Bryan says.

"You have anything else on zone thirty-two? Anything that'd help us out?" Hank asks.

"I'd rather not promote false hope, but if I was to shine a light, they're still searching for one of the bodies," Phillip says. "Compared to the others, they only found a third of the skin. Forensics is saying the edging and the st—"

"I'm feeling a little sick," I say. "It's the skin stuff." I walk to the edge of the kitchen sink.

"Here's some water." Phillip hands me a glass. "I'm really sorry I went into detail." He pats my back. "But now that I'm here, I'm ordering you to get the hell out of here as fast as you can."

"What happens once we leave?" Bryan asks.

"We have departments working on cases you couldn't even begin to imagine. They're restructuring as we speak." Phillip grabs his jacket. "By time you're at headquarters, we'll have answers and a revision from our level two and three disaster squads."

"When will our families get the alert?" Hank asks.

"We're entering code orange in exactly forty-eight hours. Their devices will sound, and they'll have to wait by the door, like they learned in training—it'll take up to four hours for their vehicle to arrive," Phillip says.

"Thanks for looking out for us." Bryan shakes Phillip's hand.

"You're my squad, and I'm impressed by the leaders you've become—you and Hank," Phillip says.

"Thanks, man," Hank says.

"Consider yourselves lucky—you'll have a simple evacuation process as long as you've been following normal protocol. Until we get to headquarters or I tell you otherwise, no more phones after sunrise. We go off grid until one of our tech departments begin production of the next generation software—should be three days from now," Phillip says.

"Roger that," Bryan says.

"Good. I might as well mention now—we're assembling a new division after the evacuations. We're forming an army of the elite, Carnage Squadron, and I'd like you, Hank, and Leslie on this force," Phillip says.

"I'm in. What about the rest of my squad?" Bryan asks.

"The others will be sent to recruitment or revival. You'll live together according to your zone, so you'll still be together. The last thing we want is to break up a squad," he says.

"Sounds like a fair deal to me," Hank says.

"Where will I be?" I ask.

"You'll be with your family in Tin City Place, training with other Interhybrids in your zone," Phillip says. "I want us out the door in under eight minutes."

"We should grab Jack," I say.

"Donavan—the kid," Bryan says.

"Donavan will be driving the first group out. I'd like Bryan, Cindy, and Sam to accompany Anna back to headquarters. Jack, Leslie, and Hank will stay back with me and my agents—we'll get everyone else out," Phillip says.

"Jack's been compromised," Bryan says.

"Then Jack goes with you, and Sam stays with us." Phillip nods. "Is my spot still around—my old hideout by the United Center?"

"Yes, we've used it multiple times. I actually made it one of our emergency spots," Bryan says.

Hank nods. "We named it Agent P—it's evolved, though. The millennials call i—"

"By millennials Hank's referring to Sam and Jack," Bryan says.

"I figured. So what do they call it, then?" Phillip asks.

Bryan points at Jack.

"A gent named P," Jack says.

"As much as we've trained the two of them, they've got their own lingo," Bryan laughs.

"It's cool—I like it. A gent named P," Phillip laughs. "Anyways, our time's up here. Get in touch with the rest of your squad. We're leaving now."

"Roger that. I'll call them now," Bryan says.

Hank looks at Bryan. "Would you be okay with me getting in touch with Les and Sam?" Hank asks. "We're about to separate and I'll be with them and—"

"I'm placing you in charge," Bryan says. "You okay with that?"

"I'll take care of everyone," Hank says.

"I know you will," Bryan says. "We're pressed for time—you know what to do … just stay ahead of the game."

"We're out of time," Phillip says.

The agents follow Phillip toward the door. Bryan shakes hands and nods at each person. I see a door swing open in the background. Agent Donavan walks Jack to the kitchen.

"Anna." Phillip walks over to me. "I'll see you at headquarters. You can introduce your family to the rest of the squad when we arrive," he says.

"Thank you." I hug Phillip. "Be sure to tell my dad and brother that I'm with the man who saved me in my car accident. That I'm with that Bryan guy who called him. He'll know who I'm talking about, and so will Jessica."

"I'll be sure to tell them, and I'll see you out there." Phillip shakes my hand.

I watch the group trickle out the door. The agents wave as they leave the apartment. Hank strides backward and stops.

"You guys be safe. I'll see you soon." Hank hugs Bryan and pats him on the back.

"You too," I say, hugging Hank.

"You're in good hands with Donavan. He's crazy, but a great driver," Hanks says.

"What did I miss?" Jack asks.

"Hank's staying and you're coming with us," Bryan says.

"Try to stay out of trouble." Hank shakes Jack's hand.

Hank turns to see Phillip standing in the doorway. He nods and walks out the door. We sit at the kitchen table in silence. Bryan dials Cindy on speaker phone.

"What's up?" Cindy asks.

"You scared for your first day at work?" Bryan asks.

"I'm ready," she says.

"You'll be taking your students on a fieldtrip this morning—alone, without chaperons. Meet me at our spot at sunrise so I can give you your lunch." Bryan pauses. "You there?" he asks.

"I'm here," she says. "Was thinking, sorry. I'm interested to see what you packed for lunch."

"You'll be happy. Oh, I forgot to tell you—your phone's due for an upgrade as we speak," Bryan says.

"Great, see you soon." Cindy hangs up.

"I'm not even going to begin to translate that conversation," I laugh.

"She'll be waiting for us," Bryan says.

"Anything you guys need to wrap up here, do it now. I want us out the door in three minutes," Donavan says. "We're pushing our luck with sunrise."

"Jack, help me sweep the place," Bryan says.

"On it—fill me in please?" Jack paces behind Bryan.

Agent Donavan looks at me. I can't decide if he's waiting for me to speak or analyzing me. He reaches inside his coat pocket and grabs a pair of leather gloves.

"Can I tell you a secret?" he asks, putting his gloves on.

"Of course," I say.

"I'm supposed to wait, as we may have a fourth evacuation joining us later in our arrival group. But we'll be joining with others like you," Donavan says.

"At headquarters?" I ask.

"Yep. We've got a thirty-three-year-old male from Glasgow, Scotland, and a twenty-eight-year-old female from Barcelona, Spain," Donavan says. "One thing you three have in common—Stags killed a parent."

"I'll be happy to meet them," I say.

"I thought I'd tell you now, so you don't feel alone. I can imagine—this isn't an easy life transition."

"You'll be bringing three people together—all of whom recently learned their parents were murdered by Stags?" I ask.

"Yes, and possibly a fourth," Donavan says.

"I guess retaliation will be our group therapy," I say.

"If you want to look at it that way. Try to get some rest on the way there," Donavan says.

CHAPTER 31

As we pull out of the garage, I'm drawn to the start of a beautiful Chicago sunrise. I see a blood-orange haze rising between city buildings. Fiery highlights of fuchsia-pink enhance its flattering effect. The blend of vibrant colors reflects off the glass buildings. I think of sherbet ice cream.

I see the bright colors mirror off the sooty sidewalk ice. What was once fresh snow looks like muddy ice mounds. The dusky morning wind hurls sideways, blowing particles from the dirt-filled snow into the air. People are up, going about their chaotic lives. They seem to be dragging to work though I'm not sure what day of the week it is. Bundled up in their warmest Windy City gear, the early morning Chicagoans walk with purpose.

I look at each person on the sidewalk as we drive by. I see a man carrying a briefcase hail a cab. Several speed walking to the bus stop, while others run to catch the L-train pulling into the stop. I watch a couple holding hands. The man's dressed neatly for the day, and the woman's in her sweats. His cab pulls up, and she turns to give him a kiss goodbye, revealing she's late in her pregnancy. What will happen to the baby inside her belly and will that baby be able to survive in this new generation? Will we be another species depleted by extinction? Will our bones be dug up and displayed another five thousand years from now, replicating our discoveries from ancient Egypt?

"Where to, boss?" Donavan asks.

"Clark and Armitage—toward Lincoln Park Zoo. There's small parking lot," Bryan says.

"Just point when I'm close to it. We'll have plenty of time to get acquainted with one another. You should try to sleep for now. You guys look like shit," Donavan says.

I look at Jack. "You look like you came straight from makeup as an extra in *The Walking Dead.*"

Bryan turns around in his seat. "You think they film that show this time of year?"

"I'm sure shows like that film year-round," I say.

"Perfect. We'll drop you off where you belong," Bryan laughs.

"You sure about that? I think I'd scare the zombies at this point," Jack says. "At least I've showered." He smiles at me.

Donavan looks at Jack through the review mirror. "I've got a better idea."

"Yeah? What's that?" Jack asks.

"I'd use you as a scarecrow—plop you right in front of headquarters," Donavan says. "You could save us some money."

"Pretty good sir—you'd get along great with my partner Sam," Jack says.

"Can't wait to meet him," Donavan says, turning on the news.

In local news, in Pilsen a family leaves town for a kayak trip, leaving their itinerary on their recording, leading burglars directly to their doors. Coming up after the break, Police Chief Harvey discusses what not to do when leaving town.

"Stupid idiots these days," Donavan says. "People lack common sense."

Jack looks at me and we burst into laughter.

"Burger, looks like you made the news," I say.

"You've got to be kidding me," Bryan laughs.

"Didn't you plan that so we'd stay out of the spotlight?" Jack asks.

"And technically we did—the fake family took the heat," Bryan says.

"It's been minutes, and you've already made the morning news?" Donavan turns the radio off.

CHAPTER 32

Cindy presses her face against the window and skims the cars parked along the street. She stares at the lakefront. A sliver from the sun gleams in the distance. Grabbing the bedroom phone, she dials the front desk.

"I'd like to check out," she says, staring at the cars parked on the street. She hangs up and walks over to a floor lamp. The cord stretches from the wall and across the room as she drags the light closer to the window. She stands in the pitch-black room and tugs the light chain. The light flashes twice in the darkness. She pauses. "One, two, three, four," she counts, tugging the chain again. The light blinks on and off.

Cindy rubs her eyes and stares at the vehicle down below. The interior light flickers on and off. Leslie and Sam signal from inside the vehicle. Leslie turns on the light once more. Sam and Leslie wave underneath the dim glow. The light goes off.

"See you guys soon," Cindy says, putting her jacket on. She walks through the dark room, feeling around for the bathroom switch. A baby cries from the next room over as she flips on the bathroom light. She jumps and holds her chest. The baby cries louder. The high-pitch scream echoes through the bathroom drywall. She exhales and turns on the faucet.

Holding a hand towel under the nozzle, she soaks the towel and pulls the drain shut. She spreads the towel across her face and rubs it around. Steam rises from the sink, adding to the soothing effect. She grabs her phone from her back pocket, snaps it in half, and drops it in the sink. The crying sound trails off as she turns off the faucet.

Gathering the pieces of her phone, she wraps them in Kleenex. Water leaks from the phone and all over the floor. She grabs another Kleenex and storms out of the bathroom, feeling around for a garbage can. The phone clunks as it hits the bottom of the can. She grabs the floor light, drags it backward, and stops. There's movement out the window.

"What the hell?" Cindy runs to the window. Two shadowy figures move down an ally. The figures glide toward the sidewalk and cross underneath a streetlamp. They're wearing hoods and dressed in black clothing. They cross under another light. "Stags," Cindy utters, skimming the cars. Leslie and Sam remain parked on the street. "No, no, no—drive away. What're you guys still doing here?"

Cindy drags the floor lamp back to the window and tugs at the chain. She stares at the vehicle. "Come on—look up." She turns on the light and lifts the lamp in the air, thrusting it side to side.

The shadows lurk down the sidewalk and split apart. They squat down on both sides of a parked vehicle and creep to the front of the car. The two Stags slither down the line of parked cars toward Leslie and Sam.

Cindy sprints toward the door, tripping on the light cord. She yanks the cord from the wall as she plummets to the ground. The room goes black. "Get up." She jumps to her feet and lunges at the light switch, slicing the top of her hand on the corner of a hanging mirror. Her hands shake as she turns on the light and grabs the phone, stretching the cable cord as far as it goes. She dials the front desk.

"You've reached the front desk. Would you mind holding for a moment?" a woman asks.

"No, it's an emergency. It's an emergency," Cindy says. An advertisement and music play in the background. Cindy grabs the cord and plugs the floor lamp back in. She lifts the lamp and jumps up and down in the air.

Fog covers the rising sun, and the darkness takes over. The Stags approach Leslie's and Sam's vehicle. They tuck behind the trunk. Cindy beats on the window. The baby begins to cry in the other room.

"How may—"

"Send someone outside right now. There's been an accident—saw it from my window." Cindy tugs the light chain.

"Out front?" the woman asks.

"Yes, please hurry." Cindy hangs up.

The fog fades and the sun inches up. A blue haze surrounds the city, and a pink glow circles the rising sun. The Stags approach the driver and passenger doors and pry them open. They drag Leslie and Sam out of their seats by their throats and cover their heads with black bags. Leslie kicks, forcing her foot on the horn. The horn echoes between buildings.

The Stags release Sam and Leslie. They take a few steps and pass out on the street. The hooded giants search the vehicle and scoop the lifeless agents off the ground, tossing Leslie and Sam over their shoulders. They walk away as the murky-gray skies lighten. The Stag carrying Leslie turns in the middle of the street and looks up. It points at Cindy.

"Oh my God," Cindy cries. "No." Cindy drops to the ground and slides against the wall. She stands up and peeks out the window. The Stags vanish down the alley.

A woman and a security guard dart outside and run in the middle of the street. They search around the premise and circle back to the entrance. The guard pulls out his radio, and they walk back inside the hotel.

Cindy runs out the door and waits for the elevator. "Come on," she snarls. Both elevators stop at the second floor. She bursts through the staircase door and staggers down the steps. Halfway through the high-rise staircase, she grabs her mouth and ruptures into tears. "Hold it in—be strong," she chokes, picking up the pace.

She thrusts herself against the first-floor door and spills into the lobby. A woman shrieks and drops her coffee on the ground. The security guard swivels around.

"I'm fine. Sorry, was doing my morning workout—I mean warm-up." Cindy runs toward the exit.

"Everything okay?" the guard asks Cindy, bending down to help the woman with her coffee explosion.

"I'm fine, and I'm sorry about the coffee," Cindy says, running out the door.

She strides toward the alley and grabs her gun from the handle. The bitter morning air hisses at her as she approaches the alley. A backstreet light flickers off for sunrise. She skims along the concrete walls, forcing herself down the unlit pavement, and stares up at a sign. "No outlet, huh?" she whispers to herself.

The wind wails through the alley, hurling dirt and ice particles in the air. Cindy points her gun and clears the corner. She peeks at her hand as she aims the gun. Blood trickles down one hand and all over the gun. The mirror ripped through her skin. She flicks the blood from her hand and adjusts her grip on the gun. The alley dead-ends.

The morning sun rises. She tilts her head in the air and looks around. The daylight enhances her view of the buildings surrounding the alley. She squints at a broken window and runs toward the building. The glass spreads across the pavement below the broken window. She looks at the glass. "Clean and minimal," she mutters to herself and picks up a piece of glass. "Recent." She squats down in the middle of the glass and looks at the hole in the window. "Not enough fragments down here—was outside in." Cindy takes off running down the alley, toward the building entrance.

CHAPTER 33

"The sun's up," Donavan says. "What would you like me to do?"

"We wait here," Bryan says. "My squad no longer has phones, and she's alone. We wait."

"We wait, then." Donavan folds back his seat.

Jack's sleeping peacefully in a reclined, middle row seat. His hands are clasped together in his lap and he's grinning. He looks handsome, even when he's out cold.

I recline my seat halfway and grab a pillow. I look out the window. The clouds cover the early morning sun. My eyelids feel as though I've got paper weights clipped to them. I take one more look at my crush and close my eyes.

"Donavan." Bryan whacks him in the arm. "It's Cindy—pull forward."

"She dove in the bush," Donavan says.

"Wait—don't move," Bryan says. "Keep your foot off the brake and turn the car off."

"What happened?" Jack darts upward in his heat.

Jack and I pull our seats up and stare out the window.

"Anna, look out the left back corner of the vehicle. Jack, you get the right side," Bryan orders. "Look for any movement. I want to know what you see—even if the wind blows snow around."

"Got it." I nod.

"Did you see her?" Bryan turns to Donavan.

"Just as she dove," Donavan says.

"She had blood all over her and looks like a mess. Something went wrong," Bryan says.

"Why did she jump in the bushes?" I ask.

"She's being tailed," Bryan says.

Donavan adjusts his seat. "She's brought them with her. Cindy should know bet—"

"She knows better than anyone, believe me," Bryan snaps. "Something went wrong, and she's covered in blood. We wait right here, until we have the green light."

"We have no choice now," Donavan says. "If we move, they'll get Anna. Cindy's the sheep."

"She's crawling toward the dumpster—my four-o'clock," Jack says.

"Oh my God. What the hell happened? I just spoke with her and everything was fine." Bryan punches himself in the thigh.

"Calm down," Donavan says, looking at Bryan. "We've all had extensive training—read people for a living." He shakes his head.

"What're you getting at?" Bryan asks.

"How long have you and Cindy been sleeping together?" Donavan asks.

"Sleeping together?" Jack asks. "They're not sleeping together."

"And you've managed to hide this from your team of CIA agents living under one roof—impressive," Donavan says.

"That's impossible," Jack says.

The truck is silent. We watch for Cindy.

"Bryan?" Jack asks.

"Not now. Keep an eye out for her," Bryan says.

"Well, you answered my question." Jack looks out the window.

"I'm going to ask her to marry me," Bryan says.

"Why would you guys lie like that?" Jack asks.

"We were ready to tell everyone, and Theresa passed. Everyone was devastated—Hank still is. We decided we'd wait longer," Bryan says.

"Did you fill out the form with headquarters?" Jack asks.

"The relationship forms? Nah," Bryan says, watching out the window.

"How long have you two been seeing each other then? Couldn't be that long," Jack says.

"Our eleven-year anniversary was last week," Bryan says.

"You're kidding?" I blurt.

"You're an outstanding agent and I admire you, so we'll keep this one to ourselves," Donavan says.

"I feel like I no longer know you," Jack laughs.

"There she goes," Bryan says. "She's turning the corner—watch her."

Cindy's holding a handful of rocks. She drops one of the rocks on the ground. Once the first rock hits the ground, she throws the next.

"Count the rocks," Bryan says.

Cindy drops the last rock and removes her shoe. She shakes out her shoe and vanishes around another corner.

"You get that Jack?" Bryan asks.

"Grab her at the beach bridge emergency spot," Jack says.

"Good job. How many rocks?" Bryan asks.

"She dropped twelve rocks," I say.

"Anna's right, I counted twelve," Donavan says.

"Multiply that by three—we wait here thirty-six minutes," Bryan says.

"How do you know where to grab ger?" I ask.

"What she did with her shoe—one of our silent signals," Jack says.

"We'll wait here for thirty-six minutes and grab her under the bridge," Bryan says.

"And she'll spend her next thirty-six minutes losing the tails," Donavan says.

I stare at the clock and cross my arms. Jack puts his hand on my shoulder. We watch people cutting through the alley. Happy people pass by, laughing alongside a friend. One man argues with his girlfriend over the phone and punches a brick wall. We watch a drunk kid break into a parked car. The kid crawls inside and passes out.

"Good thing he stopped there. We wouldn't have enough room for him in here," Jack laughs.

"Times up," Bryan says. "Let's grab her."

"You got it." Donavan starts the truck. "But let's get one thing straight. If she's not there—"

"I know. You don't need to say it," Bryan says. "Everyone keep an eye out."

Donavan steers into rush hour traffic.

"I definitely won't miss this shit." Jack shakes his head at the cars.

"There's the bridge," Bryan says, sitting up straight.

I hold my breath as we turn under the bridge. Bryan unlocks the doors.

Donavan pulls behind a car and looks around. "Thirty seconds until the light changes. Cross your fi—"

Someone runs into the side of Jack's door.

I choke out air and scream. "Lock the doors."

Cindy opens Jack's door and crawls across the floor. "Shut the door—shut the fucking door."

Jack grabs a blanket from the back seat and covers Cindy. Bryan holds her hand and gives her a water. The light changes, and Donavan turns onto Lake Shore Drive.

"Take a minute to process. You're safe now," Bryan says.

Cindy drops the water and covers her eyes. She cries. "They …" Cindy dry heaves and cries harder.

Bryan jumps over the center console and onto the ground. Jack and I move back a row.

"Jack, hand me a plastic bag from the trunk," Bryan says.

Jack opens a bag and holds it in front of Cindy. Cindy vomits inside the bag.

"What would you like me to do?" Donavan asks.

"I've never seen her like this before. I'm not sure—just get us out of the city," Bryan says.

"No," Cindy says. "You can't. Drop me off—I have to get out. Let me out." Cindy rolls toward the door.

Bryan jumps behind Cindy. He jolts and looks at me.

I cover my eyes. "You ripped your stitche—"

"Nope." Bryan shakes his head at me. He grabs Cindy and holds her tight. "You must tell us what's going on."

"She's in shock Bryan," Donavan says.

"I get that, but we need to know what happened out there," Bryan says.

"What if we stopped and called Phillip?" Jack asks. "Maybe Leslie and Sam will be able to—"

"They're dead." Cindy grabs the bag and throws up.

Donavan opens his mouth and Bryan puts his finger in the air. "Can you repeat what you just said about Sam and Leslie?"

Cindy hurls into the bag. "They're gone—both of them."

"What do you mean?" Bryan asks.

"You sure?" Jack asks.

"Stop." Bryan points at Jack.

"The Stags got them. Please don't make me say it again—drop me off so I can tell the others." Cindy wipes her tears. "I walked in."

"You don't have to say anything else.

I feel my stomach turn and hold my mouth. I cry into my hands.

Jack holds his arms behind his head, taking deep breaths. Tears fall down his cheeks.

"Jack? Can you do me a favor and grab the first aid kit from the back?" Bryan wipes his eyes.

Jack nods and grabs the first aid kit.

"Grab two pills from the yellow pill bottle." Bryan grabs the water. "Listen up—give Cindy two of these pills every six hours. You repeat this until you reach headquarters. They'll treat her when you arrive. Explain everything you saw to the doctors."

"Wait." I stop Bryan. "Aren't you coming with us?"

"I must tell the others. They're going to need my help." Bryan hands Cindy two pills. "Now listen—inform the doctors that she knows time-sensitive information and to contact Phillip as soon as possible."

"We will," Jack says. He grabs a pillow and covers his face.

"Leslie's a fighter, and Sam's smart. If there's a slight chance they could be alive, the two of them will find a way."

"Where am I dropping you?" Donavan looks in the rearview mirror.

"Drop me under the tracks—just before the highway entrance," Bryan says.

We wait for Cindy to close her eyes, and Jack and I move to the middle row seats. Bryan folds out the third row and lays a pillow and blanket on top. He carries Cindy to the back of the truck and tucks her in. Pulling the seat belts from both sides, Bryan buckles her in. He leans over and kisses her on the forehead. "Love you," he whispers.

Bryan scoots toward the front of the truck and stops at Jack. He lowers the pillow from Jack's face. "This is the worst part of our job—we're a family." Bryan hugs Jack. "Donavan will get you there safe, and I'm putting you in charge of our arrival. Get everything ready for family check-ins, and we'll see you in a few days."

"See you soon." Jack says. "And we'll take care of Cindy."

Bryan turns to me. "I'll go with Phillip to see your family." Bryan hugs me. "You'll finally get your chance to heal up—no more accidents."

I rub my eyes. "Thank you for saving my life—numerous times. I'll see you guys in a few days."

Donavan pulls under the train tracks, and Bryan hops out. "Donavan, it's been a pleasure, man. I'm going to get you drunk when we get back." Bryan leans back inside and shakes his hand.

I stare out the back window and watch Bryan walk to the traffic light. He grips the sides of his face and stares at the ground. People walk past him on the sidewalk. He wipes the tears from his eyes and waits for the light to change color. The light turns green, and Bryan takes off running.

CHAPTER 34

I open my eyes and look out the window. I see a sign for Des Moines, Iowa.

"Jack?" I whisper.

Jack opens his eyes. "Hey."

"Cindy needs the next dose. It's been six hours," I say.

"I slept?" he asks.

"Several hours."

"Sam and Leslie?" Jack turns to me.

"That happened. I'm so sorry." I grab his hand.

"I wonder what she saw?" Jack slides two pills from the bottle. "Cindy's the most calm and collected in the group. Her words were all over the place."

"I walked in—what did she mean by that?" I ask.

"Not a clue. She should've been checking out of the hotel room," Jack says.

"You kids hungry?" Donavan looks in the rearview mirror.

We shake our heads.

"Then tell me if you need me to stop at all. It looks like we might see some snow." Donavan turns on the radio.

I adjust the pillow and close my eyes.

And for your traffic, the expressways are moving along nicely, just before the afternoon rush hour.

In world news, like a wildfire overnight in Bangkok, what doctors are saying started as cold virus symptoms has hospitals overflowing with sick patients this morning.

I open my eyes. Agent Donavan steps on the gas.

CPSIA information can be obtained
at www.ICGtesting.com
Printed in the USA
LVHW110157200719
624756LV00001B/194/P

9 781545 744130